Acclaim for Rad███

"**Love After Hours**, the fourth in Rad██ evokes the sense of a continuing dr█████████ ████ ████ ██ ██████ Carrie's slow-burning romance intertwines with details of other Rivers residents. They become part of a greater picture where friends and family support each other in personal and recreational endeavors. Vivid settings and characters draw in the reader…"—*RT Book Reviews*

Secret Hearts "delivers exactly what it says on the tin: poignant story, sweet romance, great characters, chemistry and hot sex scenes. Radclyffe knows how to pen a good lesbian romance."—*LezReviewBooks Blog*

Wild Shores "will hook you early. Radclyffe weaves a chance encounter into all-out steamy romance. These strong, dynamic women have great conversations, and fantastic chemistry."—*The Romantic Reader Blog*

In **2016 RWA/OCC Book Buyers Best award winner for suspense and mystery with romantic elements** *Price of Honor* "Radclyffe is master of the action-thriller series…The old familiar characters are there, but enough new blood is introduced to give it a fresh feel and open new avenues for intrigue."—*Curve Magazine*

In **Prescription for Love** "Radclyffe populates her small town with colorful characters, among the most memorable being Flann's little sister, Margie, and Abby's 15-year-old trans son, Blake…This romantic drama has plenty of heart and soul."—*Publishers Weekly*

2013 RWA/New England Bean Pot award winner for contemporary romance *Crossroads* "will draw the reader in and make her heart ache, willing the two main characters to find love and a life together. It's a story that lingers long after coming to 'the end.'"—*Lambda Literary*

In **2012 RWA/FTHRW Lories and RWA HODRW Aspen Gold award winner** *Firestorm* "Radclyffe brings another hot lesbian romance for her readers."—*The Lesbrary*

Foreword Review Book of the Year finalist and IPPY silver medalist *Trauma Alert* "is hard to put down and it will sizzle in the reader's hands. The characters are hot, the sex scenes explicit and explosive, and the book is moved along by an interesting plot with well drawn secondary characters. The real star of this show is the attraction between the two characters, both of whom resist and then fall head over heels."—*Lambda Literary Reviews*

Lambda Literary Award Finalist *Best Lesbian Romance 2010* features "stories [that] are diverse in tone, style, and subject, making for more variety than in many, similar anthologies…well written, each containing a satisfying, surprising twist. Best Lesbian Romance series editor Radclyffe has assembled a respectable crop of 17 authors for this year's offering."—*Curve Magazine*

2010 Prism award winner and ForeWord Review Book of the Year Award finalist *Secrets in the Stone* is "so powerfully [written] that the worlds of these three women shimmer between reality and dreams…A strong, must read novel that will linger in the minds of readers long after the last page is turned."—*Just About Write*

In **Benjamin Franklin Award finalist** *Desire by Starlight* "Radclyffe writes romance with such heart and her down-to-earth characters not only come to life but leap off the page until you feel like you know them. What Jenna and Gard feel for each other is not only a spark but an inferno and, as a reader, you will be washed away in this tumultuous romance until you can do nothing but succumb to it." —*Queer Magazine Online*

Lambda Literary Award winner *Stolen Moments* "is a collection of steamy stories about women who just couldn't wait. It's sex when desire overrides reason, and it's incredibly hot!"—*On Our Backs*

Lambda Literary Award winner *Distant Shores, Silent Thunder* "weaves an intricate tapestry about passion and commitment between lovers. The story explores the fragile nature of trust and the sanctuary provided by loving relationships."—*Sapphic Reader*

Lambda Literary Award Finalist *Justice Served* delivers a "crisply written, fast-paced story with twists and turns and keeps us guessing until the final explosive ending."—*Independent Gay Writer*

Lambda Literary Award finalist *Turn Back Time* "is filled with wonderful love scenes, which are both tender and hot."—*MegaScene*

Applause for L.L. Raand's Midnight Hunters Series

The Midnight Hunt
RWA 2012 VCRW Laurel Wreath winner *Blood Hunt*
Night Hunt
The Lone Hunt

"Raand has built a complex world inhabited by werewolves, vampires, and other paranormal beings...Raand has given her readers a complex plot filled with wonderful characters as well as insight into the hierarchy of Sylvan's pack and vampire clans. There are many plot twists and turns, as well as erotic sex scenes in this riveting novel that keep the pages flying until its satisfying conclusion."—*Just About Write*

"Once again, I am amazed at the storytelling ability of L.L. Raand aka Radclyffe. In *Blood Hunt*, she mixes high levels of sheer eroticism that will leave you squirming in your seat with an impeccable multi-character storyline all streaming together to form one great read." —*Queer Magazine Online*

"*The Midnight Hunt* has a gripping story to tell, and while there are also some truly erotic sex scenes, the story always takes precedence. This is a great read which is not easily put down nor easily forgotten."—*Just About Write*

"Are you sick of the same old hetero vampire / werewolf story plastered in every bookstore and at every movie theater? Well, I've got the cure to your werewolf fever. *The Midnight Hunt* is first in, what I hope is, a long-running series of fantasy erotica for L.L. Raand (aka Radclyffe)."—*Queer Magazine Online*

"Any reader familiar with Radclyffe's writing will recognize the author's style within *The Midnight Hunt*, yet at the same time it is most definitely a new direction. The author delivers an excellent story here, one that is engrossing from the very beginning. Raand has pieced together an intricate world, and provided just enough details for the reader to become enmeshed in the new world. The action moves quickly throughout the book and it's hard to put down."—*Three Dollar Bill Reviews*

By Radclyffe

Romances

Innocent Hearts

Promising Hearts

Love's Melody Lost

Love's Tender Warriors

Tomorrow's Promise

Love's Masquerade

shadowland

Passion's Bright Fury

Fated Love

Turn Back Time

When Dreams Tremble

The Lonely Hearts Club

Night Call

Secrets in the Stone

Desire by Starlight

Crossroads

Homestead

The Color of Love

Secret Hearts

The Provincetown Tales

Safe Harbor

Beyond the Breakwater

Distant Shores, Silent Thunder

Storms of Change

Winds of Fortune

Returning Tides

Sheltering Dunes

Honor Series

Above All, Honor

Honor Bound

Love & Honor

Honor Guards

Honor Reclaimed

Honor Under Siege

Word of Honor

Code of Honor

Price of Honor

Justice Series

A Matter of Trust (prequel)

Shield of Justice

In Pursuit of Justice

Justice in the Shadows

Justice Served

Justice for All

Rivers Community Romances

Against Doctor's Orders

Prescription for Love

Love on Call

Love After Hours

Visit us at www.boldstrokesbooks.com

DANGEROUS WATERS

by

RADCLYffE

2018

DANGEROUS WATERS

ISBN 13: 978-1-63555-233-1

This Trade Paperback Original Is Published By
Bold Strokes Books, Inc.
P.O. Box 249
Valley Falls, NY 12185

First Edition: March 2018

CREDITS

EDITORS: RUTH STERNGLANTZ AND STACIA SEAMAN
PRODUCTION DESIGN: STACIA SEAMAN
COVER DESIGN BY SHERI

Acknowledgments

I am often asked where I get my story ideas, and I usually answer "from things I read in the news." Not every story I write is an action-adventure or intrigue story, though all my books are romances. Sometimes I'll read an article about the farm-to-table food movement or a study on the genetics of bird flu or the restoration of a priceless artifact, and a plot idea emerges. Then all I have to do is imagine the people involved and how they might find love in the process of solving the challenges inherent in the situation. Given the amazing response to the 2017 hurricanes in Texas and Florida by civilian and military first responders as well as ordinary citizens, I was instantly captivated and changed my upcoming publication schedule so I could write this book in the moment.

Many thanks go to: senior editor Sandy Lowe for her remarkable ability to adapt to my creative impulses and her excellent publishing expertise in support of BSB's authors and operations, editor Ruth Sternglantz for treating each book as if it were the only one on her desk, editor Stacia Seaman for an incredible job of putting this one together, and my first readers Paula and Eva for taking time out of their busy lives to send invaluable feedback. Sheri got just the right cover once again.

And as always, thanks to Lee for weathering all the storms. *Amo te*.

Radclyffe, 2018

To Lee, for every season

CHAPTER ONE

Landfall minus 10 days, 6:15 a.m.
National Hurricane Center Atlantic Ops
Florida International University, Miami, Florida

"How's the world looking this morning," Stan Oliver said as he hipped the door to the control room closed while juggling a big blue Mickey mug of coffee, a powdered jelly doughnut spewing white sprinkles on the scuffed, stained, baby-poop brown carpet, and a sheaf of printouts under his left arm. He'd almost made it to the desk he shared with the other two shift supervisors when half the stack slipped and followed the doughnut to the floor. "God damn it."

"When are you going to stop contributing to the extinction of what's left of the planet's forest cover and get a tablet like the rest of the world," Bette Jones said without turning from her trio of thirty-two-inch monitors. The muted light from the screens erased the lines around her mouth and eyes and filled out the hollows in her cheeks, giving her profile the flat perfection of a face stamped on an ancient coin.

Stan edged his mug onto the corner of the gray metal desk set perpendicular to the long row of computer banks, monitors, and communication arrays and scooped up the papers and doughnut. Dumping the pile in the middle of the desk, he settled into the chair and leaned back. "I'll start using one of those overpriced mini flat-screens as soon as someone figures out a way to scribble on one so it actually feels like writing. I think when I doodle."

Anjou Beck snickered from the adjoining station and, when Stan shot him a look, quickly bent his head over his keyboard, blue-green dyed forelock dancing above delicately arched blond eyebrows.

"Doodle," Stan repeated, "as in free-form design, coloring outside the lines, unleashing the power of the unconscious mind…"

"Doing science here," Bette said in her soft South Carolina drawl. "Facts, figures—"

"Uh-huh. Forecasting, computer modeling." Stan took a bite of doughnut and brushed crumbs from his red polo shirt with the NHC logo on the chest. "It's not all science. That's why they're called predictions."

Anjou sat up straight, his thin shoulders rigid in his plain white T-shirt, indignation coloring his pale Scandinavian cheeks a jaunty rose. "We're not witches, you know. Those forecasts are all based on billions of bytes of data and constantly refined, dynamic analyses."

"No argument." Stan propped a foot on the corner of the desk and sipped his coffee. The kid was a genius but could use a few years' seasoning to develop his instincts. Hurricane forecasting was more than just numbers and charts. "But never discount that squirmy feeling in your gut when you see something that just doesn't look right."

Bette laughed. "The udgies, you mean."

"Exactly. So…any squirmy udgies this a.m., you two?"

Anjou shook his head with a mumbled, "I don't believe you guys."

"Inez headed away from the coast an hour ago and wind speeds are dropping, just like we figured," Bette said. "New York will get some rain but not enough disturbance to cause any noticeable coastal surges."

"Good news for the UN meeting this week," Stan muttered around the last of his doughnut. He knew Inez had stormed herself out already, having logged in remotely to the research center's main tracking program at four a.m. as had been his habit for the last fifteen years, but his team didn't need to know that. He wasn't checking up on them, he was just starting his day with a clear picture of the winds and waters of the North Atlantic basin—his territory. Officially for the next eight hours or so, and twenty-four seven as far as he was concerned. Weather didn't follow a clock, and neither did he. His job was to be here, tracking the storms when they traveled. "Water temps, Atom Boy?"

"Still warm." Anjou stroked a few keys and a steadily climbing graphic appeared on his big screen. Surface temps had been rising for the last twenty years, and this year was no exception. "Too warm."

Stan grimaced. Hurricanes fed off the heat radiating from the ocean's surface. "Hot spots?"

"Nothing showing," Anjou replied.

Bette said, "Watch the coast of Africa today."

"Why?" Anjou switched screens rapidly, scanning air temp, wind speeds, ocean current graphs. "Can't see anything unusual."

"Got a feeling, Bette?" Stan asked softly.

"Mmm," she murmured. "Might talk to the hunters in a bit."

"Good idea." Stan noted the time and the key variables in their sector and programmed the satellite readouts for the far east Atlantic. Well out of range for anything likely to make it all the way to their side of the ocean, but he knew better than to ignore an udgie.

CHAPTER TWO

Landfall minus 10 days, 7:00 a.m.
Miami Memorial Hospital
Miami, Florida

Dara closed the PowerPoint slides and flicked on the conference room lights. Four eager faces, a fifth one barely awake, and the sixth unapologetically bored gazed back at her from the length of the conference table. "Questions?"

"I still don't see why we have to be able to identify poisonous snakes," Marco said with a hint of a whine. He flicked his shock of jet-black hair out of his eyes with an impatient gesture, managing to look put out and put-upon at the same time. "I'm not going to be practicing in the Everglades."

A couple of his colleagues grinned, and he laughed, enjoying the subtle applause.

Dara bit back her reflex reply: *Because I expect you to.*

Marco, who undoubtedly planned on working at one of the posh local private hospitals when he finished, was the oldest son of an influential Miami family and, like many of the sons and daughters of the privileged Dara had grown up with, hadn't yet cultivated a tolerance for frustration. Hard to do when you were used to every whim being instantly satisfied. Not his fault, really, and her job was to help him, and the rest of his group, learn to exchange arrogance for confidence in their own judgment.

"All right, let me show you why." Dara opened PowerPoint again, scrolled down to her ancillary slides, and selected one.

Kirk, the other male in the group—when had the gender ratio flipped and women begun to predominate in med schools across the country? Probably when men decided that medicine wasn't the prestigious career it used to be and definitely wasn't the most lucrative—grunted and said, "Nasty."

"Indeed," Dara said dryly. The foot in the middle of the slide was three times its normal size, fire-engine red with a hint of blue-black along the tips of all the toes, the skin peeling off in wet sheets. She picked out the resident who'd been half asleep during the lecture. "Suki, what's the pathology here?"

"Um." Suki cast wide eyes at her colleagues, barely hiding her desperation as she grasped for an answer. "Snakebite?"

"Good deduction, considering the topic for this morning's lecture was venomous bites. But that's the etiology, not the pathology."

Suki frowned, and Dara sighed inwardly.

"Anybody? The difference?"

"Cause and effect," Naomi, who'd graduated top of her class at Howard, answered quickly.

"Correct. The clinical signs resulted from the snakebite. So, Suki, want to try again?"

"Cellulitis?" she said with a hopeful lift in her voice.

"Correct. What else?" After a long silence, Suki had clearly exhausted her diagnostic acumen for the morning, and Dara shifted her focus to Consuela. "Thoughts?"

"The discoloration of her—or his—toes looks like ischemia. Early onset gangrene?"

"Good. Anyone want to venture what the cause of *that* might be?"

Six bodies shuffled in their seats.

"All right. Let's go around the table and list the causes of reduced blood flow to the lower extremity." Dara nodded to the resident on her left. "You're up first."

When she'd finally walked them through all the potential causes for toes falling off, they finally made their way to compartment syndrome, caused by swelling and inflammation from the poisonous snakebite.

"Good. Now, what antivenom should you use? Marco?"

Silence.

"There's no way to know," Kirk, who for some reason hid his

intelligence behind a perpetually bored facade, replied as if the effort was an annoyance.

"And why would that be?"

He met her gaze. "Because you don't know what the snake is."

Dara smiled. She'd been watching him since he'd first sauntered into the ER eight weeks earlier and hadn't needed long to decide he had the potential to be one of the best residents she'd trained in a long time. He underplayed his book smarts but couldn't conceal his innate clinical sensibility, something that couldn't be taught. If he wanted to cover up his native intelligence, she'd let him, as long as his practice lived up to his potential. She understood the need to wear a different public face when the private one left you vulnerable.

"What if the patient told you it was red, black, and yellow striped."

Suki shot up in her seat. "That's a coral snake!" She blushed and looked around. "I grew up down here."

Dara pointed a finger at her. "Exactly. And that's why all of you need to know what the indigenous poisonous species are in your area. With any luck, your patient will be able to describe for you what happened, and you can prescribe an antidote."

"Can't you just get somebody from infectious disease to do that?" Marco said.

Dara narrowed her eyes. "As long as you're in this residency program, you take care of the emergencies. If you need a consultant, it better be after you've made the appropriate diagnosis to begin with. All clear on that?"

Six heads nodded, even Kirk's.

Dara closed up her computer. "Okay, we're done, then. If you worked last night, get out of here. The rest of you, go grab charts."

As the residents filed out, the head ER nurse, and Dara's best friend, Penny slipped into the room.

"How are they doing?" Penny asked.

Dara sighed. "They seem to get younger and less prepared every year, but maybe that's just because I'm older and getting more tired every year."

"Yeah, like thirty-two is ancient." Penny scoffed. "Haven't you set the record for being the youngest section head ever or something like that?"

"Age is a state of mind," Dara muttered.

"Well, I'm about to make your morning even better. There's a Gold Coaster in room seven who insists on seeing an attending, and you're the only one free."

Dara gritted her teeth. Gold Coaster. Back in her residency days, she'd heard the term applied to herself when people thought she wasn't listening, as if her family's money somehow bought her a pass. Maybe it had in terms of getting into the college she wanted, which unfortunately also happened to be her father's alma mater, although she'd put her grades up against anyone's. Being a bona fide heiress—God, she hated that term—sure hadn't paved the way during her residency. If anything, training in Miami, where her family name showed up on buildings, parks, and even a road sign or two, made her life hellish. A couple of her attendings had obviously resented her presumed special status, and trying to have a personal life where her social connections didn't surface was impossible. Good thing she was too damn busy most of the time to care.

"Can you see her?" Penny prompted.

As much as she worked to distance herself from her family's reputation and the social network attached to it, she couldn't deny a patient the right to request an attending. She'd just bring a resident with her and insist they be involved in the care. "What is it?"

"A facial laceration, of course."

"And they're not requesting plastic surgery right off the bat?"

"We're trying to ward that off." Penny grinned sheepishly. "I might have suggested you were highly skilled with facial lacerations, could see her sooner, and wouldn't charge as much."

"Oh, thank you." Dara shook her head and tucked her computer under her arm. "All right, I'll be there in a couple of minutes."

"Thanks, you saved me one headache."

"How are you feeling?"

Penny made a wry face and patted her stomach. "I'm gonna have two in diapers when this one comes along. Of course I'm ecstatic."

Dara knew she meant it. Some people were born to be parents. "How about Sampson? Is he ready for the double dose of daddyhood?"

Penny rolled her deep-brown eyes in an expression of fond exasperation. "We were really happy when Evie came along, kind of unexpectedly after, you know, six years of trying and a year of considering other options, and then poof! It's like somehow we unlocked the fertility vault, and without even trying, number two is on the way. Sam has been marching around with a puffed-out chest like he's the father of the year."

Dara laughed. "If your BP gives you any problems this time, I want to know about it."

"Believe me, you'll be the first to hear." Penny waved and hurried back to the central station.

Dara exchanged her computer for her tablet and joined Vincie Duval, the chief ER resident, who leaned against the counter entering notes into a laptop. Taller than Dara by a few inches and willowy where Dara was slender at best, Vincie was a top candidate to join the ER staff at the end of the residency year if she wanted. So far she'd been quiet about her plans. Vincie's parents had immigrated from Guadeloupe when Vincie, the oldest of four, was only six. Her father had died on a fishing boat lost at sea, and she'd grown up helping to raise her sibs. If she wanted to take a job closer to her family, Dara could understand. She'd ended up staying close too, although their stories couldn't be further apart. She shrugged the past away with the realities of the moment, a habit that was second nature now. "Got a minute to see a patient who might need sutures?"

"Sure." Vincie's perennially smiling light-green eyes brightened, complementing her smooth, tawny complexion. With her boundless energy and effortless beauty—if she wore any makeup it was too expertly applied for Dara to tell—Vincie somehow always managed to look ready to take on anything.

If she'd ever been that optimistic, Dara couldn't remember when. Sometimes Vincie's enthusiasm made her feel decades older than she was. Granted, her blond hair, naturally tanned coloring, and blue eyes gave her a perpetual south Florida beach glow even without trying, but inside she was weary. And she really didn't have time for that, today or any other time. Dara pulled up the intake form on her tablet and held open the curtain enclosing cubicle seven for Vincie. Once inside, she stepped to the bedside of an elderly woman propped up on the stretcher, a small square of gauze taped to her forehead and a bruise purpling her left upper lid. She wore a red cardigan that looked like cashmere over a mismatched, incongruous stained yellow T-shirt along with an imperious expression.

"Who are you?" she demanded querulously.

"Ms. Hastings?" Dara held out her hand. "I'm Dr. Sims, and this is Dr.—"

"Finally." The woman dismissed Vincie with barely a glance and glared at Dara. "I asked for one of the attending physicians, and I don't want to see a resident."

Dara kept her smile in place. "I am one of the attendings, and this is Dr. Duval, one of our senior in-house physicians. Can you tell us what happened?"

The woman plucked at the hem of her sweater and, after a second, waved a hand toward the tablet. "I'm sure it's all in there. I already told several people."

"Perhaps you could tell me again," Dara said.

"What did you say your name was again?"

"Dr. Dara Sims."

"Sims. Sims." The elderly woman—her intake form put her at seventy-four—frowned. "Any relationship to Barrister Sims?"

An ache started at the back of Dara's head. She could ignore the question or, in the interest of time, simply answer. She surrendered, at least partially. Barrister did not deserve a mention. "Priscilla Sims is my mother."

"Oh," the woman said, her expression softening. "Well, then, I suppose it's all right."

Dara nodded, feeling her smile begin to slip. "Can you tell us what happened," she asked again as she pulled on gloves and removed the gauze. The laceration was superficial, and she glanced over her shoulder at Vincie. "What do you think?"

"I can clean it up and Steri-Strip it."

Dara nodded and replaced the gauze. "How did this happen?"

"I…I…the maid or someone must have moved a footstool. Careless of them."

"I see." Something in the woman's tone tugged at Dara's memory. The familiar *oh, it's nothing, I'm just busy* she'd heard from her grandmother so many times as her memory and awareness had begun to slip away. "Did you experience any dizziness or loss of balance before you fell?"

The patient's gaze flickered away. "No."

"Light-headedness, chest pain?"

"No, no." Another hand wave. "Oh, perhaps I was dizzy for a second."

Dara asked a few more questions as she examined her, noting how Ms. Hasting's answers changed when Dara repeated some of the same questions. She wasn't sure if the patient was being intentionally evasive or really couldn't remember.

"How did you get here?" Dara asked.

"I had the doorman call a car."

"Good," Dara said. "The laceration isn't bad, and I don't think you need sutures. While we set up to put some Steri-Strips on that, I'd like to get an MRI."

"All right," she said, strangely acquiescent.

"We'll be right back." Dara motioned for Vincie to follow her into the hall. "What do you think?"

"She's definitely confused," Vincie said. "Maybe as a result of the fall, but possibly something else is going on that caused it to begin with."

"I know. The MRI will rule out anything physical. Let's find out who's with her from her family, and if there's no one here, let's get someone. She shouldn't go home alone."

"I'll take care of it."

"Call me when you get the MRI results."

"Got it."

Dara headed for the workstation to check on the charts of patients waiting to be seen. When the clerk saw her coming, he held up the phone.

"There's a call for you, Dr. Sims," he said. "I was just about to page you."

"Who is it?"

"Brian from Shoreline Residential."

Dara's heart jumped and she held out her hand. "I'll take it, thanks. This is Dara, Brian. Is something wrong?"

"I'm sorry to bother you, Dara, but your grandmother is asking for you."

Dara checked her watch. "I'll be there as soon as I can. I just have to get things covered here."

"Sure thing. I'll be here."

Dara hung up and swung around. Penny was right behind her. "Hey, I need to leave for a while."

"I heard." Penny squeezed her arm. "Go. Everything here is under control. I'll call if anything changes."

"I won't be long," Dara said.

If she was in time at all.

Landfall minus 10 days, 1:30 p.m.
Roc Hotel
Miami Beach, Florida

"Morning, Harry." Sawyer slid onto a stool at the thatch-topped cabana next to the pool outside her room. She braced herself against the hundredth round of Jimmy Buffett singing about the mythical Margaritaville of some long-ago endless summer.

"The usual?" Harry asked.

Man, had she really had enough to drink in two days to have developed a *usual*? She squinted in the glare from the water and tried to picture where she'd left her shades. Bedside table, where she would have placed her weapon if she'd been on duty. Getting sloppy now that no one was likely to be shooting at her. "Hold the vodka this morning. Just make it hot and spicy, though."

"Like your women, huh?" Harry the bartender's sun-leathered skin crinkled around his watery blue eyes as he winked and reached for the Stoli. He waggled the bottle. "You should take the hair of the dog. Start your day off right."

Sawyer smothered a wince. Harry was wrong on several counts, but a lesson in PC-terminology was beyond her at the moment. She needed a headache remedy, true, but hair of the dog was definitely not on the menu. If she'd been enough of a drinker to handle the vodka, she wouldn't have a hangover to begin with. "Just the juice, thanks, Harry."

"You know best," he said dubiously. "I saw your blondie friend come down for a swim this morning. You don't like the beach?"

"I like it fine." Sawyer passed him a ten and palmed the sweating glass. The celery fronds drooped over the top, looking about as lively as she felt. She pushed them aside, sipped the blood-red juice, and coughed when the horseradish hit the back of her throat. She blinked tears from her eyes. "Just not before noon."

He laughed. "Late night."

"Catching up." She was only two days into her fourteen-day leave, and last night had been the first night in a year she'd said more than ten words to a woman who wasn't her best friend's wife, her CO, or her barista. Not for lack of poolside company, true, and Harry clearly had noticed the traffic to her table. But talking was not doing—at least not in her book, and she'd heard enough bragging on supposed sexcapades in mess halls and Humvees to know the difference. Last night had ended after a round of drinks in her room with Bridget from Brussels, an abbreviated make-out session she hadn't even been sure she wanted and hadn't initiated, and a hasty apology when she'd bowed out of anything more intimate. Bridget had taken the rebuff with a shrug and an air-kiss before sashaying back out to poolside. No doubt to have better company before too long.

Alone under a clear, star-studded sky, Sawyer'd stretched out in the lounge on the postage-stamp-sized patio and finished her drink and one more she really didn't need. Thus explaining waking up at noon with a crick in her neck, a tracer barrage of too-bright sun lighting up the insides of her eyelids when she tried to open them, and a deuce of 50 mm's pounding away at her cerebellum. In civilian terms, a mother of a hangover.

Stateside for less than a month and pathetically out of practice in more ways than one. Well, she had twelve more days to catch up on living in a non-war zone before the next round of reservists arrived for training on the HH-60s. Coordinating pararescue team maneuvers on the Pave Hawks wouldn't leave her much time to think about what shape her future was going to take now that she was home. Of course, she might get deployed again, and that would solve all her problems. True.

CHAPTER THREE

Landfall minus 10 days, 2:00 p.m.
Shoreline Residential Center
Miami, Florida

"How is Priscilla?" Caroline Sims asked as she carefully straightened the blanket over her lap. The typical September Miami day edged into the mid-eighties, but she wore a pale-rose crocheted shawl around her shoulders over a faded blue dress with small white pearl buttons down the center. Her white hair was recently permed in the nondescript style of so many women her age, a style Dara knew for certain her grandmother would have hated if she'd been aware of it. The dress was hopelessly out of date as well, but one of the few items her grandmother still recognized.

Dara remembered the day a decade before when she and the housekeeper had spent a frantic two hours searching for that dress while her grandmother verged on the brink of a full-blown anxiety attack, only to find it neatly folded in one of the boxes her grandmother had marked for the handyman to take to the Goodwill. No amount of explanation could convince Caroline that the housekeeper or some other member of the help staff hadn't put it there. By then, she'd been forgetting more and more, and Dara had finally been forced to consider options for the future and what would be needed to keep her safe. The task fell to her, since her mother just couldn't cope, and there was no one else, was there.

Now the dress, laundered dozens of times since, was a faded

reminder of the woman Caroline used to be, even though right at this moment, her eyes were clear and focused outward.

"She's fine, Grandmom. Busy," Dara said, searching madly for something to say about her mother. "You know, with so many of her humanitarian organizations."

Charity had lost its political correctness, even though Dara suspected that's what her mother considered anything that truly benefited those beneath her social status.

"Well, your sister always did like helping others," Caroline said.

"She's my mom," Dara said gently. Her grandmother's social worker had suggested this was a safe correction when her grandmother was lucid but still a little confused.

Caroline frowned. "Of course, I know that. Barrister's wife." She smiled. "And you're my favorite granddaughter."

Also, the only granddaughter, but Dara just reached out and took her grandmother's hand, happy to have her nearby for a few minutes. "Have you been outside for a walk lately? It's getting cool enough in the afternoons now, and I know how much you like the flowers."

Caroline nodded. "Yes, thank you for reminding me. I must tell the gardener to trim the roses. They're getting so leggy."

"You know," Dara continued gamely, "there are roses along the path. I'm sure Brian will be happy to walk with you."

"Brian. Oh, of course. He always was such an attentive son."

Dara couldn't bring herself to correct her, since thinking about her father—correction, *Barrister*—brought up too much anger. Anger she really should've let go of a long time ago and told herself she would every time the flush of old resentments rose within her. Twenty years was a long time to harbor feelings that were perfectly appropriate for a twelve-year-old, she'd told herself more than once. So what if he'd walked out, left them, started another life and another family. In his eyes, he'd always done his duty, being sure the family had everything money could buy.

"Brian is your nurse," Dara said. "The African American guy who helps you get to the dining room and your group sessions?"

"Of course, Brian." Caroline's face brightened. "But I think you're confused, darling. He's not the nurse. I'm quite sure he's the attorney."

"Would you like to go outside now?"

Caroline was quiet for a long moment, her gaze slowly drawing away, pulling back from Dara's. She shifted to glance out the window that looked onto the acres of lawn and gardens and trees behind the residence, the walkways carefully maintained so the elderly or the less than able could manage them on foot or in a wheelchair.

"I do so wish Barrister wasn't so busy," Caroline whispered. "I'm sure he'd come by more often, if he could."

Dara swallowed hard. Barrister had stopped *coming by* the moment he'd walked out the door. His checks and the dividends from the family businesses continued to flow into her trust and her mother's accounts, but his attention—the one commodity of his she'd truly longed for and never been able to capture—had gone elsewhere. A new wife, eventually a new family. Half siblings she never knew.

"I'm sure you're right," Dara said around the silent screams choking her.

Her grandmother focused on her again. "I'm so glad you decided to visit. You will come again, when I'm not so busy, won't you?"

"Of course I will." Dara kissed her cheek. "I'll see you again soon."

Her grandmother smiled, the smile she'd cultivated over years in polite society, the one she aimed at those whose faces and names she would forget as soon as she turned away.

Landfall minus 10 days, 4:30 p.m.
Roc Hotel
Miami Beach, Florida

Sawyer jolted up in bed, the sheets a tangle around her bare feet, the room a dull yellow, the air a heavy coat of grit and sweat on her skin. She'd drawn the beige floor-to-ceiling curtains across the double sliding glass doors to block out the relentless sun, the glimmering white sands, the insistent bludgeoning brightness of the holiday beach.

She couldn't quite capture the dream flickering at the edges of memory, not that she wanted to. She'd stopped dreaming somewhere in the middle of her last year in Africa. The heat, the blazing sun, the ever-present thump of ordnance in the dark had scorched the possibilities from her unconscious. Dreams were things that existed in the daylight, and only nightmares ruled the dark. Fortunately, she'd driven both away, and if the price was random stretches of near coma masquerading as sleep that didn't haunt her while awake, she was willing to pay.

She rubbed both hands over her face and through her sweat-damp hair. She needed a haircut—the back was going to hit a good inch below her collar soon. She could probably get by until she headed back to base, though. She had plenty of time—too much time. She looked at the clock. Three hours gone. She'd only intended to stretch out for a few minutes after her shower, but her body had had other ideas. At least her head wasn't pounding any longer. Still a little fuzzy, but nothing she wasn't used to. Dehydration was a familiar companion. Absently grabbing the bottled water from the bedside table, she downed half of it and checked her phone with the other hand.

As she expected, all the messages were work related: internal memos from central command, updates on regs, squad movements, activation orders, changes in schedule. Halfway down, she saw a rare personal header.

Rambo@gmail.com
How is the sun?

Smiling, she swiped to view.

Hey, Bones. How's the beach? How are the babes??
Getting anything? I mean, relaxation wise :-) :-) :-)
R
PS #2 is on the way!

Grinning, Sawyer hit Reply and typed:

Water's great, getting lots of sleep, having a great time. Congrats, what's your hurry?
B

She hit Send and leaned back on the pillows. Rambo, aka Ralph Beauregard, was about the best friend she had in the world. They'd gone through Guard ROTC in college together, ended up in the same battalion group, and deployed together. They'd both gone active Guard together too, and now he was her counterpart in supplies and acquisitions. He kept troops fed and clothed—and armed when necessary. He also kept her search and rescue teams outfitted with the latest gear and medevac supplies.

Just seeing his name made her miss the squad. Why'd she ever think a leave with nothing to do except not think about where she'd been or what lay ahead was a good idea?

The twelve days in front of her stretched longer than twelve months in the field ever had.

Landfall minus 9.5 days, 6:15 p.m.
National Hurricane Center Atlantic Ops
Florida International University, Miami, Florida

"Hey," the tech at the big screen said to the room in general, "something's cooking out there."

The evening supervisor walked over and scanned the readouts. "Huh. Wind speed above that wave formation has doubled in the last hour."

"Yeah, and the water temp's still high."

"Could be something forming," the supervisor said. "Let's send out a watch notice. I'll pull up the list of names."

"Pretty far out there," the meteorologist said.

The supervisor nodded, still watching the patterns swirl and coalesce. "Yeah, probably nothing to worry about."

CHAPTER FOUR

Landfall minus 8 days, 3:05 a.m.
National Hurricane Center Atlantic Ops
Florida International University, Miami, Florida

NOAA Hurricane Advisory
Tropical Depression Leo
12:00 a.m. AST
Location: *12°N 32°W*
Moving: *NNW at 20 mph*
Min pressure: *980 mb*
Max sustained: *35 mph*

Stan Oliver cleared his throat as he swiped his phone off the stand beside the bed, his thumb automatically repeating the action to take the call. Next to him, his wife mumbled, "Let the dog out," and rolled over, sound asleep again before Stan could mutter hoarsely, "Hello?"

"Sorry to wake you, Stan. You said you wanted to be notified—"

"No problem." Stan was operations chief at the NHC, and the only reason he still took shifts on the floor was because he liked it. He liked seeing his people at work, and he liked watching the patterns of wind and rain and life moving over the vast surface of the Earth, reminding them all—at least all of them who paid any attention—of just how very insignificant they all were, and how much they owed the planet for tolerating their presence.

"Jonas change course, did he?" Stan sat up on the side of the bed and cupped the phone in his palm, although Anna gave no sign of hearing him. They'd been tracking Hurricane Jonas, a Cat 1, who'd been heading into open water in the Gulf as it lost power throughout the evening. He'd checked on him just before he'd gone to bed a little before midnight, and he'd shown no signs of rebuilding, as sometimes happened when the speed dropped over warm waters. Inez had long since been downgraded to storm status and no longer threatened the East Coast. Unusual, to have two so close together. Ten named storms, with six progressing to hurricanes, was about average for the whole season, but it was peak week in peak season, and weather was changeable. That was a fact that never altered.

"Not Jonas—Leo. He's showing rapid intensification. Speeds have increased twenty knots in the last four hours." Claire Donahue was a seasoned meteorologist, and the faint rise in her voice hinted at excitement only someone who knew her well would pick up.

Stan heard it. An increase in speed that quickly was the hallmark of a powerful storm forming. "Is he looking like a Cape Verde event?"

Cape Verde storms formed just off the coast of Africa and the Cabo islands, and if they managed to track all the way across the Atlantic, often became the big storms—the monster storms. The hurricanes that literally rained down death and destruction to hundreds.

"He's already as big as Hugo was, with half the time forming." Claire paused. "If he keeps moving this way and the currents stay hot, he's going to be bigger than anything we've ever seen."

"I'm coming in."

Landfall minus 7 days, 8:45 a.m.

NOAA Hurricane Advisory
Tropical Storm Leo has been upgraded to a Category 3 hurricane. Five-day, tropical-storm-force wind probabilities of 90 mph winds are projected over an area ranging from the Caribbean to the mid-Atlantic United States.

Landfall minus 7 days, 4:45 p.m.
Roc Hotel
Miami Beach, Florida

Sawyer stroked underwater, her lungs just starting to burn when she hit the far end of the fifty-foot pool. A hundred laps, all of it submerged except for a breath at each turn. After the first half mile her mind emptied, even as every other sense heightened. Shadows rippled on the surface—bodies moving across the steaming patio tiles; turbulence to her left—a swimmer making a clumsy dive; a distant hum—music, not incoming. She wasn't alone anywhere, and she could never let down her guard.

When she surfaced in the deep end of the pool, she let her momentum carry her up and out, slapped both hands flat on the surround, and tucked her legs. She straight-armed into a push-up, knifed her body over the side onto the deck, and vaulted to her feet. Flinging water and tendrils of black hair from her eyes with a quick shake, she quickly focused to check her position. All clear.

She stretched, welcoming the subtle buzz of adrenaline and the undercurrent of restored control. No more alcohol, a reasonable five hours of sleep the night before, and two good meals a day put her back on an even keel. Two miles in the pool had even started to work off a lot of the nervous energy she couldn't seem to burn off anywhere else. Weren't vacations supposed to be relaxing?

Maybe they were, for most people, but not for someone who'd been in near-constant physical motion all her adult life, and the bulk of that time in mortal danger. Sitting still, even to read a book, which she'd done plenty of while deployed, was a trial.

"Very, very nice," a deep sultry voice said from behind and to her right, accompanied by soft clapping.

Sawyer pulled up a mental snapshot of the terrain even as she turned. A lone sunbather, midforties, blond, bronzed, and toned, in a white two-piece that revealed a whole lot more than it covered up.

The woman smiled slowly, removing designer shades to reveal sharp green eyes. A shapely arm encircled with a pricey-looking gold link bracelet held out a snowy white towel in Sawyer's direction. "I almost hate to cover up the scenery."

Sawyer took the towel and riffled it over her hair, letting it dangle in her right hand when she was done. The blonde surveyed her with frank interest. Sawyer hadn't worn a conventional bathing suit, just a sports top and tight black jogging shorts, which covered about as much as the cutoff T-shirts and shorts she was used to wearing in the desert for the endless days they waited for orders to move out. She'd gotten used to *not* being looked at. The brutal heat, constant stress, and insidious boredom went a long way toward dispelling physical interest. Her stomach tightened in a wholly unexpected way as the woman's gaze moved over her bare shoulders, down her nearly bare torso, lingering for a few seconds on her midsection, before slipping farther down.

"What is it exactly that you do to get a body like that?" the woman asked.

"Not a thing," Sawyer said. "Good genes."

The woman laughed and lifted a martini glass with two olives rolling in the bottom. She gestured to a lounge chair beside her. "Join me?"

"Thanks, but I gave it up."

"Drinking, or fucking?"

Sawyer glanced around, but no one seemed to be paying any attention to them. She grinned. "The first, although it's a little early in the day for the second too."

The woman tipped back her head and laughed. "Now I know you're lying." Her lips lifted in slow invitation. "I'm Catherine Winchell. I'm sure you've never heard of me, which is just as well, considering the circumstances. And who might you be?"

Sawyer strode closer, folded the towel, and set it on the chair next to Catherine. "Sawyer Kincaid."

"And what are you doing here? You don't have the look of a beach bum, and I don't see the wife and kids anywhere."

"None of the above. Just a somewhat reluctant vacationer."

"I can see that. Maybe you should learn to relax a little more. Sawyer."

Sawyer nodded. "You're right, and I appreciate the advice."

Catherine sipped her drink. "If you don't want to be propositioned, you probably should cover up those abs. I don't think I've ever seen a body like yours before."

"Uh...thanks."

Catherine laughed again. "If you change your mind, I'm in 742." Sawyer gave a slight nod. "I'm a whole lot more than flattered—"

"You don't need to be flattered, you just need to be good."

Sawyer was searching for an answer to that one when one of the pool waitstaff came toward her holding out a portable phone. "Colonel Kincaid?"

Sawyer unintentionally straightened. "Yes?"

Out of the corner of her eye, she could see Catherine sit up a little, her expression turning hawk-like, avid, as if she suddenly sensed prey.

"Emergency call for you...uh...Colonel...sir?"

"Thanks." Sawyer held out her hand for the phone. "This is Colonel Kincaid."

"Sawyer, sorry to interrupt your leave," General Jim Baker said.

"No problem, General," Sawyer said, turning her back and walking to the far side of the pool, out of hearing range of the few remaining people who hadn't gone inside to start preparing for the dinner hour. "How can I help you, sir?"

"NOAA just sent out another updated hurricane advisory. Big storm coming, and the governor has ordered us to mobilize. I want you to take ground command."

"Yes, sir. I'll be there in four hours."

"Driving?"

"Yes, sir. From Miami Beach."

"Why don't you head on out to MIA. We'll send a bird for you."

"Yes, sir."

"See you at the briefing."

"Yes, sir." Sawyer blew out a breath and glanced out toward the ocean. The sky was a gorgeous aquamarine over water almost the same color blue, with playful gulls circling above lacy froth-tipped waves, and dozens of oblivious vacationers scattered along the immaculate beach in colorful cabanas. Unsuspecting, unwary, and possibly in mortal danger. In the Keys, on islands, in cities along the coast, the same picture unfolded. Battles came in many guises.

The boredom, the aimlessness, the uncertainty of purpose fell away and Sawyer knew exactly who she was and what she was about. She strode back around the pool, and as she passed Catherine Winchell's chair, the woman called out.

"Colonel Kincaid, is it?"

Sawyer looked back. "Just Sawyer at the moment."

"Anything you care to share?"

"I'm afraid not."

Catherine rose and walked beside her as Sawyer continued toward her room. "You don't watch much television, do you?"

"Not really." Sawyer paused on her patio by the sliding glass doors. "I'm sorry, I'm a little short on time."

"I can see that. That's why I'm curious." Catherine dug in the colorful straw satchel she'd slung over her shoulder and held out a card. "Channel 10 News, Miami bureau."

Sawyer did not take the card. "Now I'm really short on time."

Catherine laughed and tucked the card delicately under the waistband of Sawyer's shorts. "I can be a good person to know."

"I don't doubt it. But I'm not the person you want to talk to you. We have a media representative, if and when there's anything to talk about. I'm sure your station will have the number."

"I'm sure one of these days we'll see each other again."

"It was nice talking to you, Ms. Winchell." Sawyer nodded and slid open the door.

"You never mentioned what branch of the military," Catherine called after her.

Sawyer smiled and shut the door, letting the heavy drapes fall closed behind her. Catherine Winchell was as persistent as she was beautiful and, if Sawyer wasn't mistaken, used to getting what she wanted. The only safe play with a woman like that was no play at all. As she pulled her duffel from the closet, her stomach tightened with an undeniable twinge of regret.

Landfall minus 6.5 days, 7:45 p.m.
Ocean Drive, South Beach
Miami Beach, Florida

Dara's cell rang as she let herself into her condo. From the door she could see across the open-floor living space to the balcony and the ocean beyond. She still had enough daylight left for a run if she hurried. She could be on the beach in two minutes once she hit Ocean Drive. Hurriedly she dug out her phone from her backpack and checked the readout. Private number. Her pent-up breath escaped. Not the hospital. "Hello?"

"Dr. Sims?"

Dara winced. Celebrated too soon. She vaguely recognized the voice but couldn't quite place it. "Yes?"

"Sorry to bother you at home. This is Victor Sanchez."

"Of course, how can I help you, Mr. Sanchez." She'd heard the hospital CEO speak enough times at staff meetings, but she didn't really spend a lot of time with the administrators. They were budget and protocol people, and she mostly wasn't. Sure, she had to deal with the financial end of things to keep the ER running, but fortunately, the medical chief of staff bore the brunt of that. As to procedure and protocol, if it didn't affect patient care, she left that to management to manage.

"You couldn't be reached, so the call got handed up to me." He chuckled. "And I am sending it back to you."

Dara glanced at her phone and saw there was a missed call. "Sorry, I was driving. I put my phone on Do Not Disturb when I'm in the car."

"Very wise of you. We've been alerted there is a statewide hurricane alert. Nothing critical at the moment, but since you're the head of the hospital's emergency response team, I thought you'd want to know sooner rather than later."

"Of course. I'll check my mail—I should automatically get an update from the state."

"Well, it is the season for these things, and I'm sure it will turn out to be nothing much."

Dara rolled her eyes. In her line of work, nothing was nothing to worry about until she was absolutely certain every possibility had been considered.

"Just be sure to keep me apprised," he said, already sounding as if he'd dispensed with thinking about the potential problem.

"I certainly will," Dara said. "Thanks. I'm sorry you were bothered."

"No trouble at all, Doctor. You have a nice night."

Dara switched to her mail program. The last message had come in just after she'd left work. An advisory from the state emergency response division alerting all level one trauma centers of an impending weather event. She scanned the details. A hurricane warning, apparently a big enough storm to warrant enhanced readiness, but still a good week away. She quickly typed a memo to the other members of the hospital emergency management team for a morning meeting and sent it out. She could already hear the complaints about a seven a.m. meeting, but that was the only way to get everyone together at such short notice. Maybe by morning, the threat level would've been downgraded, and she could cancel the meeting. These kinds of alerts were common this time of year.

Shedding her clothes as she hurried to the bedroom, she put thoughts of hurricanes aside. If she was lucky, she could still get in a decent run.

CHAPTER FIVE

Landfall minus 6 days, 5:55 a.m.
Florida National Guard, Joint Training Center
Camp Blanding, Florida

Sawyer rounded the corner to the briefing room just as Rambo approached from the opposite direction.

"Sorry about the vacation, Bones." Rambo's mildly sarcastic tone told her he knew damn well she was happy to be back. Maybe he was being just a little bit critical too. He mostly gave her the space she demanded, even from a friend, but every now and then he slipped in a gibe that maybe she could do with a little more fun and less work.

She let his needling pass, because when it counted, he'd always been there for her. When her mom died, when her family scattered at last, as if the glue holding them all together had finally hardened to dust along with her, he'd been the one to stand with her at the graveside and watch her sisters and brothers begin to drift away on the wind. He'd been the one to invite her home for a meal, and to his wedding, and to the baptism of his first child. He never pushed, but he was always there.

"How's Miko?" Sawyer asked, knowing exactly how to divert the conversation from herself.

His smile broadened, joy tingeing his creamy tan skin an unexpected and oddly beautiful rose. "Gorgeous as ever. She seems to get prettier every time she's pregnant."

"I don't think you should mention that around her. It sounds a little—" She waggled her hand.

"Macho?"

"That might be one word for it." She pushed the door to the briefing room open and let him pass by. "Tell her hello from me."

"You're overdue for barbecue."

"Uh-huh."

He didn't have a chance to bug her further. The rows of chairs facing the big screen at the far end of the long, narrow room were half full, and a dozen troops followed them in and shuffled to seats. She and Rambo settled in the first row, as was customary for the ranking officers.

She nodded to the wing commanders, who flew aerial surveillance, and her squad, the Pave Hawk helo pilots who flew combat search and rescue when deployed, and when at home, civil SAR, EVAC, and disaster relief.

"Attention!" a deep male voice commanded from the back of the room and everyone shot to their feet.

Brigadier General Jim Baker, commander of the Florida National Guard, strode to the front of the room at precisely 0600 accompanied by another officer. Sawyer had served under him for most of her ten years in the active Guard, at home and abroad. In his midfifties, he was still sandy haired and in fighting trim. He had the well-earned rep of being a boots on the ground leader. She respected and trusted him, and when he'd pushed her to go full-time active Guard, she'd found a home she could count on.

"As you were," Baker said, and everyone sat.

The screen behind him lit up with a map of the eastern United States, the Caribbean, and a portion of the Atlantic Ocean. Red circles, stacked like poker chips spread across blue-green felt, trailed across the ocean toward the islands south of the continental US. As the circles closed in on land, streamers spread out like tails on a whip, fanning out into dozens of lines headed toward the islands scattered in the Caribbean and the Florida Keys. Some drifted off into the Gulf of Mexico and others turned northeast away from the coast. The majority, however, ended up over land, stretching on a path from New Orleans to North Carolina. Baker fixed a laser pointer on one of the circles in the middle of the ocean marked with a time stamp. "This the last location of Hurricane Leo's eyewall. It's too early to tell for sure where he's headed from here." The red light danced over the many paths headed for inhabited areas. "Right now, the computer models show these as the likely paths."

"That's helpful," Rambo muttered.

"What we *can* be sure of," Baker continued, ignoring similar comments from around the room as he focused the pointer on Florida, "is he's going to hit land with a seriously big punch."

Baker handed the pointer to the officer by his side. "Major Kim is with the 53rd Weather Reconnaissance Squad and has just come back from a data-gathering mission. I'll let her fill you in on the details."

"Thank you, sir." Kim stepped forward. "The storm front is massive just in terms of sheer size. The biggest formation we've ever tracked. Added to that, the water and wind conditions are optimal for an acceleration of wind speed, which we've been seeing in the last twelve hours." She circled the Florida Keys and moved north to the tip of the mainland. "No matter how Leo tracks in the next five to six days, the Keys are likely to get a shellacking. We can expect twelve- to fifteen-foot storm surge in addition to high winds there and, if Leo makes landfall over the state, along the coasts. Because of his size, both coasts will likely be affected."

"Thank you, Major," the general said. "This could be the most devastating storm to hit this region since Andrew."

Sawyer's chest tightened and icy cold slithered through her gut. Anyone who lived in a hurricane region had weathered more than one episode of nature's fury, but there hadn't been anything as lethal as Andrew in twenty-five years. Images of torn sheet metal flying through the air like deadly scimitars, trailer homes crushed like soda cans and impaled by uprooted trees honed to lethal spear points, raging rivers of muddy water carrying everything—everyone—in their paths away. Sweat soaked the back of her shirt, and she shivered.

Baker focused on Sawyer, and the effect was like a jolt of electricity, burning the haze from her brain. She shuddered, shaking off the memories. She'd lived through it, lived through some things just as bad. She'd been a kid then, and she hadn't been in charge. She would be now.

If the general noticed her reaction, he didn't show it. "The governor's Emergency Management Division has designated Miami Memorial the medical op center. Colonel Kincaid will have overall operational command of SAR and relief preparedness, including coordinating the local emergency medical response and liaising with naval Fleet Command, which is moving a carrier into range." He looked to Rambo. "Colonel Beauregard will command supply disbursement. Questions?"

"What's the chance of a mass civilian evac?" Sawyer asked.

"The governor is waiting for a clearer indication of the storm's direction."

"Thank you, sir." After dozens of briefings like this one, Sawyer was adept at reading the unspoken messages from her superiors. Baker was a master at hiding his opinion of civilian authority, but his tone suggested *he* would have made a decision by now.

With the Guard fully mobilized, Sawyer could disperse troops into high-risk areas quickly, but she'd seen firsthand how difficult moving civilians en masse could be. Delay could be deadly. She also knew the Guard served at the pleasure of the civilian authorities, and all she could do was her job. Part of that was anticipating the next crisis and averting casualties, and she intended to do that even if she had to sidestep a little red tape or bruise a few civilian egos.

Baker's adjutant dismissed the room and Sawyer rose with the others. Her second priority after evacuating threatened communities was ensuring medical response was at full capacity. Six days might be plenty of time to gear up emergency relief centers under Guard supervision, but the readiness of the civilian medical center was an open question. A question she'd need answered as quickly as possible.

Sawyer said to Rambo as they walked out, "Let me know where you'll be setting up your main supply center."

"I'm thinking Orlando," Rambo said. "You heading south?"

"Yeah," Sawyer said. "Miami seems the most reasonable central staging point until we know where we can safely set up relief centers."

"I'll copy you in on supply assessments by end of day." He hesitated. "You okay?"

Sawyer frowned. "What? Why?"

"I don't know—I thought for a second there you looked spooked."

"I'm fine." Her tone shut him down, and he nodded silently.

"You planning to run the medical response from Miami Memorial?"

Sawyer laughed. "I wish I could. I'll have to let them think they're in charge."

Rambo grinned. "They'll probably be happy to hand you the ball. And the paperwork."

Sawyer only wished it was going to be that simple.

Landfall minus 6 days, 7:00 a.m.
Miami Memorial Hospital

"I think everyone's here," Dara said, sitting down at the head of the table with the takeout cup of coffee she'd grabbed from the kiosk down the block from the front entrance on her way in. She needed the extra caffeine this morning. The Cuban espresso she'd picked up in the drive-through coffee place on her way to work hadn't quite gotten her up to speed. The run she'd managed to squeeze in the night before hadn't helped de-stress her the way it usually did after a long day, and she'd awakened in the middle of the night thinking about all the things she needed to do thanks to Victor's call. Waiting until morning to get started had seemed like a good idea the night before, but if she was going to lie awake all night planning, she probably should have contacted some of the key people personally. Fortunately, the NHC weather update hadn't changed much from what she'd gotten last night. The predictions were still grave, but the situation was still developing and changing hour to hour.

She double-checked the roster—pharmacy, OR, trauma, ICU, and of course, the other side of the coin, legal and finance. All accounted for. "This shouldn't take too long. Thank you all for getting here on such short notice and at such an early hour."

The trauma chief, Wen Haruke, shrugged. "It's late for me."

Dara was used to Wen's cavalier attitude, and compared to some of the trauma jocks she worked with, he was on the mild-mannered side and more affable than most. "Not to worry, Wen. We'll get you upstairs in plenty of time for your eight a.m. start."

"Where do things stand with the governor?" asked Gretchen Baylor, the hospital's lead attorney, before Dara could provide any background. "Are we officially instituting emergency protocols now, or is this just a heads-up?"

"Yes," Anthony Elliott from finance, put in. "Let's not spend money we don't need to if this is all going to blow over in another day or two." A few people groaned and Anthony grinned. "No pun intended, of course."

"As you're all aware from the email I sent last night, the latest weather advisory from NHC has upgraded Leo to a Cat 3," Dara said. "The predictive models put the Keys and possibly parts of southern Florida in the red zone. I think we have to assume we'll see transfers from hospitals in the storm track as well as acute storm-associated injuries."

Anthony winced. "It costs money to bring in extra staff, pay overtime, and hold beds open for emergencies that might never arise."

"Not to mention stocking extra blood, drugs, and supplies," the pharmacy chief added.

"We'll have to scale back on our elective surgery schedule too," Angela Murdoch, the OR supervisor, commented. "That's going to pi—uh, tick off the surgeons *and* the patients."

Dara stifled a sigh. She understood that no one wanted to disrupt their routine, least of all her. She'd have to schedule extra physicians, make everyone work twelve-hour shifts, and reduce the work rotations from four days on and three days off to no days off until the situation clarified itself. No one was going to be happy. And no one could do anything about it.

"The governor made the call," Dara said, "and the ball is rolling."

"Let me talk to the adjutant general," Gretchen said. "I should be able to get the inside track on this. We"—she glanced at Dara—"might be overreacting."

"I'm not sure what good that will do," Dara said as diplomatically as she could. Gretchen prided herself on her contacts in high places and made no secret of her political aspirations. Some rumors suggested she was going to make a run for the state senate. Good for her, and irrelevant at the moment.

Gretchen gave her a smile Dara recognized well. She hadn't gone to the same private girls' school as Gretchen, but she might as well have. She'd grown up with girls—women now—who had never doubted their ability to manipulate the system and the people in it by virtue of their name, their money, or their family influence.

"The governor is the one who made the call, Gretch," Dara repeated.

"The governor has done the proper thing, erring on the side of caution. We've got time to safeguard our own interests." Gretchen shrugged. "There are many ways to interpret the word *prepared*."

Dara took a slow breath. She wasn't in the mood for sparring. "Then I think we should clarify the definition. In this situation, prepared means full readiness. We are not waiting until it starts raining to institute the emergency protocols we already have in place. Everyone knows what they are. I'll be checking in later today with everyone to make sure there are no problems. Or delays."

Gretchen's eyes glittered with irritation, but she was wise enough not to argue in a public forum. She could make all the phone calls she wanted. *If* Dara received word from the governor through proper channels that the situation had changed, then she would alter her directives.

"Until we hear otherwise, we're going to emergency operations as of now." Dara downed the last of her coffee. "Thanks, everyone. You know how to reach me."

She dropped the takeout container in the wastebasket next to the stairwell and took the stairs down to the ground floor where the ER and trauma bay occupied one full wing. She went straight to her office to clear her emails and start wrestling with the call schedule. A lot of people were going to lose their days off. Once done, she pulled up the latest purchase orders and reviewed the stock on hand. Sighing, she emailed the ER manager and asked him to prepare an urgent order to restock half their inventory. That was going to shoot her budget all to hell. By the time she looked up, it was nearly noon, and she was famished. Miraculously, no one had interrupted her. Penny must have had everything out on the floor under control. For the thousandth time, she gave thanks for her friend.

Her cell rang, and Penny's name popped up on the screen.

Smiling, Dara answered. "Hey, I was just thinking about you. Lunch?"

"I think you're going to have to postpone that for a while."

Something about Penny's tone had Dara's skin prickling. "What's wrong? I didn't hear a trauma alert. Do we have a level one on the way?"

"Not the kind you're thinking of." Oddly, Penny had lowered her voice. "I just escorted a soldier to the break room. I think you better get out here."

"A soldier? What do they want?"

"She said she was here to organize the emergency response operation."

"Did she now." A muscle in Dara's jaw started twitching.

It looked like the storm had just arrived.

CHAPTER SIX

Landfall minus 6 days, 11:55 a.m.
National Hurricane Center Atlantic Ops
University of Florida Institute

"Are you seeing this?" Bette said with a tinge of awe in her voice.

Four multicolored screens, each ten feet wide, took up one wall of the control room, and each was filled with images of Leo. Where he'd moved, how fast he'd moved, and where—maybe—he was going later today, and the next day, and the next.

Stan grinned wryly at the rhetorical question.

He hadn't been doing anything else for the last twelve hours, and wouldn't be doing anything else for the next week or two. Until Leo made landfall—somewhere—and ran out of steam, he'd be in the weather room along with most of the other members of the watch team for the duration. Some people would take breaks—he'd make them, and the aerial reconnaissance squads were required to take downtime. But he'd be right here, catnapping at his desk, drinking bitter coffee, living on doughnuts and pizza. Watching his opponent's every move. Because make no mistake—this was war, and despite all their sophisticated advances in predictions and forecasting, he and the other weather watch groups around the world were still running to catch up.

For a weatherman, this was the storm of a lifetime. Every eye in the control room was fixed on those images. Data scrolled across the bottom of the screen—storm center size and location, maximum sustained wind speed, directional movement, track, and time. Data they all absorbed by second nature. What none of them could absorb yet, or even totally comprehend, was Leo's enormous size.

"We need a better yardstick," Stan muttered. A contradictory mix of dread and excitement curled through his chest as he tracked the massive tropical cyclone moving inexorably closer to the vulnerable populations in its path.

"What do you mean?" Bette asked.

"Wind speed doesn't begin to describe the power of this thing," Stan said. "Just look at the diameter—hell, it's as big as the state of Massachusetts. Even if the eye skirts land, the rainfall and storm surge will flood areas hundreds of miles away."

"Uh, boss," Anjou said in a half-apologetic, half-enthusiastic voice, "we just got the latest numbers from aerial recon."

"Give 'em to us."

"They're recording speeds upward of 140 in the eyewall," Anjou said, his wiry frame coiled as if he were about to spring from his chair. He swiveled and stared at Stan. "Do you think he can hold those speeds?"

"We're going to have to prepare as if he could and hope that he can't. Update the advisory to Cat 4." He strode to his desk to run new simulations of potential storm tracks, pulling data from their logs and feeds from the European and World Weather Watch systems. He sat back after mapping, adjusting, and adding a little bit of intuition, and studied the most likely storm path over the next five days. The surrounding cone of uncertainty covered damn near the whole southern US. Then he picked up the phone to call the governor's office.

Landfall minus 6 days, 12:04 p.m.
Miami Memorial Hospital

Dara stopped in the entrance to the break room to assess what she was walking into. For some reason, she'd expected more than one soldier, a show of force, but only one person waited. Maybe she'd been hasty in suspecting a hostile takeover, and she cautiously relaxed. The rangy soldier leaning against the counter contemplating a Styrofoam cup glanced up, her swift, intense return appraisal belying her relaxed pose.

"Unless you're desperate, I wouldn't recommend it," Dara said.

"Six hours old?" the soldier asked in a husky alto.

"Try ten."

A quick grimace, a flick of the wrist, and the sludge masquerading as coffee hit the sink.

Dark eyes, more black than brown from this distance, settled on Dara's. "Thanks for the warning."

At first glance, the woman was pretty much what Dara expected—*soldier* always conjured up the impression of short-haired, suntanned, stone-faced men and fit, capable women who'd obviously worked hard to carve out a space in the very system that often rejected them—she'd experienced similar skepticism and casual dismissal of her career by friends and family as well as thinly veiled suspicion and barely concealed ostracism from colleagues. Her mother's voice echoed unbidden. *Really, darling, why do you need to work at all? I'm sure your father would be happy to have you in the business, in some suitable area. And if you must have a* job, *why on earth choose something so plebian? Medicine, after all, is not exactly a prestigious profession these days.* And then there were the so-called colleagues, who still congregated in the men's locker rooms and country clubs and gentlemen's bars to make referrals and deals and alliances. The military had to be several magnitudes worse—after all, the very fabric of the organizations was built on power and prowess.

Dara had learned very quickly, personally and professionally, not to rely on first glances. She'd been wrong enough times to learn. Friends turned out to be opportunists, lovers had agendas, and parents abandoned their offspring without a backward glance.

Though she didn't even need a second look to know this woman had nothing to prove. The soldier looked completely comfortable in her tan camo BDUs and sand-colored leather boots laced above the ankle. Dara couldn't decipher the significance of the patches sewn on both sleeves, but the name and rank stenciled in block letters above her left breast were clear enough. Her jet-black hair was longer than Dara expected, curling ever so little on her collar. Her face bore the requisite tan, with fine squint lines around her inquisitive eyes and faint creases resembling parentheses bracketing her full mouth. This was no desk jockey. She spent a lot of time in the sun. Her skin, though, was unblemished and smooth. Probably good genes. The rest of her body certainly suggested that. Muscled broad shoulders, trim waist, long legs.

The soldier tossed the cup in the trash. "What do you recommend for a refill?"

"There's a good kiosk half a block down from the ER entrance." Dara held out her hand. "I'm Dara Sims, the ER chief."

"Colonel Sawyer Kincaid."

Firm, warm grip to go along with the confident demeanor, just as Dara expected. Dara had had her measure taken enough times to recognize Colonel Kincaid was assessing her in the same way she'd just done. Her gaze was unapologetically appraising, direct and intense enough to be palpable. Neither confrontational or congenial. Under other circumstances she might be intrigued or interested by the attention. Kincaid was good-looking, actually *very* good-looking, and her confident easy charm was just as attractive. But this wasn't a casual encounter, more like two competitors each sizing up the other before the big game. Dara held Kincaid's gaze and let her look. She knew what she'd see. A woman in navy-blue scrubs and a white lab coat, average height, average build, shoulder-length wavy blond hair, blue eyes, a body that said she worked at staying fit, and an attitude that announced she was in charge because she'd earned it.

Once Dara had decided Colonel Kincaid had discovered all she was likely to discover from her scrutiny, she said, "What can I do for you, Colonel?"

"You're aware of the situation with Leo?"

"I am. We were alerted last night. I wasn't told to expect the Army."

"National Guard." Sawyer heard the annoyance in the ER chief's voice and registered the undercurrent of irritation that went along with the wary posture. This woman did not like being taken off guard and was used to being in charge. Not that much of a surprise, considering her position. Might be a problem if—more likely when—the situation went critical, but as long as Dr. Sims's resistance was matched by her competence, Sawyer could handle it.

Dara shrugged. "My apologies. Military, I should say."

"I'm probably ahead of the memo," Sawyer said, "but we're going to need to get coordinated ASAP, which is why I decided to come down personally."

"Memos aside," Dara said dryly, "I think you'd better fill me in on where you fit in all of this and what I can help you with."

"I'm in charge of the Guard's disaster preparedness planning. I don't know how much you know about how these things work—"

"It's not my first hurricane," Dara said evenly, while reminding herself Kincaid's authoritative—actually, commanding—tone was just habitual. Probably everyone in the military talked that way, as if they alone understood the intricacies of the situation, especially to those they outranked. Well, she wasn't one of the soldiers in Kincaid's command, and she sure as hell wasn't outranked. "I grew up down here. I know what we're facing."

"I'm not sure you do—not from a relief and recovery standpoint." Something hot and wild flickered through Kincaid's eyes for an instant and then disappeared. "How many times have you run search and rescue and emergency medical evac for a major disaster with mass casualties?"

Her voice was just as cool and even as it had been before, that brief spark of fire extinguished as if it had never existed. But Dara had seen the flame, and the rage that fueled it. Interesting. The colonel wasn't granite after all, more like molten lava simmering beneath the surface. "I've got close to ten years' emergency medicine experience, Colonel. There isn't much I haven't seen."

"I don't doubt your medical ability, Dr. Sims, but we're talking mass casualties—the possibility of dozens, even hundreds of displaced people, many of them injured, ending up right here or in whatever aid facilities we can establish before things go south."

"Colonel," Dara said, gathering all the restraint she could muster on a bad day rapidly getting worse, "I suggest you—"

Dara's cell phone emitted a long, loud, harsh sound that echoed instantly from somewhere on Kincaid's person. She pulled her phone from her lab coat pocket. "Sorry."

Sawyer yanked her phone out of her uniform pocket. "Excuse me."

NOAA Alert

Hurricane Leo has been upgraded to a Category 4 hurricane. Predictions indicate a northwesterly track toward Barbuda, the Virgin Islands, Puerto Rico, and south Florida. Florida

Governor Phillip Valez has mobilized 6000 National Guard troops and issued a state of emergency, including mandatory evacuation of the Florida Keys.

Dara looked up. "You're reading what I'm reading?"

"Yes." Sawyer's jaw set. "There are three hospitals in the Keys. If they evacuate, can you handle their patients here?"

"They're all smaller regional places. It depends on the numbers and how many will need ICU beds," Dara said. "We'll need to coordinate with them if they decide to evacuate. We also need to reserve beds for later emergency admissions here as well."

"Let's get whoever's in charge down there."

"I'll call them." Dara pictured the chain of islands with the string of bridges and causeways connecting them. "How will you transport? There's only one highway in and out of the Keys."

"C-130 transport planes can handle the critical patients. Ground vehicles for the others."

"We could be talking about dozens of patients."

"And we're going to have to gear up the op now." Sawyer hadn't expected the first test of the situation to escalate so quickly, but that was the way of war. Endless waiting exploding into the chaos of flame and fire in an instant, demanding every sense, every instinct, every skill be at peak efficiency before the mind even registered the assault. React or die. But she was a soldier, and Dara and most of the others dealing with the crisis were civilians. For now, at least, she could wait and watch and hope they were prepared. "I can make the calls to those hospitals if you need to organize your people here."

"No. I'll do it." Dara let out a breath. The evacuation changed everything in the blink of an eye, but that was no different than a dozen situations she faced every day in the ER. She was conditioned to go from readiness into action in a heartbeat. She'd just have to see that everyone else at the hospital was too. "I'll be better able to judge how many will need in-hospital transfers."

"All right. Is there somewhere you can set up a command post here?"

"We can use our conference room. I'll give you a quick tour of our unit before you leave." Dara grimaced. "You should be able to find me there for the foreseeable future."

"Good. For now, I'll be staying. I need to meet with your emergency response team."

Dara's spine stiffened. No wonder Kincaid had shown up unescorted—she was a whole force unto herself. "Maybe we should be clear about the chain of command first, Colonel."

Kincaid's dark eyebrows arched, and for an instant, Dara would've sworn she saw a smile. Then it was gone and the square, strong jaw tightened again.

"I wasn't aware there was anything to clarify, Doctor," Sawyer said.

"This is my emergency room, and unless I'm mistaken, I'm also the emergency medicine doctor here."

"I am a certified paramedic. Most search and rescue personnel are," Sawyer said easily. The temperature in the room had just dropped thirty degrees. If Dara Sims had fur, it would be standing up on the back of her neck. So, the doctor was territorial, it seemed. Not a bad thing, if she matched her possessiveness with the skill to go with it. Sawyer didn't have a problem backing down when a fight would solve nothing. As long as Sims didn't let her pride get in the way during a crisis, there'd be no contest. "I've seen more battlefield injuries than you have, unless there's something in your bio I'm unaware of, but I'm not questioning this is your ER."

"What bio?"

Sawyer shrugged. "All personnel involved in disaster management at the state and local level are profiled in the protocols. Since you're in charge at one of the largest level one trauma centers, you made the list. I'm probably in there too."

"So you checked up on me." Dara's temper frayed. What the hell was in the bio—and why didn't she even know about it? She'd spent her entire life fighting for independence, working to shed the reputation that followed her name and the assumptions that went along with it. The idea that Sawyer had formed perceptions of her based on those kinds of expectations bothered her more than it should have, considering she didn't care a fig what the overbearing and borderline-obnoxious soldier thought of her. But just on principle, to be measured by anything other than her actions and her accomplishments was insulting.

"When I'm going into the field, Dr. Sims, I want to know who's on my team, and who I can count on. You were one of the first people I looked at."

"Well, I certainly hope I met your approval," Dara said, not caring that her tone was laced with sarcasm.

"Why does it bother you?"

"I'm not bothered," Dara said, despite being irrationally annoyed. By now she'd gotten over being sensitive to the opinions of people who didn't know her. Hadn't she? "I've got more important things to think about."

"Fair enough."

Sawyer sounded as if she didn't actually believe her, which just added to Dara's annoyance. She mustered her most reasonable tone, the one she used with overbearing colleagues and VIP patients who attempted to direct their own care. "Since we're going to have to work together, we should just agree right now to let each other do the jobs we're trained for."

"Six thousand National Guard troops are on their way to Orlando," Sawyer said evenly. "I'm responsible for all of them, and possibly thousands of civilians who may be in danger soon. In the heat of battle, Dr. Sims, there can be only one leader. In this case, it's going to have to be me."

"I won't argue that, Colonel," Dara said. "But inside these walls, and any other place I am called to care for patients, I am in charge."

Sawyer didn't like it, but she also respected rank, and Dara had a point. "We'll be staging relief and recovery from a local command post, but this hospital and your ER are our field hospital. We may have to share command."

Dara laughed and shook her head. "You are as likely to do that as I am."

Sawyer smiled. "How do you know? You haven't even read my bio."

"I don't have to." Dara shook her head. "Unless there's something in there besides you being one hundred and ten percent soldier."

"Not a thing."

Sawyer's expression shuttered closed, and Dara instantly knew there was something Sawyer Kincaid wanted left in the past. Knowing that made her a little more human, even if it didn't make her any less arrogant and irritating.

CHAPTER SEVEN

"How about that tour?" Sawyer said.

Dara almost laughed. Obviously her little show of temper, what she'd managed not to contain, hadn't fazed the good colonel a bit. Confident was probably too mild a word for her. Or maybe she just ignored what she didn't agree with and figured when the time came, she'd do whatever the hell she wanted. Well, she'd be in for a surprise if she thought she'd be taking command in this ER. All the same, something about Kincaid's arrogant charm was appealing, as much as she hated to admit it. She'd always been drawn to self-assured women, in and out of the bedroom. And, whoa, what murky subterranean cave in her subconscious had *that* non sequitur crawled out of? Sawyer Kincaid and sex did not belong in the same universe. Doing business without fireworks was going to be hard enough, let alone juggling anything personal.

Full stop. End of that line of thought STAT.

What had Kincaid just asked? Tour. Like this was an amusement park or something. Okay, now she was just being snarky because the woman had gotten under her defenses and made her lose her temper. Really, she never let anyone close enough to do that. She must just have been taken by surprise. She wouldn't let that happen again. "Sure, why not. Let me email the ERT—sorry—emergency response team, and set up another meeting. It'll take at least half an hour for them to get back down here."

"Let me guess, administrators?"

"Most of them, but they're all highly qualified and serious about their responsibility," she said, mentally crossing her fingers when she thought about Gretchen, whose interests leaned more toward self-promotion than upholding the hospital's mission, "but they're used to taking more time to make decisions than we are. All except Wen, the trauma chief."

"I understand," Sawyer said as they walked out into the hall. "A lot of the people making decisions for the military have never stepped onto a battlefield."

"It makes a difference, doesn't it," Dara said softly.

"You mean when you actually get your hands bloody?"

"Yes."

Sawyer nodded. "You have to experience the way time collapses, as if every second lasts an hour and every minute goes by faster than a heartbeat, to understand what it's like to make critical decisions that mean life or death for your troops."

"Or your patients," Dara said softly.

"Pretty much the same thing," Sawyer said thoughtfully.

"That's why we do what we do, right? Because we can."

Sawyer smiled, a half smile that held as much pain as truth. "Because we have to, maybe."

Dara's breath caught. How could she be having a conversation with a near stranger that she'd never been able to have with anyone close to her, even some of the women she'd had relationships with? Maybe that was why they never lasted very long. "I guess that's why we need to keep clear boundaries—we each may have tough calls to make, and we can only do that alone."

"Believe me, Dr.—"

"Dara," Dara said, "since we're going to be on the same team, more or less."

Sawyer grinned. "Then you have to call me Sawyer."

"I dunno." Dara tilted her head, pretended to consider. "I rather like calling you Colonel. It's all stiff and proper sounding."

Sawyer laughed. She didn't mind being typecast, although the playful note in Sims's—strike that—*Dara's* voice took any edge off the assessment. Dara's teasing smile was as unexpected as the curling heat stirring in her belly. She liked the smile, wouldn't mind instigating a repeat. Too bad she probably wouldn't get much of a chance. Still, she could enjoy it now. "If it suits."

"Oh, believe me, it does." Dara heard the slightly flirtatious tone in her voice and wondered where the hell that had come from. What was she thinking? She never flirted, not even when she'd been young enough and hormonally immature enough to want to capture a girl's attention. She had just resolutely refused to use one of the tools every other girl she'd known, and a lot of her mother's set as well, had employed by second nature. Maybe their teasing looks and playful banter had been harmless, but she'd needed to break free of the mold, and the expectations that came with it. At the moment, though, poking a bit of fun at Colonel Sawyer Kincaid was surprisingly enjoyable, especially when Kincaid grinned back at her as if amused, and…pleased. The dancing humor in Kincaid's eyes and the way the corner of her mouth broke the harsh line of her jaw, softening it in an incongruous, almost vulnerable way, felt like a reward. Dara blinked the vision away. "No insult intended, Colonel."

"None taken. I was about to say, *Dara*," Sawyer said, with an emphasis on her name, "that I…" She frowned, dark brows lowering over her eyes. "Hell. I can't remember."

Dara laughed, delighted. At least something could put the stoic colonel off her stride, although she never expected it would be teasing. Did the woman never relax? "Come on, I'll point you in the direction of good coffee."

"For that, I would be eternally grat—"

Penny rushed around the corner, calling, "Dara! Two level ones coming in back to back. Gunshot wounds."

"How soon?" Dara said, already moving down the corridor in the direction of the three trauma bays.

"ETA two minutes out. They were practically around the corner from us."

"What's open?" Dara pulled off her white coat as she half ran past the receiving area and treatment cubicles, some with curtains drawn, the rest standing open in wait.

"One and two are both clear," Penny said. "We're setting up in there now."

"All right, get anesthesia down here and put trauma on standby. Who else is free to take one of them?"

"Carla has an MI who's crashing and can't leave him. Jeremy is just finishing up a lower extremity cast. The resident ought to be able to do that."

"Good—get Jeremy into two and find me a resident. We're good enough for now. Let's go."

She was turning the corner toward trauma admitting before she remembered Sawyer. The double doors from the ER receiving area slid open, and paramedics pushing two stretchers poured through, wheels clattering, monitors beeping, several of them already shouting vital signs to the ER staff who met them in the hall.

Battle engaged. Everything else would have to wait now.

Dara grabbed a cover gown and pulled it over her arms, letting it hang loose in the back, as she ran to meet the first stretcher.

"In one," she called to the young red-haired paramedic who pulled the stretcher at breakneck speed. The paramedic's stethoscope jumped around her neck with every stride, a frantic metronome ticking off precious seconds, all that might remain for the patient.

The patient's face was obscured by the tape encircling an endotracheal tube and a wad of blood-soaked gauze over his lower jaw and neck, but at a glance he looked to be a young Caucasian male. More blood saturated the sheets beneath his head and shoulders, and a crimson trail of fresh droplets followed the stretcher down the glaringly lit hall like a line of lost children. Bright red blood spurted from beneath the bandage the second paramedic, a burly Latino with a grim set to his jaw, pressed to the man's throat. Arterial and profuse.

"GSW to the neck," the big guy said. "I'm not sure the tube's in. We couldn't see a damn thing, too much blood in the airway."

Dara cut a quick look at the O2 monitor. Seventy. They weren't aerating him.

"We might have a lung down," she said, "or the tube slipped out of position. Let me have a look down there." She caught Kirk's eye. "Get an endotracheal tube and a trach tray ready. We need to be sure we're in the trachea."

Kirk, the first-year resident who rarely seemed to break a sweat over anything, nodded, his face pale and his quick breaths pulling the cotton fabric of his mask in and out in erratic bursts. He found an intubation tray on a shelf behind them and ripped open the sterile covering. He moved aside as Dara pushed to the head of the table and grabbed gloves from a box on the counter.

"Hand me some suction," she said, sliding the lighted retractor into his mouth and toward the back of his throat. Blood and bits of bone immediately flooded her field. "Penetrating wound here. Get trauma down here right now. He needs a trach."

"Wen's on his way," Penny called.

"Dara," a man shouted from the doorway, his voice barely carrying above the din of monitors, ringing phones, and staccato orders. "Patient in two is crashing. Jeremy needs to put in chest tubes and needs more hands."

"Kirk—go," Dara said without looking up from the debris field. If she could just get a clear look past the epiglottis—

"We lost his pressure and his pulse," the female paramedic announced.

"Damn it," Dara muttered. "We need more lines. Where's the damn blood? Pen?"

"On it," Penny replied.

From beside her, Sawyer said calmly, "Where do you want me, Dr. Sims?"

Dara looked up. Sawyer was gloved and gowned.

"Can you get a big line in him?" Dara said after only a second's hesitation. Right now, the only thing that mattered was the patient, not protocol, and she was short of hands. "He's bleeding out."

"Femoral good enough for you?"

"Just give me a hose in there," Dara snapped.

"Done."

Sawyer looked over her shoulder and caught the eye of the nurse who seemed to be everywhere at once. "Cut down tray?"

"Here you go." Penny wheeled over a stainless steel tray and tore open the instrument pack. "Penny Arnaux."

"Sawyer Kincaid."

"What do you want for a line?"

"IV tubing." Sawyer made a five-centimeter incision just below the groin crease on the patient's right thigh. As she worked her way down through the fatty tissue, Dara's voice overrode all the chaos, issuing instructions, maintaining order, keeping everyone on task. Calm, controlled, certain. Sawyer relaxed into the zone—focused on her mission, confident in the command.

The femoral vein came into view and she picked a large branch just below the half-inch-wide blue ribbon as thick as her thumb. Beside it, the femoral artery lay pale and weakly fluttering. No blood to pump.

Pretty soon his limbs and organs would begin shutting down, then minute by minute, his body would die. Hands steady, she uncovered a major branch off the femoral vein.

"Get the tube ready," she said.

"All set to go." Penny pressed so close to her side, Sawyer could feel her heartbeat.

She nicked the side branch, held it open with forceps, and slid the sliced-off end of an IV tubing directly into the vein.

"Open it up," Sawyer said. Clear fluid began pouring through the quarter-inch tube directly into the patient's main blood vessels. It wasn't enough, he needed blood, but it was what they had. "Got something to tie this in with?"

"Here you go." Penny dropped a suture pack into her field. "Pretty work, Colonel."

"You've done this a time or two yourself." Sawyer tied the IV tubing in place and straightened. "Thanks."

"Run saline straight open in there until we get blood." Dara slid a new endotracheal tube into the patient's airway. Blood spurted out the top of the tube and streaked her mask. She quickly suctioned out the tube and hooked it to the ventilator. The readout on the O2 monitor started to climb. "Call the blood bank again, Pen."

"I'm on it," Penny said.

Sawyer closed the skin incision in the leg with a couple of staples from the instrument pack.

"Damn it, there's a lot of blood down there." Dara suctioned the endotracheal tube again and fresh blood poured out. "Where the hell is it coming from?"

"Probably hit the trachea on the way through his neck before going up and out his jaw," Sawyer said. "Either that or he's bleeding from a branch of the carotid in the back of his throat."

Dara met Sawyer's gaze. She didn't say what they both knew. If he was bleeding in the mess of torn and swollen tissue in the back of his throat, they'd never find it. They wouldn't have time.

"We're not losing this one," Dara said. "We'll just have to keep up with the blood loss until—"

"What have you got for me," a cheerful male voice said from behind them.

Dara said, "Hi, Wen. Gunshot wound to the neck, took out part of his posterior mandible. Blood everywhere. Can't tell if the trachea's nicked or not. There's too much blood in the airway."

"Got a chest X-ray yet?" The trauma guy sauntered over to the table, pulling on gloves. He was shorter and lighter in build than Sawyer, but he gave off an air of being much bigger. His cover gown hung loose off his shoulders, his mask untied and dangling around his neck. Cavalier—relaxed. Looking like he was on his way to a party. He glanced at Sawyer, took in the oak leaf on her collar above the gown she'd pulled on, and raised his brows.

"Welcome to our little corner of the war, Colonel," he said. "Major Wen Haruke, Army Reserve."

"Pleased to be here, Major."

"Permanent deployment?" Wen said as he reached for a headlight hanging from a hook above the counter behind them.

"Short-term placement."

"If you two are done bonding," Dara said dryly, "can we get this guy out of here and up to the OR?"

"I've got blood," Penny said, dropping six units of whole blood onto the bed. She read off the name on each one: John Doe, patient number 20144479. "All match."

"Go ahead, Pen, hang it," Dara said, and she hooked a bag to the right arm IV. "Sawyer, can you hang one in that leg line?"

"Copy that."

With three units of blood pouring in, his pressure crept up.

Wen edged the paramedic aside, replacing his hand on the bloody gauze, and peered underneath at the neck wound.

"Yep, that's a gusher," he said, as if describing the weather. "Must've just nicked the external carotid, or he'd have bled out by now. Put your finger back on there, buddy."

"I'll take that, Major." Sawyer put pressure on the wound. The artery beat feebly beneath her fingers.

"Thanks." The paramedic stepped back, sweat streaming down his face, and let out a long breath. "Man, it's going to be a long day."

Sawyer wished a long day was all they faced, but then, that's why she was there. The battle was just beginning.

CHAPTER EIGHT

Landfall minus 5.5 days, 2:30 p.m.

Dara pulled off her cover gown, wadded it into a ball, and tossed it into a laundry receptacle by the door. She stood in the doorway of trauma bay one, pulse racing, skin as sensitive as if an electric current raced beneath the surface, listening to the clatter of wheels and receding jumble of voices as Wen, Penny, and one of Wen's trauma fellows pushed the patient's stretcher down the hall toward the elevator. Behind her, the housekeeping staff had already begun the task of gathering the discarded package wrappers, empty IV bags, and bloody sponges littering the room before mopping and disinfecting the bloody tile floor. She'd always thought of the aftermath of an alert like the abandoned battlefield, and conscious of Sawyer beside her, wondered if she'd even been close to imagining the reality. How could she really know?

"Was it anything like what you're used to?" she asked.

"In some ways," Sawyer said from beside her. "You'd do well in the theater, Dr. Sims."

Dara snorted. "I'm not sure about that, not if people were shooting at me at the same time."

"Sometimes they are," Sawyer said. "Other times, you're in the belly of the Black Hawk, the gunners are firing, the air is rushing through the open ports, and you can't hear anything except your own heart beating in your ears."

"That must be terrifying," Dara said.

"It probably should be, but there's just no time for fear in the middle of a firefight." Sawyer shook her head. "That comes later for most of us, if we're lucky. If you wake up in the middle of the night afraid of the next callout, that's bad for everyone."

"If you falter, someone dies," Dara murmured.

"Yes," Sawyer said.

Dara pictured what they'd just been through taking place in a helicopter, surrounded by smoke and fire and death on the wing. What kind of training would it take to enable someone to ignore their fear, to disregard the possibility of their own death and make critical decisions under those conditions? Or did only those who already kept their emotions under lock and key ever make it that far? She'd always thought she'd chosen emergency medicine for its immediacy—for the satisfaction of solving a problem, administering treatment, and bringing closure to the situation. Endings were important to her—clean and sharp and certain. Maybe she'd been fooling herself—maybe she chose to live with death as a sign of her failure because somewhere in her past, she'd closed off the part of herself that wept for loss.

Dara rubbed her eyes. What did it matter, after all this time, why she was here? All that counted was that she did what needed to be done. "I need to check on Jeremy and the other trauma patient."

"Sure."

Dara stuck her head into trauma bay two. Jeremy Gold was an experienced ER physician, ten years her senior. She trusted him to handle just about anything, but every patient who came through their doors was ultimately her responsibility. "Everything under control, Jer?"

"All good." Jeremy—tanned, blond, buff, and looking for all the world like a stereotypical beach bum—stepped away from the table and pulled down his mask. He looked as fresh as if he'd just arrived, not having just ended a grueling alert. Only the patina of sweat on his forehead revealed how hard he'd been working. "He's probably got a perforated lung. Lotta blood coming out of the chest tubes, but his pressure's holding and the O2 sats look okay. They're getting another trauma room ready for him upstairs. Angie Eastwood is on her way down."

"Great," Dara said. Angie was a young trauma attending, capable beyond her years. "I've got a meeting—call me if anything comes up."

"Will do."

Dara continued down the hall and said to Sawyer, "If you want to take a break—"

"I'm good," Sawyer said.

Dara laughed, a peculiar lightness chasing away the ghosts of doubt and sadness. "You certainly are. We were lucky to have you in there. I couldn't have gotten that line in faster myself."

Sawyer grinned. "Now, there's a compliment."

"True." When Sawyer laughed again, the lightness in Dara's chest expanded and she had an inkling of the high some people chased with drugs. For a minute, she floated, absolutely certain she'd never felt so good. Oh yes, she could get used to that sensation. Too bad the chances of that were slim, considering what was ahead. Neither of them was likely to be laughing much. Despite the grim forecast, her second wind was coming back, and with it, the elation of the win. At least, she hoped it was a win. They'd done their part and gotten the GS patient off the table and on the way to the OR in stable enough condition for Wen to have a chance at repairing the damage and keeping him alive. "We won that round."

"Yep," Sawyer said. "That just shows why we're flying into a firefight with a fully equipped trauma bay in the belly of a Black Hawk. The save rate is ninety-seven percent if we get them to the field hospital alive."

Dara slowed. "Huh. Those stats are better than ours—if multiple trauma patients make it to a level one alive, their survival rate is a little shy of ninety percent."

"Bet they'd be better if you age-matched the samples," Sawyer said, hitting the door release on the wall. The double doors swung open into the main hospital corridor. "Remember, our patients are young, in peak condition, and usually suffering from major blood loss—either amputation from IEDs or penetrating trauma. We've got blood in the Black Hawks now."

"So you're a jump ahead of us," Dara murmured. "I wish sometimes—"

"No," Sawyer said quietly, "you don't."

Dara shot Sawyer a look. Sawyer's ability to know where Dara was going with a thought was disconcerting. She'd never been obvious to anyone in her life. "How do you know what I was going to say?"

Sawyer shrugged, not looking the least bit repentant. "You're a trauma doc. You like the challenge. You want to be tested, don't you?"

"I want to be the best," Dara said.

"More ways than one to get there," Sawyer said. "You don't need people shooting at you."

"No—I guess a hurricane will do just as well."

Sawyer grimaced, a ghost of something flickering in her eyes again. This time Dara couldn't pretend she hadn't seen it. "What?"

"Nothing," Sawyer said quickly.

And there was the denial again, so automatic maybe Sawyer had come to believe it herself. And none of Dara's business. "At least we know we can work together when we need to."

"Looking that way."

Dara lifted a brow. "Surprised?"

Sawyer shrugged. "I might've been, if we hadn't had that little chat beforehand about who's in charge."

Dara shook her head. No way was she going to believe they wouldn't cross swords at some point when a crisis arose. Sawyer was used to being in command, just like her. "Probably the first of many little *chats*, since we both like to be in charge."

"I guess we'll take it as it comes."

"Good plan," Dara said. "How about we get that cup of coffee, if you still want to stay for the ERT meeting."

"Like I said, I'm here for the duration, one way or the other."

As they neared the exit, Penny came through the stairwell door. "Hey—coffee run?"

"Yep," Dara said. "Want anything else?"

"Bagel with cream cheese if he's got any left. And decaf for me."

"Right. Everything okay upstairs?"

"The patient was good when Wen took him back. He'll call down when he's finished. Jeremy's guy okay?"

"Yes. Two for two."

"Gunshot wounds in broad daylight." Penny shook her head. "Can't wait till the sun goes down. It's a full moon."

Dara frowned. "Really?"

Penny nodded.

"Crap," Dara muttered and glanced at Sawyer. "You see the same thing—people going crazy on the full moon?"

Sawyer shook her head. "That's about the only time we relax a little. Terrible conditions for an ambush."

Dara tensed. "I'm sorry. I know it's not the same."

"Not so different." Sawyer shrugged. "Except for the bullets."

Dara's stomach tightened. "Except for the bullets. At least, most of the time."

"Is now the time for me to ask why you're here, Colonel?" Penny asked.

"Perfect timing. A hurricane is gonna wallop the Keys and maybe parts of south Florida. Evacuations have started." Sawyer nodded toward Dara. "You all are our medical command center. I'm coordinating the military response."

Penny glanced at Dara. "We're in for a deluge, then."

"That's a perfect word for it. I'm sorry, but we're going to have to adjust the call rotations until this is over. As soon as I've finished getting emergency response protocols geared, we'll start working on it."

"Okay," Penny said steadily.

"Are you okay?" Dara asked.

"Absolutely. Go." She made shooing motions. "Go get some food while you still can."

As they headed toward the exit, Sawyer murmured, "Some problem there?"

"I don't think she'd mind me telling you," Dara said. "She's pregnant. She had preeclampsia last time and had a pretty tough go of it."

"She's good."

"The best."

"Good friends?"

Dara nodded. "The best."

"Double bonus, then."

"Yes." Dara weaved through the midafternoon crowds. Most dressed in shorts, breezy tops or tanks, and exuding *tourist* from every pore. How many people just like these were only now beginning a hurried exodus from the Keys, rushing to get airline tickets, gas for their cars, and new reservations somewhere on higher, safer ground? "I feel like I should be doing something more than going for coffee right now."

"You are." Sawyer halted by the open-air coffee kiosk as Dara got into line. Colorful signs announced a dozen different blends and coffee concoctions, along with sandwiches and pastries. "I'll have what you're having?"

"Double caramel soy latte with whipped?"

Sawyer chuckled. "No. Large dark roast, light on the cream. And one of those sandwiches—surprise me."

"That's annoying, you know?"

"Which part?"

"The psychic part."

"I would take credit, but I saw an empty coffee cup in the break room with your name on it."

"And you remembered?"

"Coffee choices say a lot about a person."

"Oh? And what did mine say?"

"Practical, professional, and unfussy."

Dara narrowed her eyes. "Is unfussy code for boring?"

Sawyer's gaze grew just a little heavy, and her mouth quirked at the corner. Just a little. "Anything but."

Dara blushed. She felt the heat and could practically see her skin brighten. *Oh my God. I am so humiliating myself.* "You're getting turkey, Swiss, and sprouts, like it or not."

"Sounds great."

Dara gave Sawyer the eye. "Sprouts?"

"Love 'em."

Laughing, Dara turned away to order. Oh yes, Sawyer Kincaid could be addicting all right.

3:35 p.m.
Emergency Medical Command Center
Miami Memorial Hospital, Miami, Florida

Sawyer's phone buzzed and she pulled it out of her pocket, checking the text under the edge of the table as men and women, in suits for the most part and a white coat here or there, filed into the room. When she saw the secure link, she punched in her access code and orders scrolled down the screen.

Central Command to Kincaid, Col. Sawyer, ANG.
EVAC support orders—establish forward operations staging
center Homestead Air Reserve Base. Charlie Squadron to
proceed 2000 hours to Key West International Airport in
relief capacity, Key West Memorial Hospital. Hospital to
hospital transfer, Miami Memorial.

Sawyer acknowledged and sent out a quick alert to Charlie Squadron to report at 1900 hours for preflight briefings. Homestead was thirty miles south of Miami—close enough to coordinate relief and rescue with Dara. Sawyer slid her phone away and Dara caught her eye, one eyebrow raised in question. Sawyer, sitting on Dara's right at the end of the table farthest from the door, leaned close. "Orders. Patient transfers out of Key West Memorial Hospital."

Dara nodded and Sawyer returned to watching the members of the ERT as they entered. Body language, who paired off with whom, could often reveal a lot about how a team would come together, or not. She'd seen it time and time again in tents and mess halls and ready rooms. Who played cards with whom around a makeshift table by the glow of a lantern in the middle of the night, who picked which side to join for an impromptu game of football on a dusty parade ground, who sat alone reading and writing letters, who drank alone. Who stared into the dark, contemplating drifting outside the wire.

This was different, of course. These people didn't depend on each other to survive, at least not yet. That might happen before this was over, and when it did, it was always good to be forewarned about who to trust and who not to. More importantly, she needed to know who might break, and who would stand.

When she'd first met Dara, she'd known only one thing—Dara was well trained on paper. She'd attended excellent schools, from a private girls' preparatory school through university and finally medical school. Her emergency medicine residency at Jackson Memorial was one of the best in the country. All top-tier, and now at a young age, head of her own division. That told her a lot—Dara was smart, most likely driven, and either very hardworking or very well positioned. Her bio had been bare-bones, and judging from Dara's heated reaction to Sawyer having read it, probably held only a fraction of what really lay in Dara's past. The same was true for her, and she respected Dara's privacy. What she'd read in Dara's bio, though, was at odds with what she'd learned of her, which only made Dara more intriguing.

Sawyer'd grown up not far from Miami and had hung out on the beaches and along the strip as a teen whenever the confines of the tiny house she shared with her mother and three sibs started to feel like a prison. She knew who the Simses were. It would be hard not to when a boulevard, a few parks, and even a pier carried their name. If that's all she'd known about Dara Sims, the heiress to the Sims fortune as some tabloids referred to her, she'd be way off course. The Dara Sims she'd met and seen in action was confident, cool in a crisis, a little competitive—no, actually, a lot competitive—and maybe most important of all, proud. Proud of what she did, proud enough to want to do it better than anyone else. Pride and sense of duty counted for a lot, and the kind of stubbornness that often went with it could also be a pain in the ass. She ought to know, since Rambo accused her of it on nearly a daily basis.

A slim brunette in a tailored suit, a red silk power shirt open at the throat, and a few well-placed expensive-looking gold bracelets faced off against Dara down the length of the table. The woman's gaze slid over Dara's, pausing just long enough to be assessing, then landed on Sawyer. Interest flared in her eyes, and she unapologetically took her time appraising Sawyer.

After half a minute or so, she smiled slightly and turned away. Opinion formed.

Sawyer catalogued her read. CEO…no, probably COO or hospital attorney. Ambitious, playing a long game, playing dirty if need be. Sawyer had sat in on enough planning sessions to know the type. The brunette might not necessarily be an obstacle but was definitely likely to be reluctant to expend resources unless necessary.

"Everyone," Dara said without any kind of preamble, "the governor has ordered the Keys evacuated. Colonel Kincaid is commanding the National Guard's support and relief operations. Miami Memorial is the official medical command center."

A quick round of introductions followed.

"What does that mean?" a trim blonde in surgical scrubs asked.

"We're first in line to receive patients," Dara said.

"How long before we know for sure if the hurricane is actually going to create problems?" asked a slightly fidgety man in a well-cut three-piece suit designed to hide his soft midsection.

"There's no doubt the Keys will be impacted," Dara said. "The storm advisories out of the hurricane center are very clear on that. The only question remains exactly how big and how far the hurricane will extend."

"So we've got time," Gretchen said.

"No," Dara said, with more patience than Sawyer would've mustered at this point, "evacuations have begun from at least one hospital. I'll know within the hour how many patients we'll need to take."

"What about Blake?" the OR supervisor asked. "They've got almost as many beds as we do. They ought to have room."

Dara glanced at Sawyer. "Colonel Kincaid, do you want to take that?"

"Right now, our evac plan calls for transport to central locations—one here in the state, and the other beyond the potential range of significant storm fallout. Between the two centers, you're better positioned and equipped to take regional transfers. We'll reserve transport to the Alabama hospital until numbers demand it."

"How much leeway is there to"—Gretchen smiled at Sawyer—"massage that plan a little bit, to keep our beds free. Transferring patients from other hospitals is costly, and the reimbursement situation is a nightmare."

The three-piece-suit guy added, "Worse than a nightmare. It's a money-losing proposition."

Sawyer said, "The operation is already ongoing."

A frown formed between Gretchen's elegantly arched brows. "I understand from a contact in the governor's office that the evacuation orders were issued with an abundance of caution. That being the case—"

"Ms. Baylor," Sawyer said, "the governor's orders are clear. The Guard has been mobilized to institute a statewide support and relief plan. Our operational plan is engaged. If the ongoing situation changes, I'll alert Dr. Sims."

Gretchen's lips pressed together. She looked at Dara. "Please advise my office as soon as you've determined how many patients we'll be accepting in transfer. There will be paperwork."

"Isn't there always." Dara shouldn't be enjoying Gretchen's annoyance, but she was, a little bit. Not many people disregarded Gretchen with quite the ease that Sawyer had. Appealing on one level, but a warning on the other. Sawyer was unbendable when it came to carrying out her orders. Dara could hardly fault her for that. She only hoped their duties never put them at cross purposes. "I'll keep everyone informed as the situation unfolds."

With some grumbling, everyone rose and filed out.

Dara let out a long sigh. "I hate these meetings."

"The military is a lot simpler. Someone gives orders, someone else carries them out."

"There must be someone who has to sit in a room like this and play politics. Or at least make nice to preserve peace."

"Thankfully," Sawyer said, "way above my pay grade."

"Does it ever bother you, taking orders even if you question them?"

Sawyer shook her head. "If it did, I wouldn't wear the uniform."

"I'm sorry, that was a rude and intrusive question."

"It was personal," Sawyer said, "but not a question I mind answering."

"You like being a soldier, don't you?"

"I *am* a soldier," Sawyer said quietly.

"Yes," Dara said quietly as she rose. "I can see that. I need to call those hospitals."

"I'll wait while you do. I'll need to put together a medevac team. We're getting ready to fly south to start moving patients."

"I want to come."

"Not possible."

Dara smiled. "Colonel, you'd be surprised what's possible."

CHAPTER NINE

"In this particular case," Sawyer said, "there is no possibility."

"Why not?" Dara said in a deceptively innocent tone.

Sawyer squeezed the bridge of her nose. *Civilian*, she repeated to herself mentally, *civilian, civilian, civilian.* "It's a military operation."

"So?"

"What part of that wasn't in English?"

Dara settled a hip onto the corner of the table, folded her arms across her chest, and smiled. "I heard all the words. I'm just not sure of their significance."

Sawyer leaned back against the doorway and checked the hallway outside in both directions. Clear. She didn't want any unauthorized personnel overhearing them. Whatever lines of command she and Dara needed to work out were between them. When the time came to give orders, and her gut told her that time would come, they both needed to be obeyed. A united front. For now, though, she needed to inject a little reality into Dara's inexperienced picture of just how bad things might get and why she was unprepared. "We're flying into uncertain conditions. High winds, low visibility, unpredictable updrafts and air currents—all of which can change minute to minute. Our pilots are the best, but any flight can get into trouble. Even if it were a bright sunny day, it's not a pleasure trip, it's—"

"Why do you make the assumption that you're the only one who appreciates the seriousness of this situation?" Heat started to rise on the back of Dara's neck. "Do I look like I spend my time painting my nails on the beach?"

Sawyer frowned, trying to make sense of that. "Where'd you get that from?"

"You really don't get it?"

"Would I ask if I did?" Sawyer didn't usually have a problem communicating, although come to think of it, she mostly gave orders, responded to orders, or communicated in the kind of offhand dark humor common to those who lived with death up close and personal every day. After the scene in the trauma room she'd almost forgotten Dara wasn't a soldier. But while Dara might be able to handle a trauma case as well as a field surgeon, she didn't think, or feel, like Sawyer. And Sawyer didn't think like her. Not even a little. "So what did I say?"

Dara rolled her eyes. "The only thing missing was the unspoken *little lady*, because you certainly sounded like that's who you were talking to."

"You've got to be kidding."

"No, I'm pretty sure about that."

"Trust me," Sawyer said, trying hard not to laugh. "You are so far from that, it's not even in the same universe as how I see you."

"If that's true, what's the problem?"

"You're just not...trained for it."

Dara straightened and stepped closer, searching Sawyer's genuinely confused gaze. Sawyer really didn't get it. How was that possible? "Okay—let me spell it out, because you're missing the point. I'm a professional, and I'm just as responsible—even *more* responsible—for those patients in need of evacuation down there than any of you." When Sawyer opened her mouth to protest, Dara poked an index finger at her, stopping just short of her perfectly pressed camo shirt. To her satisfaction, Sawyer's eyes widened and she swallowed her objection. Good. She'd surprised her. Obviously, a good offense was the only way to impress her. "I'm totally qualified to care for them during transport, which frees up some of your people if we have an emergency in flight. Besides that, I'll need to make decisions about who goes where that are going to impact everything that you and your—" She paused. "What do you call them these days? Soldiers?"

"Troops, usually." Sawyer's throat was oddly dry, as if she'd been swallowing dust for a week on patrol. She heard the words coming out of Dara's mouth, but she had trouble absorbing just what Dara was saying. Her brain—no, not her brain, just about every *other* part of her body—was totally fixated on Dara. The way her eyes flashed, the intensity of her voice, the waves of passion and strength that rolled off her as she closed in on Sawyer. Even the threat—or maybe the promise—of that finger poking into her chest was mesmerizing. What the hell was happening to her?

"Okay," Dara went on as if she hadn't noticed Sawyer paralyzed like a green recruit in her first firefight. Stunned to inactivity, disoriented, and in danger of getting blown all to hell. "If we start getting casualties and evacuees from all over the state, I'll need to make decisions that will affect your troops and what they'll need to do. It matters that I know what's going on. You can't run this operation all on your own."

Sawyer managed to shake off the weird paralysis, even if she couldn't suppress the fascination twisting up her insides. She had better control than this—she'd spent her life honing the ability to bury her fear and think, act...*lead* in the face of any horror. She'd frozen once and it had cost her everything. She couldn't forget those few moments, couldn't forgive them, but she would never repeat them. No matter what the cost. "That's not how command works."

Dara sighed. "I get that. I do, but you said yourself, it's different when you're on a battlefield. When people are shooting at you. One voice—I get that too. And I wouldn't want it any other way." Her heart was actually racing, which was really strange. Thinking about Sawyer surrounded by enemies, people intent on killing her, actively trying to kill her, was terrifying. It wasn't as if she'd never thought about the realities of war before, but standing there looking at Sawyer, alive and solid and adorably perplexed, the thought of her in danger made her throat ache. "But this isn't like that. This is a combined—okay, wait, maybe you'll get this—this is like a task force. You do that, right, with the UN and things like that?"

Sawyer winced. "Oh yeah, and it's a clusterfuck." She flushed. "Sorry."

Dara grinned. "Oh, believe me, I've not only heard the term, I've said it, and I've actually been in the middle of one."

Sawyer grinned. "Well, then you know what happens when you try to deal with an emergency by committee."

"I do. Completely. And if anybody ever tried to do that in the middle of a trauma when I was running a resuscitation, I'd have their ass. But that's not what we're doing, right? This is like—oh God, why don't I watch military movies—reconnaissance. I need to change my viewing habits."

"You know, you're not making a whole lot of sense all the time?"

"What makes you think it's me? Maybe you're just not following." Despite the seriousness of her argument, Dara was actually having fun. Everything to do with Sawyer was a challenge—when she wasn't irritated, she was strangely, inexplicably exhilarated. And she had no time to consider the weirdness of that. "Look. I'm trying to figure out a common language here. You know, in the interest of communication and cooperation."

"I think we're doing pretty well," Sawyer said, that slow, easy heat slipping into her voice.

Dara's pulse skittered again, and this time, fear had nothing to do with it. Damn it, Sawyer was sexy when she sounded like that. Terrible, inappropriate timing. Instinctively, she backed up. "You do understand what I'm saying, then?"

Sawyer blew out a breath. "I understand. You're a hands-on person. You don't want to make decisions based on information you haven't assessed yourself. You want to see what you're up against for yourself."

"That's it exactly!" Dara beamed. "So—when…What? Why am I still reading a big no in your expression?"

Sawyer hesitated, not totally sure herself why she didn't want Dara to come along. There was precedent, sure—if she wanted to take Dara, she could. All kinds of people were embedded with far less justification—photographers, journalists, reporters. Even biographers, for crying out loud. Plus, she was in command, after all. But she didn't know what she was flying into, or worse, what she might be flying out of eight or ten hours from now. They should have a clear window of time, but she knew better than to trust predictions. And once they were airborne with patients aboard, they wouldn't be turning around.

"Is it because you don't trust me?" Dara asked after the silence went on too long. "You think I'll panic in an emergency?"

"No," Sawyer said instantly. "No, I know you can handle yourself under pressure. I'm just not sure I can guarantee your safety."

Dara froze. There it was—the real minefield that stretched

between them. Sawyer seemed to think her authority extended to Dara. "This is my decision. I know the risks. You're not in charge of me, Colonel."

"Up there, anywhere in the field, you're my responsibility," Sawyer said. "That's not negotiable."

Dara struggled to keep her emotions out of her argument. If she let her temper talk for her, they'd just end up with headaches. No one had time for that. "Can you guarantee the safety of everyone else you'll be flying down there with?"

"That's different. They wear the uniform, they accept the risk."

"Well then, so do I." Dara wouldn't let Sawyer make her decisions or assume responsibility for them, but she had no problem telling Sawyer the truth. "Besides, I trust you."

Sawyer almost warned Dara not to be so quick with her trust. She wasn't afraid of shouldering the responsibility for her troops. If she had been, she would never have joined the service. She cared about all of her squad, would put herself on the line for any one of them—or anyone who fought beside her. She'd risk her life for Dara too, but that wasn't the point. The uniform they all wore wasn't just symbolic. Their colors, their insignias, their stripes and bars and stars, announced their acceptance of the risk that went with them. Dara wasn't one of them, and that was all the more reason Sawyer needed to keep her safe.

"What are you afraid of?" Dara asked quietly.

Sawyer stiffened. "I don't know what you're talking about."

"Then you don't have any reason to say no." Dara shook her head. She was done with compromise and rationales. "We're wasting time. Gretchen would love to call the governor or your commanding officer and argue the best interests of the hospital are only served if I go along. She hasn't had a chance to make a personal splash yet today. It would be just like her to send a sound bite to the press."

Sawyer winced. The last thing she wanted was to turn a simple medevac operation into a political battlefield. "I have a car outside the ER. I'm leaving now and I can't wait."

"I understand. I'll have Penny arrange coverage for me. Everyone is going to be working overtime for the foreseeable future anyhow. How long do you think we'll be gone?"

"Possibly until morning. Flight time shouldn't be more than an hour down if we can maintain normal cruising speed, but we've got to allow for delays at that end from weather or general inefficiency."

"I'll be ready to leave in ten minutes." Dara eased past Sawyer and disappeared down the hall.

"Right." Sawyer closed her eyes and let out a long breath. She hoped to hell she wasn't making a big mistake.

Dara slung her overnight bag over her shoulder and walked out into the ER receiving lot. Sawyer waited outside, leaning against an idling vehicle. For some reason, Dara had expected a car of some kind, although now that she thought about it, that made no sense. The Humvee, tan and huge, stenciled with an American flag and the words *Florida National Guard* in black block letters, looked tough and imposing—just like the woman standing beside it. Sawyer wore her uniform cap now, the bill squared and low on her forehead. Her hands were clasped behind her back, her legs slightly spread. Her gaze fixed on Dara and never wavered as Dara approached.

Dara's skin prickled. Her insides tightened. Her reaction was completely reflexive, totally visceral, and absolutely unlike her. She did not invite glances from sexy women, although Penny never failed to point them out when she did not return them. She noticed good-looking women, of course—beating heart and blood still flowing, after all— but she was always so busy and…busy…the moments were fleeting. Sawyer Kincaid was hard not to notice, and the more she did, the more annoying her unbidden, out-of-character reactions became. She did not have the time or the desire to be attracted to anyone, especially not now and not…*her*. Not when the only thing she should be thinking about was the job she had to do. And most especially not when she seemed to have nothing at all to say about the attraction. No. No. A million times no.

"All set?" Sawyer asked.

"Yes," Dara said abruptly. Okay, that sounded just a bit rude. Not exactly Sawyer's fault she exuded potent pheromones, any more than it was hers their chemistries seemed to mesh. Simple biology and just as simply ignored. "Thanks."

Sawyer opened the rear door and gestured for Dara to climb inside. When she did, Sawyer followed and pulled the door closed.

"Homestead Air Force Base, Corporal Nomura," Sawyer said to the driver.

The young soldier behind the wheel looked to be in his early twenties, clean-shaven, short-haired, and square shouldered. "Yes, ma'am."

"I don't know why it didn't occur to me you'd have a driver." Dara looked for a seat belt and didn't find one. Sawyer wasn't wearing one and neither was the driver.

Sawyer must have seen her looking. "They're not much use if we were to get hit by anything strong enough to flip us. And they get in the way of our equipment."

"Right." Dara had seen live feeds from the front—war was something news stations brought right into people's living rooms. She also had seen what it took to destroy one of these vehicles. Her chest tightened. Being in the armored vehicle, being reminded of the authority Sawyer wore like a second skin, brought home to her exactly how much she was out of her element. She was now part of something bigger than the world she usually inhabited. For the first time in a long time, she felt out of place. Not intimidated, not uncertain, simply a stranger in this new landscape.

Sawyer glanced over at her. "Are you all right?"

"Yes." *When out of your element*, Dara thought, *deflect*. "Tell me what's going to happen when we get to the airfield."

"I'll—we'll—meet with the other members of the medevac planning team to coordinate ground support, establish rendezvous points for frontline patient transfer, and set flight plans. Our aviation team will coordinate with the FCC and local domestic airports to clear airspace. Charlie Company has six Black Hawks, including two HH-60 medevac units. We'll brief the pilots on the mission objectives, review weather projections, set rendezvous points with ground transport, and assess patient needs before we head out."

"Where will I be?"

"You will stay with me the whole time. And as long as you are with me, you'll follow orders."

"Understood." Dara had no desire to complicate the evacuation mission. She wasn't going along because she wanted an adventure. She needed to know what she might be facing in the next few days, and she needed to see for herself the condition of the critically ill patients in need of transfer. "When I was getting my overnight bag, I tried to reach the ERT chief at Key West Memorial. He was supposed to get back to me and hasn't yet."

"He's your opposite number?" Sawyer asked.

"Yes—an anesthesiologist. I don't know him well—in fact, I don't think we've ever met." Dara fished her phone out of the back pocket of her scrubs. "I'm hoping he's got a handle on the transfer now and can give me a report."

"Good idea," Sawyer said. "The more information we can get on the patients to be evacuated, the better we can plan and allocate resources."

"I want to try reaching him again. Is it all right if I make a call from here?"

"Go right ahead," Sawyer said. "The advance intel will save us time."

"Just making myself useful," Dara muttered as she dialed the number she'd saved into her phone. This time a secretary answered, and she explained who she was and why she was calling.

"Just one moment, Dr. Sims. Dr. Randall should be here any second…yes, here he is."

"Josh Randall here."

"Josh, this is Dara Sims. I'm an emergency medicine attending and the head of the emergency response team at Miami Memorial. How are things down there?"

"Right now, pretty quiet. Cloudy, but not much else happening. The local weather people tell us we're going to get hit pretty hard pretty soon."

"I'm flying down with the National Guard to assist in the transfer of your critical patients. Can you tell me what we're looking at?"

"We're discharging all stable medical and surgical patients who can go home within the next twenty-four hours. I just came from a walk-through of the ICUs. We've got another thirty or so who will need ground transfer, and we're organizing ambulances for them now. That's going to take all night and probably most of tomorrow."

"Hold on a second." Dara said to Sawyer, "Will you be assisting ground transfers too?"

"Yes—we have transport vans standing by."

"Okay, I'll tell him." Dara filled Randall in, and he said he'd be in touch when he knew how many local ambulances they could get.

"What about the critical patients?" Dara asked.

"The surgical intensive care unit has six patients, all of whom need continued unit monitoring—an aortic aneurysm repair, a liver resection patient, a septic postop colon resection, two vascular bypass patients, and a multiple trauma patient on a Stryker with a cervical spine fracture."

Dara's stomach clenched. "You've got someone with a spinal cord injury in your unit? Why hasn't he been transferred to a regional spine center already?"

"Boating accident—he just came in this morning. We were able to get him stabilized and his spine immobilized, but moving him is going to be tricky."

"What do the neurosurgeons say?"

Randall gave a laugh that sounded entirely without humor. "About what you'd expect. They want to operate and fuse the spine before he's moved."

"How long?"

"They say eight hours once they get started. I've seen it take longer."

"What's your opinion?"

"From an emergency management point of view, the faster we evacuate the critical patients, the better. The patient's family wants him operated on here. I think they're gonna put up a fuss about him being moved unless we do. What's your timetable?"

"Hold on for a second." Dara leaned closer to Sawyer. "Can you give me an ETA they can work to?"

"Tell them we want to be in and out by zero thirty hours."

"Twelve thirty." Dara shook her head. "If we don't get there until ten p.m., that's awfully fast turnaround."

"If they expect to move quickly, maybe they actually will."

Dara informed Randall they'd be there between nine and ten p.m. "We're going to want to get the critical patients moved out quickly."

"What about the spinal injury?"

"Keep me updated."

"You got it."

Dara ended the call. "You might have to leave me there and take the other patients back first."

Sawyer shook her head. "That's not happening."

"There's a spinal cord injured patient who's probably going for emergency surgery. If I'm there, I can facilitate getting him ready for transfer, and you can get us on a second evac run."

"Right now we don't know there will be a second run, and I'm not leaving any of my team behind."

Dara wanted to plead her case but thought better of it. She'd save her energy and her arguments for when it really mattered. One way or the other, she'd see every patient out safely.

Chapter Ten

Landfall minus 5 days
Homestead Air Reserve Base, Homestead, Florida
Flight path to Key West 130.6 miles
Flight time 52 minutes, cruising speed 150 mph

Sawyer checked her messages during the remainder of the drive to the airbase, while Dara did the same. Despite the silence, she was acutely aware of Dara just inches away. Distractingly aware. She always knew the exact position of anyone in her radius, but she could actually register the warmth, the energy, of Dara's body within touching distance. If she stretched out her hand...

"Who are we meeting?" Dara asked suddenly. "Besides the pilots, I mean."

Relieved, feeling almost as if she'd been given a reprieve and having no idea why, Sawyer said, "Medevac missions require coordinating a number of different sections. Since the weather is against us, we'll keep this briefing lean and fast—just the battalion support chief, battalion support medical company commander, and the task force medical platoon officer."

Dara stared. "Translation, please."

Sawyer laughed. "Ground and air transport and supplies, medical supplies, and corpsman."

"How many helicopters?"

"We've got two HH-60 Black Hawks—fully medically ready. Two corpsmen each."

"Plus me."

"Advisory only," Sawyer clarified. "You won't be familiar with our equipment or protocols."

"No problem. I'll be most useful working with the hospital staff anyhow."

"Good. That will help speed things along." The latest weather advisories indicated rain and fog moving in ahead of the advancing hurricane, and she wasn't sure how long they'd have before they had to get airborne or risk being stranded in the Keys. "We'll be running this more like a casevac than a medevac."

"Sorry?" Dara said. "I don't follow."

"Casualty evacuations usually happen under fire—on the ground and in the air. In and out as fast as possible is the best way to get everyone, including the crew, out alive. Medevacs are more often transfers from the frontline hospitals to a regional base or hospital. Much more controlled circumstances."

"So we're somewhere in the middle—the hurricane won't be shooting at us but could be deadly all the same."

"That's about it," Sawyer said, pleased by Dara's calm tone. Dara might not be battle tested, but she was no stranger to working under fire, just of a different kind.

The driver pulled the Humvee down an access road and stopped behind a large shedlike building made of steel and concrete, its large hangar doors closed, the only light coming from a series of square windows set high along the sides beneath the domed metal roof.

"Thank you, Corporal," Sawyer said. "That will be all for tonight."

"Yes, ma'am."

Sawyer climbed out and held the door for Dara.

"Are you hungry?" Sawyer asked. "We've got a couple of minutes, and it may be a while before we have a chance to get anything to eat."

"Food is fuel," Dara said. "I can do with a sandwich."

Sawyer led the way toward the hangar. "We'll grab something from the canteen. I can't promise anything fancy."

"Believe me, I've had many a vending room meal in my life. If it's fresh, I'll be happy."

The selection wasn't nearly as bad as she'd expected, and Dara grabbed a turkey sandwich from the machine.

Sawyer pulled out another sandwich and unwrapped it. "There'll be coffee in the briefing room."

"It's not really so different than the hospital," Dara murmured, making quick work of the impromptu meal.

"How so?" Sawyer ate with similar economy.

Dara tossed her trash and walked beside Sawyer down an empty corridor, their footsteps echoing in the cavernous space above them. "This place is impersonal but strangely comfortable at the same time. I've never been here before, obviously, but I still feel at home."

"Sometimes it's the rest of the world that seems strange," Sawyer said. "Unreal, almost."

"I know. More than once I've walked outside in the morning after working all night, and the sun is shining and people are strolling along the sidewalks and cars are driving by. All completely normal. Except I feel as if I've stepped into an alien universe. I'd almost rather turn around and go back into the ER again and wait for the next emergency. That's where I know exactly who I am."

Sawyer gave her a long look, another tendril of understanding forged between them so effortlessly all she could do was wonder at how easily they connected. She hadn't imagined civilians could feel that way. She'd given up trying to explain why the military felt more like home than any other place she'd ever been, at least since the only place she'd called home had disappeared. The people she cared about—other soldiers—already understood, and as the years had passed, she found less and less in common with anyone outside. "I know exactly what you mean. I think that's why a lot of us re-enlist or stay in. This world makes sense."

"To us," Dara said.

Sawyer stopped in front of the plain door with a simple placard announcing *Briefing Room*. She reached for the handle and paused before pushing it open. "Do you think we were made for the work, or the work makes us?"

Dara shrugged. "I was thinking about that earlier. A little of both, I guess. But it doesn't really matter, does it? We're here now, and that's where we want to be."

"Someday," Sawyer murmured, "you'll have to tell me why."

Dara's eyes widened, the dark pupils making the rim of blue

stand out so much brighter that tiny flecks of gold flared like specks of sunlight in their depths. "Why what?"

"Why you do what you do, instead of so many other things you might have."

"Is that what you think?" Dara heard the staccato of footsteps in the distance. This brief intermission was about to disappear. "Don't believe everything you read, Colonel."

"I never do."

"Then maybe I'll tell you one day."

Sawyer nodded, her gaze raking Dara's skin so intently her skin burned. The murmur of voices grew louder. Whatever private door they'd nearly opened would have to stay shuttered a while longer, but for the first time in her life, Dara wanted to let someone inside. Foolish, given the circumstances. More foolish still given how easily Sawyer Kincaid seduced her into wanting to expose her secrets.

When Sawyer pushed the door open, Dara took a breath, switched gears to professional mode, and stepped inside. Her comfort level instantly climbed. They could have been back at Miami Memorial. The windowless room looked much like the ER conference room, with a large table occupying the center, metal chairs surrounding it, a blank screen at one end, and a counter along one side with a pair of stainless steel coffeepots on a dual burner beside a stack of Styrofoam cups. The coffee even smelled identical—just short of burnt but appetizing all the same. Pavlov's dogs, all of them.

"Want to chance the coffee?" Sawyer said, already headed that way.

"Why not," Dara replied, smiling to herself. Yep, just like home.

Sawyer poured a couple of cups and handed one to Dara.

"Thanks," Dara said absently, already engrossed in the large-scale map of the state spread out on the center of the table. She recognized the general outline but not the many lines, site designations marked with symbols, and time stamps at various places along a heavy dark line connecting a series of red circles over the Atlantic Ocean. She pointed to the circles growing closer as they neared the islands. "Leo?"

"His location as of nineteen thirty hours," Sawyer said, pointing to the log on the bottom of the huge map. "This is the field of operation. During the briefing we'll finalize flight routes, confirm airspace and evac routes, and make sure everyone involved agrees on the mission plan. This way we can be sure not to overlook any key elements and be prepared to make adjustments if the situation changes."

"It's pretty much like running a mass casualty drill, coordinating all the moving pieces," Dara said. "Of course, that makes sense. A big part of civilian trauma care is based on military medical advancements."

"We're not so far apart," Sawyer said, no longer surprised at how similarly they approached a problem.

"I guess not." Dara smiled.

Sawyer turned as the door opened, grinning as Rambo walked in. "I didn't expect to see you."

"Hey, Bones. Figured you'd need a hand."

Sawyer caught his gaze assessing Dara. "Dr. Dara Sims. Colonel Beauregard."

"Hello," Dara said.

"Ma'am." He looked at Sawyer. "As soon as we got the evacuation orders, we relocated ten transport trucks to Homestead. It looks like you're going to need them."

Sawyer asked, "You planning to ride along?"

"Thought I'd make the run," he said.

She knew why he was going. The same reason she was. Conditions were not yet critical, but they soon could be. This was a mini-drill for what was likely to be a huge operation in a few days under much worse conditions. Better the snafus happened now than when hundreds of lives were at stake. "Good to have you."

"We'll need the local authorities to keep civilian traffic moving or we're going to get bogged down on the causeways."

"Ground command will handle that," Sawyer said.

Rambo nodded. "Let's just hope Leo's timetable doesn't accelerate."

Within ten minutes, half a dozen soldiers crowded around the big table. Sawyer introduced Dara and took the lead in reviewing the mission details. Once everyone agreed on the operational details, she said, "Dr. Sims will assist in patient triage to air or ground transport at Key West Memorial Hospital. She has preliminary information on the critical patients. Dr. Sims?"

Dara quickly filled in the officers on the medical condition of the critical care patients, adding, "We will have to review their conditions on arrival. There may be one, possibly several acute postop patients to transport by that time."

"Dust off at twenty-two hundred hours," Sawyer said when Dara finished.

As the others filed out, a female lieutenant entered with a familiar blonde by her side.

"Colonel, the captain requested I escort Ms. Winchell. She's with Channel 10 News."

"Ms. Winchell," Sawyer said flatly, hiding her surprise. The reporter looked nearly as casually seductive in her wine-red suit, pearl-gray shirt, and low dark heels as she had in her white bikini. The amused smile hadn't changed either. "I wasn't aware you were here. How can I help you?"

"Colonel Kincaid," Catherine Winchell said in her smoky voice. "How nice. I didn't expect to see you again so soon."

Dara stiffened, a completely irrational surge of dislike taking her by surprise. Her usual habit of not prejudging people on appearances went right out the window as she watched the way the newcomer's gaze traveled over Sawyer, like Sawyer was a tasty offering at a buffet. She could feel her teeth grinding.

"My apologies," Catherine said, sounding not the least bit sorry. "I didn't want to miss you, and your media liaison was most accommodating in allowing me to intercept you before you got official word."

"Official word of what?" Sawyer asked. She knew but would have to see the order before she'd comply. She'd never been a fan of noncombatants on missions outside the line, and this operation was beginning to look like one.

"The governor feels that the more up to date the coverage of developing events, the safer the public will be. I'll be accompanying you to report on the evacuation efforts and storm conditions." She glanced at Dara and held out her hand. "We haven't met."

"Dara Sims," Dara said. "I'm with the medical team."

"Sims." Catherine smiled. "I thought you looked familiar." Just as quickly, her smile faded and she returned to Sawyer. "I'm looking forward to working with you, Colonel."

"I'll assign you an aide who will escort you during the mission."

"Thank you," Catherine said, "but you do understand I'll need access to the person in charge, which, as I understand it, is you."

Sawyer had plenty of practice keeping her feelings to herself, but she needed all her effort not to growl. "Lieutenant, see that Ms. Winchell is properly outfitted and escort her to the flight deck."

The lieutenant saluted. "Yes, ma'am."

When the door closed behind them, Dara said, "Friend of yours?"

"No," Sawyer said. "Recent acquaintance. Come on. I'll get you a flight suit."

Dara followed, secretly pleased Sawyer hadn't sent her off with an escort too. And that she had quickly dispatched Catherine Winchell— even if she doubted they'd seen the last of her.

8:45 p.m.

NHC Storm Advisory
Hurricane Leo's storm track has shifted 15 degrees, WNW, at 15 mph. Winds at 160 mph. Projections include possible landfall in south Florida in four days. Storm center 120 miles in diameter, storm surge estimated at 15 feet in the Florida Keys.

9:48 p.m.
National Hurricane Center Atlantic Ops

"Stan," the communications chief called from across the storm control center, "I've got a call for you."

"Take a message." Stan spread his legs and planted his hands on his hips, staring at the images of Leo that filled the big screen nearly from side to side. The worrisome fact was the damn image was to scale—Leo was so big he dwarfed everything within three hundred miles. The eastern Caribbean islands in his path looked like pebbles tossed into the bottom of an enormous swimming pool. Insubstantial and inconsequential. Only the numbers told the true story: Barbuda, population 100,000; Antigua, population 11,000; St. Martin, population 40,000; Puerto Rico, population 3 million; Florida Keys, population 73,000.

"Stan, it's the governor's office."

"Tell them I'll get back—"

"It's the governor on the line."

Stan sighed. "Right." He crossed the room and took the phone. "Yes, sir. Stan Oliver here."

"What does this latest advisory mean for Florida, Stan?" Governor Phil Valez asked.

"I wish I could tell you that for sure, sir." Stan turned to watch the live feed of the swirling storm mass. "At this point, our predictions are just that—every hour the accuracy increases, but we're still a long way from knowing where he's going."

"Time is one thing we don't have," Valez said. "My highway people tell me we'd need four days minimum to evacuate south Florida, and that's assuming best case scenario and people actually leave when we give the orders."

"Yes, sir," Stan said.

"Well? What do I tell the citizens?"

"We're sure about the Keys—they're going to get wind and major storm surge."

"What about the coasts?"

"He's picking up speed." Stan watched Leo's huge center moving westward, pictured the trajectories the major storm models predicted—all with substantial error bars—and listened to the churning in his midsection. "Everyone in the low-lying coastal areas along the west coast should head for high ground."

Valez cursed under his breath. "Right. Thank you. Keep me informed."

The governor hung up and Stan rubbed his gut. He needed two more days to be sure of what the bad feeling meant, and he didn't have them.

CHAPTER ELEVEN

Landfall minus 4 days
Flight deck, Homestead Air Reserve Base

"Sergeant Jones," Sawyer said, addressing a young soldier with close-cut red hair, bright blue eyes, freckles, and a round boyish face that made him look about fifteen, "this is Dr. Dara Sims. She heads ERT at Miami Memorial. She'll be riding along."

"Ma'am," he said seriously, making Dara feel a decade older, and she already felt at least forty after the last couple of days.

"Jones is the corpsman who'll be flying with us," Sawyer went on. "Ordinarily we'd have two medics on board if we were flying casevac, but with medevac, in order to free up a bit more room for more patients, we'll fly with a smaller crew. Besides the pilots, there'll just be you, me, Jones, and Sergeant Brianna Norton, the crew chief. She's responsible for everything about the aircraft except the actual flying."

From behind them, a cultured, smoky voice added, "And don't forget me."

Dara caught Sawyer's expression morph through a series of changes so quickly she would have missed it if she hadn't been staring right at her, and if she hadn't gotten used to the subtle reflection of her moods in the set of her mouth and hard glint in her eyes. Yep—Sawyer was annoyed, aggravated, and something else—distrustful, maybe—about Winchell's presence. Dara wished she could tell if Sawyer just disliked the idea of an embedded reporter riding along on principle or if there was something else going on. She'd have to be unconscious to miss the seductive tone in the blonde's voice whenever she spoke to Sawyer or the way Winchell perused Sawyer's body as if she was visually undressing her. Not subtle at all—avaricious and confident. Nope, wasn't hard *at all* to figure out where Winchell's thoughts were headed or what she'd like to do upon arrival.

The idea of Winchell getting her hands on Sawyer curdled Dara's stomach. Not that that was any of her business and for sure none of her concern. Still, she had a very strong urge to hang a sign around Sawyer's neck: *Not safe for consumption. Sample at your own risk.*

As if she'd ever be that possessive even if she did have some right. Dara stifled a snarl when the reporter joined them and managed to position herself directly in Sawyer's line of sight. Yeah, real subtle.

Catherine pointed to the ID card she'd already been assigned by someone in the media affairs office, proclaiming her official status. "General Baker assured Les Bennett, my producer, there'd be no problem getting me access to your operations. After all, it's in the public's best interests to be properly informed in a timely manner."

"It's in your best interests," Sawyer said in a flat voice Dara recognized as the one that usually meant Sawyer was working hard not to explode, "to remain safe and capable of filing your reports."

Catherine laughed, a throaty sound that might have come off as practiced if it didn't suit her sophisticated persona so damn well. "I have no doubt you'll be able to keep me perfectly safe and…"

Don't say satisfied, Dara fumed inwardly. *Just do not go there.*

"…secure."

"I plan to keep everyone safe," Sawyer said with no trace of a smile. "Just follow my orders and you'll be fine."

"I wouldn't dream of doing anything else." Catherine's smile was luminous in the dim light of the hangar.

Dara resisted rolling her eyes. Barely. The woman was damn beautiful, she had to admit, but did she have to be aiming all 1000 kilowatts directly at Sawyer?

Sawyer merely nodded and focused on Dara, somehow managing to ignore all that heat surging her way. "Dara, Sergeant Jones can give you a tour of the medical facilities on board before we take off. I'll be back after I check with Charlie Tango 2."

"Of course." Dara looked around for Sergeant Jones in the hopes of making a quick exit. Sawyer no doubt had a million details to review before the mission began, so she had a very good excuse for disappearing. Dara, on the other hand, couldn't think of one fast enough, and Catherine Winchell effortlessly intercepted her before she could search out the corpsman.

"How did you come to meet Sawyer?" Catherine asked.

Sergeant Jones had unobtrusively slipped away. Wise man. Dara wished she could follow. She couldn't see a recorder anywhere, but she bet there was one somewhere in the pocket of the tan flight suit Catherine Winchell somehow managed to wear with a stylish flair. Dara was pretty sure she just looked shapeless in hers. Like she really should be worrying about that now. Although she *had* noticed how good Sawyer looked in the equipment-laden vest and BDU pants that hugged her thighs. Thankfully the poor illumination hid the flush she felt creeping up her neck at the image.

Dara hoped a noncommittal answer would shut down further questions. "Colonel Kincaid, as I'm sure you already know, is heading up the rescue and recovery arm of the National Guard's operation in response to Leo. Miami Memorial is the medical command center. We're coordinating efforts."

"And you got a ride-along on the first wave. Nice work."

Dara's back teeth started to ache, a sure sign her temper was about to fray. "I'm not sightseeing. We've got critical patients to move. The first run of many, probably."

"So tell me," Catherine said conversationally, relaxed and friendly, as if they were sharing a pre-dinner glass of wine at poolside, "what's it like working with the military? You seem like someone who likes to be in charge, and I assume you'll be taking orders now."

The woman was uncanny in ferreting out the sensitive buttons to push. Fortunately, Dara had had a lifetime filled with dodging intrusive personal questions from celebrity hounds and hunters and paparazzi. She smiled. "We each have a job to do, and right now, I want to go over the medical equipment with Sergeant Jones. So if you'll excuse me."

"Of course," Catherine said, falling into step beside her as Dara headed for the helicopter. "By the way, how much do you know about Sawyer's history?"

"I'm sorry?" Dara found the question so unexpected, she slowed without thinking and stared at the reporter.

"Well, I assume there's a story there, don't you? There's always a story." Catherine smiled. "I'm certain *you* have a very interesting one. For instance, how do your parents feel about you doing the work you do? I would have expected you to take a position in one of your mother's philanthropic organizations. Or there must bc a scat with your name on it in your father's boardroom."

"I make my own choices," Dara said, the shards of glass lining her throat threatening to turn her sentences into flying razor blades, "and I didn't ask my parents' permission."

"Well, see? There's a good story right there then too, isn't there. Let's talk again when it's not so noisy. Somewhere private," Catherine said, that honey-soft, irritatingly seductive tone slipping back into her voice again. "I'll buy you dinner and we can get to know one another."

Dara almost laughed. Only years of hiding her feelings allowed her to keep her thoughts to herself. As if she would ever be attracted to Catherine Winchell. Oh, she was beautiful, and undoubtedly intelligent and accomplished. But every single thing about her reminded Dara of her mother and the social set she'd fought to escape from her entire life. A quick image of Sawyer leaning against the counter in the coffee room where she'd first met her flashed through Dara's mind. Now, there was an attractive woman. Confident, capable, charming in an altogether unpolished way. That was a woman who could hold her attention. "I'm sure we'll be far too busy for the foreseeable future for any kind of conversation, let alone dinner. Besides, I have nothing to contribute to your story. I'm not the least bit interesting."

Catherine laughed and shook her head. "Oh, you clearly have no idea how interesting you are. But as I said, we'll wait until we have some privacy for that." She glanced toward the helicopter and then toward the rear of the hangar where Sawyer was just visible talking to the crew of the second helicopter. "In the meantime, we'll see what kind of story Colonel Kincaid has to offer."

Dara swallowed a dozen retorts, ranging from *leave her alone* to *not on your life*. Sawyer could handle herself. Winchell was just being a reporter—always on the hunt for a juicy story, a scoop, the next big ratings sweep. One of the big reasons Dara had wanted out of the privileged life to which she'd been born was the constant scrutiny, by peers, by family, by strangers—if she could have been anonymous, she would have been. But despite turning her back on her father after he'd so easily turned his back on them, she couldn't fault her mother for clinging to what remained of her life in a world where a woman was often judged by the status her husband provided, and most important of all, she couldn't hurt her grandmother by walking away from her family. All she could do was insist on being her own woman, no matter the cost.

With a tremendous effort of will, Dara turned her back so as not to see Catherine Winchell making her way over to Sawyer, and climbed into the open body of the helicopter.

"Sorry," she said to Jones. "I got held up. Want to give me that rundown now?"

"Sure thing!" Jones eagerly pointed out the surprising amount of state-of-the-art medical equipment on board for in-flight patient care—oxygen, defibrillators, refrigerated plasma and blood, instrument packs, intubation capability, even a battery-powered ventilator.

"You can do a full-scale resuscitation here if you need to," she said.

"Totally," he said with unmistakable pride. "Most of the time, we're just stabilizing blood volume and cardiac output. The blood makes a huge difference there. But sometimes, we're full-out resuscitating by the time we get to the frontline hospital."

"How long have you been doing this?"

"I've been in the Guard six years, and active for the last eighteen months. I just came back from a year's deployment." He looked out the open bay doors in the direction of the second helicopter where Sawyer stood with the crew. "I was with Colonel Kincaid in Africa."

"I imagine it's good to be back," Dara said, not quite knowing how to talk about something she'd never experienced and suspected could only be understood firsthand. Aware of Sawyer only a short distance away, preparing to lead a dangerous mission with lives at stake, she wanted to know what Sawyer had faced. What that had cost her.

"Most of the time," he said, a musing note in his voice as if he wasn't quite sure. Then his eyes brightened. "It feels good to set up on a mission again, though. Especially with the colonel."

Dara smiled at the obvious hero worship in his voice. "I know what you mean. It's what you're trained for, right?"

"Yeah," he said, suddenly shy again.

"Ten minutes, Jonesie. Button her up," a female soldier with a tablet in her hand, squint lines radiating from her cool gray eyes, and a thousand-yard stare called from the hangar floor.

"On it, Chief," Jones snapped.

Dara had barely finished her quick review of the equipment when Sawyer reappeared in the open hatch with the same woman. "Dara, this is Crew Chief Norton. She'll be in command of the aircraft during our flight."

"Dara Sims," Dara said.

Norton nodded to Dara's greeting and climbed in, talking into her radio as she ran through the preflight check. "You and Ms. Winchell will take the seats next to Sergeant Jones. Go ahead and strap in."

"Right," Dara said, picking the spot on Jones's left.

Sawyer turned to the reporter. "Ms. Winchell, ready to go?"

"Can't wait." Catherine Winchell put a hand on Sawyer's arm and climbed into the helicopter.

Sawyer settled opposite Dara, Jones, and Catherine, next to Brianna Norton. The rotor noise picked up and Dara sensed forward movement. Her stomach flipped at the realization she was about to embark on a lifesaving—potentially life-threatening—mission. She'd flown medevac shifts before, but only short distance and under optimal conditions. This was worlds different. Across from her, Sawyer looked relaxed and still totally focused.

Sawyer pointed to the headphones she took down from a hook behind her head, gesturing for everyone to do the same. Her voice came through Dara's headphone.

"Everyone, make sure you're buckled in. We should have a pretty smooth ride going down." She smiled. "If you have to vomit, you won't be the first. Try to miss your boots."

Dara grinned and mouthed, *like hell* when she caught Sawyer's eye.

Sawyer looked at Norton. "Chief? Are we clear to dust off?"

"That's a go, Colonel."

Her gaze on Dara, Sawyer touched her mic. "This is 1-4 Charlie Tango 1. Commence liftoff, over."

"Roger, 1-4. Charlie Tango 1, over."

"Roger, 1-4. Charlie Tango 2, over."

The nose of the helicopter tilted, the engine roared, and adrenaline pounded through Dara's bloodstream until her head swirled. She kept her focus on Sawyer, the calm at the center of the storm.

CHAPTER TWELVE

Airborne over the Atlantic Ocean
Visibility: Amber Illum, Moon angle 25 degrees, illumination 35%

The crew chief's voice came over the com. "We're coming in over the Atlantic side of the Keys. Weather boys report winds have picked up and we'll have some turbulence. Nothing the pilots can't handle."

As if on cue, the Black Hawk bucked and swayed, forcing everyone to hang suspended in their webbing by their shoulder harnesses for a few long seconds.

When the turbulence quieted, Sawyer clicked her mic to Dara's channel. "How are you doing?"

Dara fumbled for a moment, then mimicking Sawyer's movements, activated her headset. "Hell of a ride."

Sawyer smiled. She was tough all right. "Ought to touch down in ten. Just do what the chief tells you, when she tells you, and you'll be fine."

"No problem. Where are we landing?"

"The LZ is in the parking lot closest to the ER to make transfer easier."

"Good. It's raining, isn't it?"

"Looks like it, but that's mostly just atmospheric stuff freezing and melting on the airframe. Fog is coming in, though. We won't see much from the ground." Sawyer didn't see any point in mentioning the fog was likely to stick around and get denser, and the longer they stayed, the tougher the flying conditions would get. Her job was worrying about that—Dara's was helping to get the patients out as quickly as possible. "You'll triage with the hospital ERT leader once we land and coordinate transfer with our corpsmen."

Dara nodded. "Got it."

They'd already reviewed all this and Dara knew her job, but Sawyer figured the diversion would make the bumpy ride more tolerable. The bird jumped up a dozen feet and dropped just as fast. Outside, the night was black and getting blacker. No lights below for the pilots to fix on, and even with night goggles and infrared, there'd be nothing to see. She'd made plenty of runs in red illum conditions in Africa, where the moon provided no ambient light, the desert below was a void, and the pilots had to fly without infrared to avoid turning the bird into a target to enemy on the ground. Being confined in the endless dark was disorienting and quickly could become panic-inducing, even when the chance of being fired on was slim. Never zero, though; never safe. She'd learned to trust the pilots and close her eyes, escaping to a place of calm inevitability. Tonight she'd kept her eyes open, aware Dara was watching. She'd never detected a second's panic in Dara's eyes. She would have made a good soldier.

"Enjoy the rest of the ride." Sawyer grinned when she saw Dara laugh. Out of the corner of her eye, she caught Catherine Winchell intently following their silent exchange, obviously trying to figure out what she was missing. Winchell, to her credit, was holding up. She had a job to do too and was probably good at it. Too bad part of that job went beyond simple reporting, and that was the part Sawyer wanted to avoid. She intended to follow orders to the letter where the reporter was concerned, and not one syllable beyond that. She'd already gotten a taste of just how easily Catherine Winchell inserted herself into any situation and would undoubtedly charm any number of soldiers into providing her with sound bites before this operation was over. Sawyer didn't plan on sacrificing her privacy for politics. She'd keep Catherine informed as to mission status and update her on evacuation bulletins, storm path, or any other intel that impacted civilian safety, but beyond that she'd have nothing to say.

The bird dropped altitude steadily, and the crew chief came over the com again. "Three minutes to landing. Maintain your position until cleared to disembark."

The pilots set the Black Hawk down on the parking lot with the barest of thuds, and the in-flight vibrations rapidly diminished. Unlike in many other helicopters, the engine and rotor noises never varied much between idle and flight, so conversation was still limited by the continued roar even after the chief signaled them to remove their headgear and release their harnesses.

When the chief slid open the bay doors, Sawyer gestured to Dara and Jones to go ahead, and waited for Catherine to give her a hand down.

"Doing okay?" Sawyer asked. Despite her personal feelings about having a reporter along, Catherine was her responsibility.

Catherine held on to her arm as they walked. "Just a little off balance. Not exactly luxury accommodations. Somehow I thought they'd be...fancier."

"Nope—they're workhorses. Have been since the seventies."

"Combat and medevac, correct?"

Sawyer nodded. "That's right. Depending on the configuration and equipment, assault or recovery."

The second Black Hawk landed a hundred feet away, its rotors whirring, and one of their team jumped out and jogged over to join Jones and Dara. The hospital was a smallish one-story affair arranged in a T with the short arm running along one side of the parking lot. The illuminated red sign noting the emergency entrance was hazy and blurred in the thickening fog.

"Stay with me," Sawyer said.

"Don't worry," Catherine said, "I don't intend to let you out of my sight."

Just inside the ER entrance, Dara and the corpsmen were met by a slender man with round, gold-rimmed spectacles, a close-cut salt-and-pepper Afro, and a worried expression.

"I'm Josh Randall," he said to the group, "and mighty glad to see you."

"How are we doing?" Dara said, shaking Randall's hand.

"We've got the five critical earmarked for you just about ready to go," he said, "but the neurosurgeons took the spinal cord injury up to the OR right after we last talked. Too soon to tell how long they're going to be, but at least a few hours."

Dara glanced at Sawyer. "I'll review the ICU transfers with Dr. Randall and give you the order of transfer as soon as I can."

"All right." Sawyer addressed the medics. "Jones, Sun Li, go with Dr. Sims."

"We've got another problem," Randall said.

Dara paused. "What?"

He winced. "An MVA on the way. Two multiple trauma victims, one with a possible pelvic fracture."

Dara squeezed the bridge of her nose. "You didn't close to trauma?"

He raised his hands. "I did, but what can I do? There's no other hospital for fifty miles, and even if the patients are stable enough to make the trip, the roads are clogged with evacuees. I couldn't tell them not to come."

Dara glanced at Sawyer. "Can you evacuate them directly to the mainland?"

"Unless one of them needs immediate OR." Sawyer turned to the corpsman from the second helicopter, an Asian woman who stood half a head taller than Jones and had him by about forty pounds of what looked like solid muscle. "Sun Li, this has just become an official casevac mission. Get your bird ready. Take Jones."

"Yes, ma'am," the medic said. She and Jones jogged away.

Randall looked from Dara to Sawyer, his expression relieved. "I'll head up to the ICU and get the other patients ready for transfer."

"Good," Dara said, as the sounds of approaching sirens grew louder. "I'll be there as soon as I can."

Dara and Sawyer hurried outside, Catherine close behind, the red light on Catherine's minicam blinking as she captured the ambulance, red lights swirling and sirens blaring, emerging from the fog like an injured beast.

The rear doors of the ambulance flew open as soon as the vehicle careened to a stop. Two patients occupied stretchers side by side with a pair of blue uniformed paramedics crouched between them.

The huskier of the two, a sandy-haired guy with shoulders nearly as wide as the space between the two stretchers, looked out, took in Sawyer's uniform and Dara in a flight suit, and said, "Hey, you guys the Guard?"

"That's right," Sawyer said, making room for Dara to climb in first.

"Sweet. We just got orders to head back to Marathon and assist in their patient transfers. We're not going to be able to take these two anywhere from here."

"What have you got," Dara said, dimly aware of Catherine Winchell leaning into the ambulance with her recorder. Ignoring the distraction, she quickly scanned the two car-crash victims. Both were young, late teens or early twenties, a male and female.

The younger of the two paramedics, a slender man with deep brown eyes to match his burnished gold skin and impossibly long lashes, said in a surprisingly deep baritone, "One-car accident—rollover. He's the driver. Both were seat belted, but from what we could put together, the passenger"—he indicated the woman with the tilt of his chin—"had her feet or her knees braced against the dash. Bilateral femur fractures and likely compression pelvic fractures. Her blood pressure's been all over the place."

"Airbags deployed?" Dara asked. If they'd been restrained and protected by airbags, the risk of head and neck, abdominal, and long bone injury was reduced by nearly fifty percent. Unfortunately, if the female had her legs up, the airbags would be much less useful.

"That's affirmative on the airbags," the younger paramedic said.

Dara crouched to make a quick assessment. The male had what was probably a forehead laceration, judging by the gauze bandage nearly soaked through with blood wrapped around his forehead. He was breathing on his own, though, and a quick glance at the monitors revealed stable vital signs. His right arm was splinted in an air cast. "I'm Dr. Sims. Can you tell me your name?"

After a few seconds, he managed to focus on her face. His pupils were large and dark, but even and responsive when she flicked a penlight into them. "Um...where...what happened?"

"You were in an accident. Can you tell me your name?"

"Brad...Brad Ames. Where's...Ellie?"

"She's here. We're going to take care of you both." Dara pulled a stethoscope from a tray above the stretcher and listened to his chest. Clear. Although disoriented and dazed, he had no apparent major injuries. Under ordinary circumstances, he'd be evaluated in the ER and, if nothing else developed, admitted for treatment of his fracture and observation. He was stable enough to be classified as a Class III trauma and could wait the hour flight time for further care.

The girl, Ellie, was another matter. Her lungs sounded congested, possibly from direct thoracic trauma resulting in fluid buildup in her chest or potentially fatal fat emboli from the femur fractures infiltrating the lung tissue. She was at risk to crash and would need careful monitoring and immediate critical care.

"What's the status on fluids so far?" Dara asked.

"They've each had about two liters of saline. The girl is getting tachy," the lead paramedic said, pointing to the rising pulse readout on the portable EKG screen. "She's gotta be losing a fair amount of blood around the fracture sites."

Sawyer squatted behind Dara. "We've got blood on the Black Hawk, but without a type and cross, she'd have to get O-neg. We've got plasma substitutes that ought to be enough for a quick ride back to the mainland if we get going now. Visibility is getting worse all the time."

Dara's chest tightened. She heard the unspoken message. They might not all be leaving tonight, but the girl at least needed to. If she decided to transfer her immediately, and she went bad en route, the corpsmen might not be able to stabilize her. On the other hand, if the patient stayed here with the hospital evacuating, she'd need to be transferred by ground, an even longer process if complications developed. Dara considered what Sawyer had told her about battlefield casualties and their low mortality rate if evacuated immediately. This certainly fit that scenario, and this was what Sawyer's SAR personnel were trained for.

"Let's get her out of here," Dara said.

"Might as well take him too." Sawyer jumped down and jogged across the parking lot to the Black Hawk.

Dara waited for Jones and Sun Li while Sawyer conferred with the Black Hawk crew chief and pilots. The two corpsmen, working together as if they'd done it a hundred times, and maybe they had, got the stretchers out of the ambulance, across the empty parking lot, and into the waiting helicopter in a matter of seconds.

Dara followed and caught up to Sawyer. "Should we wait for the other ICU patients?"

"We can handle six in our bird, but if Jones goes back with these two, that will leave you and me as the only medics."

"We can handle that," Dara said.

"Then let's get this bird in the air." Sawyer motioned to the crew chief and pilots to take them up. She backed up as the rotors increased speed and the bird lifted off, vanishing within seconds into the fog.

Catherine suddenly appeared at her side, holding her recorder in one outstretched hand as she panned Sawyer and Dara. The only illumination came from the flickering red ER sign and the running lights on the remaining Black Hawk, casting them all in eerie shadows. "In situations like this, how do you decide who takes priority? After all, isn't it possible that one of the other patients might not be evacuated in a timely fashion with only one helicopter remaining?"

Dara bristled, resenting the implication she would compromise any patient's survival under any circumstances. While she was reminding herself Catherine was asking a valid question and trying to give her the benefit of the doubt, Sawyer spoke up.

"First responders make that kind of decision every day," she said looking directly at Catherine and, as a result, at the camera. "We're trained to make decisions on the battlefield or in the midst of a mass casualty situation, and that's exactly what Dr. Sims did. That's why our medical response during the next few days will be a joint venture."

She turned aside and started for the hospital. Dara wanted to follow, but Catherine thrust the recorder closer.

"As the physician in charge—"

"No, I'm not," Dara said. "You heard what the colonel just said. This is a team effort. Colonel Sawyer is in command of this mission. She's more than qualified. Out here, I'm the medical consultant. If you'll excuse me." She skirted around Catherine and hurried to catch up to Sawyer. She took in the set of Sawyer's jaw and silently appreciated her restraint. "How do you keep your temper when someone is intentionally trying to instigate like that?"

Sawyer laughed, although she didn't sound at all amused. "I try not to be bothered by uninformed people."

"Oh, that's a really nice way of saying ignorant buttheads."

Sawyer grinned. "Them too."

Dara pointed to the sign indicating the ICU down an adjacent hallway. They headed for it. "I think I'm getting to like working with you."

"I like your style too."

Dara flushed, aware the remark was not really supposed to be a compliment, but she couldn't help but like it. Even the sound of Catherine's boot heels hurrying to catch up to them couldn't dampen the surge of pleasure.

CHAPTER THIRTEEN

Landfall minus 4 days, 12:22 a.m.
National Hurricane Center Atlantic Ops

Stan's phone roused him from an uneasy sleep. He rolled over on the cot he'd been using since he'd returned to the weather command center what felt like a month ago. He hadn't been home since. Soon after he'd arrived and gotten a good look at what Leo was turning into, he'd put his wife on alert to call the property manager to prepare the house for the storm. She'd informed him on one of their twice daily phone calls that everything at their waterfront condo was good. They had hurricane glass and shutters on all the windows, remember? Besides, she also reminded him with the tiniest bit of heat, she'd been through this before without his help. As she was right, and perfectly capable of handling unpredictable weather like everyone else who decided to brave the Florida mosquitos, alligators, and temperamental climate for the idyllic conditions most of the year, he only suffered a few moments of guilt over leaving everything to her. He sat up, rubbed his face, and said hoarsely, "Oliver."

"Hey, boss," Anjou said, sounding almost as groggy. "Got something I think you're gonna want to see here. Leo has kicked it up a notch."

Stan was suddenly totally awake. "Not unexpected. The water's warm everywhere and the surface winds are quiet enough that he can take his time collecting a little more juice."

"Yeah, well, he's collected a *lot* more juice. And there's something else."

Now Stan's chest tightened. "What?"

"He's changing course."

Stan was on his feet. This was why he never went home when a hurricane was blowing in. "On my way."

12:58 a.m.
Key West Memorial Hospital

"What's the update from neurosurg?" Dara asked as Randall hung up the phone. From her perch on a stool behind the semicircular desk in the ICU, she could watch the nurse and PA moving between the five patients in the row of beds along the opposite wall. She'd been there for the last hour, feeling a little like she was back in her residency again—sitting up half the night waiting for lab results or a bed to open or a patient to declare which way they were going to fly, down the tubes or over the hill to recovery. She'd been an attending for five years, and though she spent many a night without sleep, she hadn't been this close to the ground in a long time. As tired as she was, the charge of being right on the front lines was energizing. She could see why someone like Sawyer, and corpsmen like Jones, would want to stay in the thick of that action. She would too in their place, except for the bombs and the bullets. War had never seemed as immediate, or as cruel, as it had since meeting Sawyer. War had become personal, and the thought was frightening. With a deep breath and a silent reminder to keep focused on the job, she added, "ETA?"

Randall grimaced. "They say two more hours before they're done. They had to bone graft the C-spine to stabilize it."

"Two hours probably means three minimum." Dara scanned the five other patients in the intensive care unit. One was an elderly postoperative ortho patient on a ventilator. Luckily, she was cardiovascularly stable. The only reason the woman still needed respiratory assistance was resolving postoperative pneumonia. Still, she was too critical to send in an ambulance that might get stuck in a backlog of traffic. One big reason the Guard had sent helicopters to both Key West Memorial Hospital and Marathon was the lack of alternate ground routes north. The Keys were like a chain of beads, with only one major highway and a series of bridges connecting them to each other and the mainland. With hundreds, probably thousands of cars heading toward south Florida, the congestion was bound to bring traffic to a standstill in places. She didn't even want to think about what might happen if those cars were still on the bridges and causeways when the hurricane arrived. One thing was for certain. They couldn't have ambulances on the road with critical care patients trapped inside when Leo hit. They'd have to wait for the neurosurgeons to finish and then move all the remaining ICU patients on the Black Hawk.

"We'll need to hold him here for at least an hour postop before we attempt to transfer," Dara said, keeping her misgivings to herself. Randall wasn't to blame for the delay. "So we're looking at close to five a.m." She sighed. "Maybe we'll have some light by then at least."

Randall, his face ashen with fatigue and his eyes morphing from blurry to barely focused, nodded. "I'd tell you to go now, but we can't risk putting this fresh postop in an ambulance and we can't rush him out of here. If he bleeds around the bone grafts, he could end up a quad."

"Don't worry. We won't leave here until he's stable." Dara eyed Randall. "How long have you been up?"

For a moment, he looked confused, as if he couldn't quite decipher her question. "Oh. Uh—since the day we got word to evacuate. I was on call the night before and just never went home."

"Why don't you go get some sleep. Do you have someone who can cover in here for you?"

He winced. "Most of our staff have been here as long as me. We've been trying to rotate them home as soon as the patients in their sections have been transferred so they can take care of their families." He gestured to the two ICU staff looking after the five patients. "Ordinarily there would be at least four nurses and/or PAs in here. Jeff and Phyllis volunteered to stay until we're clear up here, and then they're both slated to go home. They're on their fourth back-to-back shift already."

"Why don't I cover here in case they need backup, and you can grab a couple hours. We could be in for a long wait, and you've still got the rest of the hospital to worry about."

"What about you?" he said.

"I will if I can, but I'm okay for now."

"Thanks. I'll take you up on it, then. I can wait until you make a coffee run. You're going to need it. If you and the rest of your team get a break, rooms 110 and 111 are free to crash in. 110 has bunks, so you ought to have enough room."

"Thanks." Dara got up to hunt for Sawyer. The last she'd seen her, she'd been on her way outside to brief the Black Hawk crew. "I'll be back in ten minutes."

"I'll be here." He dropped into a chair in front of the monitors as Phyllis, the ICU nurse, came over to ask him a question.

Coffee first. Dara headed for the conference room that doubled as a break room around the corner from the intensive care unit. The door was open, and as she rounded the corner, she heard voices. Catherine and Sawyer. If she hadn't heard the question quite so clearly, she wouldn't have stopped just before she reached the doorway.

"So how does it feel," Catherine Winchell asked, "facing the kind of hurricane that almost destroyed your whole family?"

"I don't know what you're talking about."

"Really, Colonel," Catherine said, her voice teasingly reproachful, "did you think my research assistant couldn't pull up those stories in a matter of minutes?"

"I was a kid. And I have nothing to say."

Sawyer's tone held a raw edge Dara hadn't heard before, but she recognized barely contained fury and something else. Pain. She'd heard it in the voices of those who'd lost patients, lost loved ones, lost the battle with death on so many fronts. Whatever memories Catherine was determined to reawaken, they were painful ones.

Heart pounding, she stepped inside, propelled by an overwhelming urge to get between Catherine and Sawyer, as if her physical presence could somehow stop the verbal assault. Of course, Sawyer didn't need Dara to defend her, but that didn't make the urge any less intense.

"Sawyer," Dara said as she walked in, "I've got an update for you."

"What's the word?" Sawyer grabbed the chance to deflect Catherine as Dara strode in, fire in her eyes. If Dara'd had a sword, it would've been raised and aimed at Catherine's head. The image of a Valkyrie riding into battle passed through Sawyer's mind, fierce and fearless and fearsome. She'd seen the expression on warriors she'd led into battle, but she'd rarely seen that impressive power unleashed in her defense. Oh, she'd known with absolute certainty her troops would have her back—in battle, yes, but personally? Other than Rambo, she'd never let anyone know enough about her to realize she might need defending. And even he didn't know where her deepest wounds and greatest vulnerabilities lay. Not his fault. She kept her secrets close and her weaknesses hidden.

Catherine had ambushed her and, until Dara walked in, had her cornered. Dara's appearance gave her the chance to regroup, and she needed it. Her past had no place here. Not anywhere anymore.

Dara stopped a few inches away, pointedly ignoring Catherine. "We're looking at three more hours at least. Most likely four."

Sawyer grimaced. The last weather report indicated winds continuing to increase. Cloud cover was thickening, and visibility had fallen. At the very least, they'd need a new flight route home, and if the new path took them too far outside the planned route, they might be looking at refueling along the way. But their mission was to evacuate these patients and get them to Miami safely. Whatever needed to be done, she'd have to figure out a way to do it. Letting Catherine throw her off task had to stop.

Catherine smiled at Dara as if Dara hadn't just interrupted her. "I was just asking Colonel Kincaid about the similarities between this situation and the one during Andrew. You must be aware of that story." She tilted her head toward Sawyer. "She was quite famous for her heroics, even back then."

Sawyer's jaw tightened. "That has nothing to do with what's happening here."

"Doesn't it?" Catherine said. "You might think that who you are, what you've experienced, doesn't matter, but the people need a hero. They need to believe in their saviors."

"I'm neither of those things. I'm a soldier, just like the six thousand other soldiers who are down here fighting to make sure everyone is safe."

"Yes," Catherine said, her honeyed voice vibrating with conviction, "and every one of those six thousand soldiers needs a face, and we can't show them all. Yours will be the face that stands for each of them. They deserve that."

Oh, she was good. Dara was torn between disagreeing and empathizing. Her personal feelings for Catherine's blatant personal interest in Sawyer aside, she was familiar with Catherine's reputation.

She was an influential and respected reporter, and a popular one. And she probably had a point. As much as Dara wanted to argue, she couldn't really, not with the theory at least. Up to a point. Yes, every person, civilian or military, deserved to be recognized for risking their lives to benefit others, but Catherine's questions crossed the boundary from the professional to the personal, and whatever she'd discovered about Sawyer had the power to wound. Nothing else mattered to Dara.

"Catherine," Dara said, as if she didn't know she'd just derailed Catherine's interview, "they've given us the use of the on-call rooms. 111 is right down the hall. You might want to catch some sleep."

"I appreciate your concern." Catherine gave Dara a long, appraising glance. "Since I know you can't leave without me," she said with an amused smile, "I might just take you up on it."

"I told Randall I'd relieve him," Dara said to Sawyer as Catherine turned and left. "Do you have time to go over the patients in the ICU now?"

"Of course." As they walked out into the hall, Sawyer murmured, "Thanks for the save."

"Anytime," Dara said.

Sawyer's grin was the single bright spot in Dara's long night.

Sawyer followed Dara from bed to bed in the ICU, making mental notes as Dara gave her a thumbnail sketch of each of the patients they'd need to transport. All required monitoring, but fortunately three of the five were awake and able to communicate. The fourth was sedated and the fifth intubated. When they moved back to the desk she said, "We should be able to handle all of them with no problems. I can keep an eye on these five for the length of the flight, which will leave you with the postop patient."

"That's a lot for you," Dara said.

The ICU nurse came over as they talked and held out a hand to Sawyer. "Colonel, Lieutenant Phyllis Zywicki. Navy reserve. I can go with you if you need me."

Sawyer glanced at Dara. "We have room."

"I thought Dr. Randall said you were due to go home," Dara said.

Phyllis shrugged. "I was planning to go down to the ER and lend a hand anyhow. I've got no family to worry about down here, and my roommate already left with her cat and my parrot. You'd be doing me a favor with the lift."

"Then we can use you," Dara said. "Thanks."

Sawyer said, "Who do we have to clear it with?"

Phyllis waved a hand. "Honestly, probably no one. I'm sure Dr. Randall will agree, and since the evacuation orders, he seems to be making all the decisions. I think the other members of the ERT are all administrators." She laughed a little wryly. "And I think they've all left town."

Sawyer nodded. "We'll talk to Randall."

"Great," Phyllis said. "You've got a couple of hours before the postop patient comes back. Might be a good idea to get some rack time."

Sawyer said, "Up to Dr. Sims."

"Are you okay with that, Phyllis?" Dara said.

"Totally. Everyone here is stable and you'll just be down the hall. You'll both be pulling the heavy load once we're airborne. Go while it's quiet."

Dara glanced at Sawyer. "Can't argue the logic."

Nodding, Sawyer followed Dara out into the hall. "110?"

"Unless you want to share with Catherine," Dara said dryly.

Sawyer snorted. "I'll pass."

Chuckling, Dara entered 110 and paused in the doorway of a typical on-call room—eight by ten, tile floors, nondescript furniture, plain narrow bed. In this case, bunk beds. Efficient use of space, and not uncommon if not particularly comfortable. Comfort and on-call were not generally associated states. "Top or bottom?"

Sawyer gave her a look and Dara rolled her eyes.

Grinning, Sawyer said, "I'm good with the top."

Of course you are. Dara carefully didn't look at Sawyer as Sawyer vaulted past her onto the top bunk. Appreciating the fluid way she moved, the absolute confidence in her every step, the muscular silhouette of her form passing through the sliver of light in the dark room—no, not thoughts she should entertain. That way lay dragons, and she had enough to worry about. She sat on the bottom bunk and kicked off the boots she'd been given along with the flight suit. It had been a long time since she'd doubled in an on-call room with anyone, but somehow, with Sawyer, sharing the small space felt perfectly natural. Neither of them had bothered to turn on a light, and a bar of gold sneaking through the crack beneath the door was the only illumination. She stretched out and stared at the underside of the upper bunk. Sawyer didn't move. Didn't turn over, didn't make any sound at all. Dara wondered if she was asleep already, or if she was staring into the dark. Finally, she had to know.

"Are you okay?"

For a long moment, Sawyer didn't answer. "Yes. I'm used to not getting much in the way of sleep."

"Same here," Dara said, although that wasn't what she'd meant, and she knew Sawyer knew it. "I was thinking more about Catherine Winchell. She seems awfully interested in you."

Sawyer hesitated. She could shut down the conversation with a word or two. If she did, she'd be sending a signal, closing a door, drawing a line—a line she drew with ease and regularity with everyone in her life.

"Sorry," Dara said after the pause drew on. "None of my business."

"Reporters are always digging for a story," Sawyer said quickly, feeling her way along the unfamiliar terrain. This time the silence hadn't fit as comfortably as it always had before. Once, silence had protected her. Now the looming distance between them left her feeling as if she was about to go into combat unarmored and alone. If she wanted to hold on to the threads that connected her to Dara, she'd have to weave some of them together herself. "We bumped into each other completely by accident in a hotel I was staying in right before I got recalled from leave for Leo."

"You're kidding. Before all this started?"

"About the same time."

"Are you sure she wasn't stalking you?"

Sawyer laughed. "Positive. I'd have noticed. I'm always aware of anyone in my vicinity, particularly on my six."

"At your back, right?" Dara said.

"Right, sorry."

"Do you come with any kind of glossary or code book I could study up on?"

Sawyer grinned. "I could probably dig you up a manual of some kind."

"That would be appreciated. So you were saying, you met

Catherine, and then she suddenly appears embedded—that's the right word, right?"

"Correct."

"Embedded in your command." Dara huffed. "Wow, tell me that's a coincidence."

"What else would it be?"

Dara groaned. "You can't see me, but I'm head-smacking down here."

Sawyer frowned. What was she missing? Dara sounded—irritated. "Why?"

"Really, you can't see it? She's, um, interested in you?"

"Oh. Well, I gathered that. She's a reporter, and she wants a story, and she's starting with me. When she doesn't get anywhere, she'll move on."

"It's not just the story, you get that, right?" Dara kicked the underside of Sawyer's springs. "She'd like to get a little more personal with you."

"She did suggest something like that," Sawyer said, beginning to follow the direction things were going and enjoying the by-play, "but I already declined."

Sawyer could hear Dara sitting up on the bunk beneath her.

"You're kidding."

The edge in Dara's voice made Sawyer smile again. Dara was also repeating herself, and she never did that. Concise, certain, sure of every word. "Nope."

"How many times did you run into her?"

"Just the once, for about ten minutes by the pool."

"And in that period of time she made a move?" Dara's voice rose.

Sawyer rolled over and leaned her chin in her hand. "She's very focused."

Dara snorted. "Well, there's a word for it."

"Anyhow," Sawyer said, "I think her interests are professional at the moment."

"I hope you don't mind I barged in."

Dara didn't sound exactly apologetic, but she did sound a little unsure again. As if possibly she *had* been interrupting.

"I'm glad you did." Sawyer came to another crossroads. She liked talking in the dark like this, imagining the expression on Dara's face, feeling the buzz of pleasure at the heat in Dara's voice when Catherine's name came up. If she went any further down this road, though, she would be outside the wire, beyond the zone of safety, with no one to watch her six. "Catherine was getting a little too personal, even if she was doing it for a story."

"You don't have to tell me," Dara said softly.

"I know," Sawyer said. "But I want to."

CHAPTER FOURTEEN

Hurricane Andrew, landfall minus 47 minutes
August 24, 1992, 4:05 a.m.
Naranja Lakes, South Dade County, Florida

"Jim," her mother said frantically. "We can't stay here. People are leaving, almost everyone's gone."

Sawyer's mom held her baby sister in her arms, jiggling her to soothe her fretting. Her little brother was only four, but old enough to tell something bad was happening. He clung to her dad's leg, his thumb in his mouth.

The walls of the trailer shook and screeched with a tin-can rattle that sounded like people pounding on the outside with hammers. The howling noise was the wind, her dad said, but Sawyer had never heard the wind roar like the motor on her dad's motorcycle—even louder every minute too. She tried to look out the windows, but the rain was so heavy the sheets of water, like the plastic they tacked up around the window frames in the winter to keep out the cold, made everything blurry.

Being the oldest, Sawyer watched and waited for what she should do, jiggling from one foot to the other.

Her father tugged at his hair, and that must have hurt because he made a face like it did. "There's not enough gas in the truck to get very far, Kimmie." He looked like he was mad, but he didn't sound mad. He sounded...kind of scared, which was scary, because he wasn't supposed to be afraid of anything. Her mom seemed scared too.

"The radio said the hurricane's coming this way," her mom said, "and now the power's out, and I can't get any kind of signal."

Sawyer's heart pounded. She knew what a hurricane was, kinda like a thunderstorm only a lot bigger. She wasn't sure why everyone was so excited about this one. Andrew, its name was. She thought that was funny, how they named storms. Why would they do that? She'd have to ask when her mother and father weren't so busy.

"Oh my God, Jim, look," her mother said, pointing. "The water's coming underneath the door."

"Get dry clothes, food, and water together. I'll start the truck."

"No," her mother said, "don't go out alone."

Her father crouched down next to Sawyer. "I'll be right back. You help your mother with the little ones."

"Can I come with you?" Sawyer said. Her dad might need help too.

"You stay inside." He kissed her forehead. "Everything's going to be all right."

But he'd been wrong.

"We lived in a mobile home park in Dade County," Sawyer said. "We didn't evacuate—hardly anyone did. No one appreciated how big Andrew was going to be, and he came ashore pretty much right on top of us."

"How old were you?"

"Seven." Sawyer's throat was dry and she swallowed. "We tried to leave, but it was already too late. My dad…he went out to get the truck. My mom and my sister and brother and me stayed behind. Then the trailer started blowing apart."

"God." Dara's sharp intake of breath sounded loud in the still room. Like the rush of wind through blown-out windows.

Sawyer shivered. "We waited half an hour, but the water was getting higher and higher inside the trailer. The door gave way, and mud and branches gushed in. We all climbed on the couch. Then Andrew made landfall and the wind took everything. We were lucky—the trailer didn't blow away, and a lot of them did. The roof came off, and two of the walls went. A lot of the furniture too, but my mom got us all under mattresses in the bedroom."

August 24, 1992, 6:15 a.m.

The screaming wind went on forever, clawing trees out of the earth and sending them thundering through the air, turning signposts and metal siding torn from trailers into lethal sails, skittering along on the floodwaters and slashing through fences and foliage. Water soaked through the mattress where her mom huddled over the little ones, Sawyer pressed tight against her side, their arms linked.

She must've fallen asleep, and when she woke, the water was up to her knees. She shook her mother. "Mom, Mom, we have to move. We have to get out of the water. There's things in the water." She'd seen them swimming and slithering.

"There's nowhere to go, baby," her mother said, trying not to sound scared.

Neither of them mentioned her dad. He'd come back. Soon.

"We can get on the roof," Sawyer said, pointing to the remaining portion that hadn't blown away. "You can use the bookcase to climb up on maybe, and I can hand you the kids."

"All right, yes."

"You have to go first," Sawyer said, even though she didn't want to stay behind. She couldn't climb up all by herself, but she could help with the little ones and her mom could pull her up.

When they reached the roof, they were in the middle of a muddy swirling ocean of junk and other things Sawyer didn't want to look at. The truck was underwater. Only the very top showed, and she couldn't see her dad.

"Our trailer was pushed off its foundation and half buried in mud and debris. We were marooned for two days. We heard helicopters, but there were so many people stranded everywhere, and so many roads were blocked the first responders had trouble getting through. They had helicopters, but not as many as we have now, and not as many SAR teams. The ones that were flying search and rescue didn't get close enough to see us."

"That's so horrible."

"I don't know why," Sawyer said, "but I thought if we could fly a flag they would know we were there." She thought of how her mother had climbed down into the trailer and pawed through the debris that was all that remained of their possessions. "My mom slogged through storm water up to her chest looking for something to use and found a big white tablecloth in a plastic bin that was just floating in one corner of what used to be the kitchen—no idea how that hadn't floated away. I was good at climbing trees, and my mother couldn't leave the little ones in case they fell off into the water. It wasn't that far to swim."

"You went into the water?" Dara's voice held horror and awe. "And you were seven?"

"Like I said," Sawyer said, blocking out the memory of the things that floated and glided through the water, "it wasn't very far. Then I just climbed as high as I could and tied a corner of the tablecloth to one of the branches. I didn't want to go back into the water, and I could see my mom. So I waited, and the next time I heard a helicopter, I made sure they could see us."

The days and weeks after that melted in her memory into one long gray stretch of fear and misery. There had been TV cameras and reporters and strangers wanting to talk to her, but mostly there had been her mother's hollow eyes and the noise and smell of the shelters and the pervasive atmosphere of dread and desperation.

"No wonder Catherine said you were a hero! You were amazing."

"There were plenty of other stories just like mine." And she'd failed at the biggest job of all, hadn't she?

"What about your father?" Dara asked softly.

"He never came back."

Landfall minus 3.5 days, 4:10 a.m.
Key West Memorial Hospital, Room 110

Dara probably wouldn't have slept anyway, but she couldn't sleep after hearing Sawyer's story. She kept seeing a young child, far too young to be the oldest in any situation, dealing with such terrible trauma and loss. Surviving all that and still risking her life to aid and defend others. Her heart hurt at the same time as it filled with wonder.

Sawyer might've been sleeping, but Dara didn't think so. That preternatural stillness had settled over her again. She didn't turn over, she didn't shift around, she didn't make a sound in her sleep. Dara wondered if that was some kind of learned vigilance that soldiers acquired, or if it was just Sawyer, so contained, so controlled that even in her sleep there was nothing random, nothing unintentional about her actions. Did she ever deviate from her plan, did she ever allow for the unexpected? Of course she did, she had to. She'd have to be able to respond in the midst of chaos to any new threat, any shift in the momentum of the battle. But none of that was random. That was training, precision thinking, instinct honed to the razor's edge.

Sawyer wasn't a machine. She was something far more intricate and powerful.

Dara let out a long breath and hoped she hadn't been tossing and turning and possibly keeping Sawyer awake, but her blood was racing and her heart pounding. She'd been five during Andrew, and she barely remembered it. She couldn't remember being afraid or even seeing her parents acting as if anything was wrong. Of course, her family had had every advantage and convenience available to escape the disaster. She did remember they had flown in her father's helicopter to their summer home out of state. What had been a vacation to her, an exciting trip, had been a nightmare for thousands, and a devastating horror for so many like Sawyer. She wanted to ask Sawyer more— where they'd gone after the shelter, how they'd lived, and where the rest of her family was now, but she couldn't bear to press her for any more details, not when the memory was so clearly still painful, still fresh. There were moments, when Sawyer had been speaking softly in the dark, Dara had felt she was reliving the events rather than just remembering them.

God, she wished she could reach out, comfort her somehow. But she couldn't, could she. Something so personal, so intimate. So risky. Especially when a big part of her wanted to do more than comfort her. She hadn't had a serious interest in anyone in a long time—she'd been too busy, too cautious, too careful about leaving herself open to disappointment. And now, in the worst of circumstances, Sawyer came along and unleashed a storm of emotions and desires she hadn't even realized she'd locked away.

"Are you awake?" Sawyer asked quietly.

Dara caught her breath. Thank goodness Sawyer couldn't have been reading her face in the dark, although she sometimes seemed to be reading her mind. "Yes. Am I keeping you up?"

Now the springs above her creaked for a few seconds, and she imagined Sawyer turning on her side, perhaps looking down in the darkness as she was looking up, as if they could see each other somehow. The image made her smile, and the now familiar heat surged through her again.

"I got some rest. You?"

Dara chuckled. "My feet feel better."

"That's always a good start."

"I'm sorry, terribly sorry," Dara said, as inadequate as the words might be. She had to say something. Had to let Sawyer know she'd been heard, deep down inside. "For everything you and your family went through."

"Dara," Sawyer said so gently the word floated down like spring rain in the mist. "I don't want you to be sorry or sad. I wanted to tell you. I didn't want it to be a secret."

Dara's heart beat so quickly she was afraid her voice would tremble. She swallowed. "Then thank you."

"You're welcome."

"Catherine is wrong to drag that up now. I'd be happy to tell her so."

The bedsprings creaked again, and Sawyer flipped down onto the floor, landing almost soundlessly next to Dara. An instant later, her weight settled on the end of Dara's bed, just an inch from the bottom of her foot. In the light from beneath the door, all Dara could see was the silhouette of Sawyer's form, straight and strong. They weren't touching, but her body tingled.

"I wouldn't recommend taking her on," Sawyer mused. "She would be a formidable opponent, I think. And she's not going to get anywhere with it. I'm not gonna talk to her about it."

"You realize she can still write your past into the story. It's a matter of public record, I imagine."

"No doubt. Nothing's private anymore, even our suffering. If she does, then antagonizing her won't change anything." Sawyer's hand curled around the top of Dara's foot and squeezed gently. "But I appreciate you wanting to stand up for me."

"I don't understand how some people feel it's okay to encroach on other people's privacy." Dara's ire was irrational—she knew that. She'd seen the way her mother had been deluged with gossip hounds and even so-called friends when the scandal of her father's affair, quick divorce, and quicker remarriage had made headlines. Not the same thing as what Sawyer endured, not even close, but she'd been caught in the backwash at school, in her group of friends, and in her relationships for a long time after. She'd learned to ignore the invasion by putting walls between herself and everyone who saw her only as her father's daughter. The heiress to an empire.

"I guess Catherine sees the news as her battlefield," Sawyer said. "She's the standard bearer, right? The truth teller."

"Please," Dara muttered. "Acting in the name of some greater good sounds lofty, but I bet she's watching the ratings more than anything else."

Sawyer laughed and gave her foot a shake. "Hey. It's okay."

Dara blew out a breath. "Sorry. I just have a thing about reporters who think they have a right to dig around in your private life. Especially when things are messy or painful or, in your case, tragic."

"I guess you've had a lot of that."

"Oh, poor me." Dara snorted. "Sorry about my little burst of self-pity."

"I don't think that." Sawyer rubbed the top of her foot in slow, easy circles. "If I had to put up with people dissecting my every move my whole life, I'd be pretty damn angry."

Dara didn't want to move. If she did, Sawyer might move her hand. Despite the light sheet and the fact she was still wearing socks, she could feel the heat of Sawyer's hand racing up her leg, stirring places that absolutely should not be stirred here and now or probably ever. But damn, she liked it. "As long as you're okay with Catherine bringing up the past, I promise not to gag her."

"You know," Sawyer said, "I feel better about the subject coming up than I ever have. I've never actually told anyone the whole story before."

Dara couldn't resist any longer and sat up, bending her knees a little and ducking her head so she wouldn't hit it on the underside of the upper bunk. She reached out in the semidarkness and found Sawyer's hand. Their fingers entwined almost naturally, as if they'd done it a hundred times before. "I'm glad it was me."

"So am I."

CHAPTER FIFTEEN

NOAA Hurricane Advisory
Storm Path Update
Hurricane Leo
5:00 a.m. AST
Location: 17° N 61° W
Moving: *NNW at 12 mph*
Min pressure: *980 mb*
Max sustained: *130 mph*

"Anna," Stan said when his wife answered the phone on the second ring.

"You're early," she said, sounding awake even though she didn't usually get up until seven.

He was always the one to make the coffee and take the dog out, and he realized with a pang he missed it. He missed being home, and the routine of their days. "You too."

"Watching the news. The governor sounds pretty doom and gloom. How bad is it really?"

"That's why I'm calling. He's about to sound a lot more dire pretty soon. The storm trajectory has shifted a few degrees."

"I don't suppose that means out into the Gulf?"

Stan snorted. "That would be nice. No. Leo's shifted north. His path is tightening up and wind speed is climbing. He's a Cat 4, and he's headed for us."

"*Us*—us as in Florida, or…"

"Us as in Miami." Stan tried not to sound worried, but he was plenty worried. The time frame to landfall was getting shorter, and five million people lived in the Miami metropolitan area. "You need to leave now. The governor will be issuing a mandatory evac order any minute, and once he does, the highways will be a mess."

His warning elicited nothing but silence. "Anna? You there?"

"Where are you going to be?"

"What? Me? You know where I'll be."

"You know how bad Willis is on long car trips."

Stan rubbed his neck and winced. He was going to be permanently impaired after sleeping on that rollaway for two weeks. "Just put him in his crate and stick him in the back seat. He'll be fine."

"Jeremy assures me the condo is perfectly secured. He even said he could put metal sheets over the doors and storm shutters. I'll call him."

"Jeremy is the property manager—of course he says everything is fine. And metal shutters won't do a damn thing in hundred eighty mile an hour winds."

"We'll be fine. We're on the second floor."

"Anna—"

"We don't have a basement or a roof to worry about, Stanley. We'll be fine."

"God damn it, Anna."

"I'd rather be here than on the road for who knows how long and still run the risk of getting caught. When's landfall?"

She was too damn smart after all these years. Everyone wanted him to say exactly when—to the minute—and where—pinpointed on a map—and how big—pretty goddamned huge ought to cover it—Leo was going to be, as if radar and satellite and pilots flying through the eyewall were the equivalent of a crystal ball. They weren't, and three days might as well be a month in storm tracking terms. The NHC had the best forecasters and computer models in the world, but the weather was the weather. Nature forged its own destiny. "Thirty-six hours, depending on…well, you know that story. Depending on a lot of things."

"Mmm. I'll talk to you tonight. And don't worry. We've been through plenty of hurricanes before."

Not like this one. Stan sighed and said, "I'll call you. Love you."

"I love you too. Don't drink too much coffee."

5:10 a.m.
Key West Memorial Hospital

"How is it looking?" Sawyer asked the crew chief as Norton slipped out from under the tail of the Black Hawk where she'd been checking the mechanics.

"We're ready when you are," Norton said. "Any update on ETD?"

Sawyer resisted the urge to swipe at the water running down the back of her neck from the thick mist that had condensed in her hair on the short walk across the parking lot. The fog hung low, obscuring the horizon, and dawn hadn't done much to improve visibility. The cloud cover, intensified by the outer bands of Leo's advancing storm wall, blotted out the sun, and only pale gray light penetrated. The pilots would be dependent on their embedded global positioning air control systems to navigate them back to Homestead.

"They brought the surgical patient down about fifty minutes ago," she said, "so as soon as the neurosurgeon gives us the green, we're good to go. All the rest are packed up and just waiting for us to transfer them out."

"Good. I was just about to call you," Norton said.

Sawyer glimpsed Jeff, one of the two pilots, hustling his way from the ER. He'd probably taken advantage of the downtime to catch some sleep in the on-call rooms they'd been provided. His face was puffy and his jaw shadowed. Not a lot of sleep, it looked like. This didn't look good. If the crew chief wanted to brief them, something had changed in the mission directives. Sawyer readied herself to face the problem. Out here, whatever decisions needed to be made were on her back.

"Hey, Chief, Colonel," Jeff said, pushing wet strands of blond hair off his forehead. "Mariann's grabbing some chow. She'll be right out. We all set?"

"Not quite," Norton said. "I just got off the radio with Homestead. They're rerouting us. The storm front is making the air too choppy to reverse course and come in from the east on our return. We're going to swing out over the Gulf and cross the mainland west to east on our way home. Flight time's going to be about forty minutes longer. I sent the new coordinates to your onboard flight control computer."

Jeff shot Sawyer a look. "Your patients going to be able to handle the longer trip?"

Sawyer read in his eyes he wasn't happy, and she didn't blame him. Dara wasn't going to be pleased either. The long loop away from Leo's outer bands added time and mileage to their trip. An extra forty minutes might make a critical difference if one of the patients got into trouble. "Can we trim the time down any?"

"Maybe, as long as we don't run into even more turbulence or heavy air we have to maneuver around." He grimaced. "And I wouldn't bet on any of that. We're going to be cutting it close on fuel reserves as it is. But we'll give it our best shot."

"That'll do fine, then." Sawyer didn't need to tell the HH-60 pilots what was at stake. Time was the enemy on casevac runs. And these were experienced pilots. "I'll brief the medical people and tell them we need to get moving."

"Yeah," the pilot said. "That'd be a real good idea, Colonel."

Sawyer jogged toward the hospital, passing the second pilot on her way inside.

"Morning, Colonel," the pilot said, looking more awake than her copilot had.

"Lieutenant," Sawyer replied, returning the second pilot's salute.

On her way to the ICU, Sawyer paused by room 110 and, on impulse, pushed the door open, even though she knew Dara wasn't going to be inside. She'd last left Dara drinking coffee in the break room, waiting for the neurosurgical patient to arrive in the ICU from the OR. She was probably in there with him now.

As she expected, the room was empty, the rumpled sheets on the bunks the only signs anyone had been there. Crazy to be disappointed. She'd been hoping for a minute or two, just to…just to see her, to connect, to recapture the feeling of those moments they'd spent talking in the dark. She couldn't recall when talking to anyone had felt so right, so easy—even when the words had been so hard. Not the saying so much as the remembering, and the haunting regret that lingered still. She hadn't told Dara everything, about the guilt she'd never been able to shed, even when she'd gotten older and understood her seven-year-old self couldn't have made a difference. Some part of her would never be sure. She'd helped her mom and siblings survive, hadn't she? And no one had helped her dad. She should have gone with him. Maybe if she'd been there she could have warned him about whatever danger had caught him unawares. Because he would have come back, she knew that in every atom of her being, if he could have. He'd never leave them alone.

You didn't leave the ones you swore to protect behind.

Sawyer let the on-call room door swing closed, leaving the memories, painful and pleasurable, to the silence inside. There wasn't time to pull Dara aside now, to tease a brilliant smile and raised brow from her, to soak up the attention that seemed aimed only at her. She didn't know when they'd have a chance to be alone again. Possibly... probably...never. And if that was true, she'd be sorry. The ache in her chest was unexpected, and she struggled to lock it down tight. Usually she could. Closing Dara out was pretty much impossible, and she wasn't even sure she wanted to.

The intensity of her connection to Dara had just caught her off guard, that was all. She didn't have trouble talking with women. Sure, those were rare occasions when she took time from more important things to even be in a situation where she needed to socialize. Usually some barbecue or birthday celebration Rambo dragged her to. True, she never talked about personal things, just the kinds of surface things you talked about with strangers. And, of course, what she did for a living was always good for at least an hour's worth of conversation. She smiled to herself. The uniform came in handy sometimes, although her occupation hadn't seemed to impress Dara. No, the superficial things wouldn't impress her. With Dara, only the flesh and bone would do, and somehow, she'd bared it all in those few quiet hours in room 110.

Slapping the red button on the wall to open the ICU doors, Sawyer put aside the churning in her belly along with thoughts of the past and Dara. All the lights were on in the ICU, the artificial glare reminding her of the parade ground at night—stark, harsh, isolated from the world beyond the wire. Phyllis and the PA, a guy named Tom, moved efficiently from bed to bed, disconnecting lines and tubes, hooking up portable monitors, and getting the five relatively stable patients onto gurneys for the trip outside to the Black Hawk. Dara, Randall, and the neurosurgeon conferred beside the bed with the postop patient, a twenty-three-year-old who'd missed a turn on his motorcycle and, if it hadn't been for his helmet, would've died when he was thrown twenty feet into a stand of trees. Fortunately for him, he didn't hit any of those, but not so good news, he broke his neck when he landed. Currently he was intubated with an external cranial fixator encircling his head like a torturous halo. According to the neurosurgeons, the metal frame secured to his skull with screws drilled into the bone would prevent torsion on his spine and needed to stay in place at least six weeks until the bone grafts they'd placed along his pulverized spine fused in place and offered him some degree of safety.

"He's looking good," the surgeon said, her wrinkled scrubs in distinct contrast to her perky expression and bright gaze. She looked as if she'd just come in from an afternoon at the beach—relaxed and ready for a night of dinner and dancing. Since she looked about twenty, the image didn't seem too far off. "As long as the ride's not too bumpy, and you keep his pressure stable, he ought to be fine."

Sawyer didn't see any point in mentioning the obvious—they were flying along the edge of a storm wall with a hurricane coming in behind it. It might get a bit bumpy. "The external fixator ought to protect him, shouldn't it?"

She got another bright smile. "It should."

Dara said, "Well, let's get him ready, then. Thanks, Dr. Myers."

"I'll wait till you get him loaded. You can let me know when he's tucked away at your place, and I'll update the family," Myers said, making a note in the patient's chart. His parents had refused to evacuate until his surgery was completed. Dara and Myers had finally convinced them that remaining at the hospital any longer was not necessary, and they'd left a few minutes before.

"Are you leaving town, Susie?" Randall asked the surgeon.

"Nah. Bet you a dollar we're back in business in three days, and I've got patients scheduled." She sketched a wave. "I'll catch you outside."

Sawyer figured the jaunty surgeon would lose that dollar if anyone took the bet, but probably 30 percent of the population in the Keys agreed with her and would ignore the evac order. Unless local law enforcement went door to door enforcing the order, which wasn't going to happen, all she could do was get these patients to safety and hope she wouldn't be heading up another SAR run down here in a few days.

Phyllis said, "We're ready with the first one."

Sawyer took one end of the stretcher as Dara grabbed the other. As they pushed the patient out through the ICU doors into the hall, Sawyer asked, "Have you seen Catherine?"

"Not since we all grabbed coffee in the break room," Dara said. "I thought she was outside with you."

"Nope. Haven't seen her."

Dara frowned as they approached the family room at the end of the hall. "Sounds like she's up here. I thought everyone was gone."

Sawyer glanced in and slowed for an instant. Catherine was talking, all right, on the big flat screen on the wall. The Channel 10 logo ran across the bottom of the screen, the wind blew Catherine's blond hair into artful disarray, and a shot of Sawyer and Dara leaning into the ambulance filled the background.

CHAPTER SIXTEEN

Landfall minus 2.5 days, 5:00 a.m.
Channel 10 News Storm Update
Miami, Florida

"This is Catherine Winchell, reporting live from outside Key West Memorial Hospital, where evacuation has been under way since early yesterday. Behind me is the National Guard Black Hawk helicopter waiting to take the last of the most critical patients to Miami Memorial Hospital. The Florida state disaster management division designated Miami Memorial, under the direction of Dr. Dara Sims—a noted area physician—as the medical command center for the upcoming crisis. By this time tomorrow, all hospitals in the Keys will be closed. Hundreds of tourists have rushed to the local airports in an effort to escape the oncoming hurricane, and thousands of residents have already begun the arduous journey to the mainland along the single highway linking the Keys.

"This just in. The National Hurricane Center reports Hurricane Leo has changed track and is now on course to make landfall on the east coast of southern Florida. The storm has been upgraded to a Category 4 hurricane, and some models predict Leo will be a Cat 5 by the time the storm comes ashore. Governor Valez, in conjunction with Mayor Santos of Miami-Dade, has issued a mandatory evacuation order for coastal areas in Zone A and the eastern part of Zone B. This includes low-lying areas of Miami Beach and the county's other barrier islands.

"The governor states, *This storm has the potential to cause more damage than Andrew and over a much wider area. Do not ignore orders to evacuate. If you are in an evacuation area, seek shelter at designated areas in your county now.*

"Stay tuned for more up-to-the-minute updates as I follow the emergency response to Leo, live with the Florida National Guard."

Catherine, wearing a red windbreaker, her shoulders hunched against the wind and steady rain, intercepted Sawyer on her way back to the hospital to pick up the next ICU patient for transfer to the helicopter. "The pilots tell me we're taking a different route home."

"That's right." Sawyer didn't slow down, not because she was trying to avoid the reporter but because there was work to be done. If Catherine wanted to tag along, fine, but she wasn't going to stop for a photo op. Not that the rain-drenched parking lot was a great place for one. Although given her brief glimpse of the TV news feed with Catherine reporting while being buffeted in the foggy, wind-lashed ER lot, Sawyer figured Catherine was likely capable of doing most anything anywhere. She was a pro.

Catherine kept pace easily and Sawyer had a quick mental snapshot of her in the white bikini. Yeah, she was in good shape. Either she was naturally fit or she worked out, or both. If she hadn't been so ruthlessly fixed on getting her story, she'd be the kind of woman Sawyer admired. Unlike Dara, though, who was just as professional and determined, and light-years more beautiful, Catherine's motivations never seemed selfless. Maybe that's why Sawyer didn't find her attractive personally. Unlike Dara.

Catherine held out her recorder as they trotted along side by side. "Colonel Kincaid, what advice can you give people about evacuating?"

Sawyer slowed. Part of her rescue and recovery mission was to get the civilians to safety before they needed her aid. She spoke as she walked. "If you're in an evacuation area, don't wait, hoping the storm might turn out to be less serious than predicted. It's going to be every bit as bad as you're hearing. Our forecasters are experts, and this is going to be a dangerous event. Go now."

"Excellent advice. You would know how important it is to heed the evacuation orders, especially after the tragedy you suffered when your family failed to evacuate in time during Hurricane Andrew. What prompted your family to delay?"

Icy cold slithered down Sawyer's spine, and a rage so deep it burned roiled inside. "No comment."

"Colonel," Catherine said, "you survived a terrible ordeal when only a child, and now you're out here trying to prevent others from suffering the same tragedy. Your story might save lives."

"Right now, I have a helicopter crew and critical patients to secure." Sawyer yanked the ER doors open and Catherine followed her inside.

"All right, then, off the record for now." Catherine put the recorder away. "But will you agree to an interview, one-on-one, when we land? People will listen to you. You know I'm right." Catherine pulled out the big guns. "It's part of why you wear the uniform, after all. You hold a position of authority and it's your duty to keep the public safe."

"I know my duty." Sawyer's chest cramped with the effort to hold back her anger.

"Then give me a five-minute interview when we land."

"I'll think about it." Sawyer slowed outside the ICU. "How did you get that broadcast out from here anyhow?"

Catherine smiled. "Ah. The wonders of modern technology and excellent station editors. A smartphone with video capability and a portable tripod is more than adequate for live scene clips. Any blips in the quality just add to the drama and realism. I send the clips plus my voice recordings to the station, and they do the rest. All I need is a thirty-second shot of me to go with my voice-over. There are always plenty of people around who want to be interviewed, and if I have to, I ask them to shoot a few minutes for me. An ER nurse was more than happy to record me outside in the parking lot after I asked her for a few quotes."

"Smart." Sawyer shook her head as she punched the auto open button for the ICU. "I'm impressed with your resourcefulness. No recording in here."

"I'm thrilled to finally get your attention," Catherine said, a hint of laughter in her voice. "And it's our policy when showing sensitive clips to blur out faces to protect individual privacy."

"Good to know."

Dara met them just inside the door. When she smiled at Sawyer, her welcome cooled the last embers of unrest simmering in Sawyer's midsection. The punch of awareness was so intense, and so new, she shivered.

"Hey," Sawyer murmured.

"Hey," Dara said, her gaze fixed on Sawyer as if Catherine wasn't following alongside. "Myers is just signing off."

"Great."

Dara asked quietly, "You okay?"

Surprised, Sawyer nodded. No one else ever noticed if she was upset. Maybe she hid her distress really well, but not from Dara. She didn't mind, which was surprising too. "Sure."

"Good." Dara glanced quickly at Catherine before turning her attention to the last patient in the ICU. The other cubicles stood empty, bedraggled bedding, discarded IV tubes, and blank monitors standing silent witness to the hasty retreat.

Catherine was good to her word and stayed back as Sawyer, Phyllis, and Dara readied the neurosurgical postop patient for transfer. Myers accompanied them out to the Black Hawk for final check once he was aboard.

When they reached the helicopter, Norton leaned out the bay doors and Sawyer lifted her end of the stretcher up into the bird. After climbing in, she helped secure the stretcher in the cargo area as Dara and Phyllis checked on the other patients.

Myers knelt to evaluate the stability of the external frame holding his head and neck still. After a minute she shifted into a crouch and turned to Sawyer. "Okay—he ought to be good even if you get a little bumpy weather."

"Thanks, Doc." Sawyer hoped a little weather was all they ran into.

Myers scanned the interior. The metal frame was unadorned, with every available nook filled with equipment and IV bags, pressure lines, and tubes hanging from the roof. The pilots were sequestered in their armored cabin in the far front. With patients and crew, it was cramped in the main body. "Cozy. Too bad I can't ride along."

Sawyer shook her head. "You ought to jump in your…Jeep…and head to the mainland. The hospital isn't going to be operating at full tilt for a while."

Myers grinned, and looked again like a college senior with nothing but fun on her mind. "How do you know I have a Jeep?"

"'Cause you need it for your surfboard."

"You're scary." Myers sighed. "If only…"

"We're all set," Dara said, easing in beside Sawyer. "I'll take over here now."

"Good luck. Ta all," Myers called as she hopped out. She looked up at Sawyer. "Wish I flew your way." With that, she waved and, head down, sprinted back to the ER.

Sawyer frowned after her. "I missed something."

"She thinks you were flirting," Dara murmured.

"Huh?"

Dara shot her a half-exasperated, half-fond look. "You weren't?"

"No." Why would Dara think she was flirting with a woman she didn't even know? She didn't flirt with anyone. And she wasn't interested in starting. Frowning, she hunkered down by the stretchers. Teasing Dara to get her to laugh was different.

"For someone so on top of everything…" Dara shook her head.

Sawyer would have protested further, but Norton gave her the two-minute sign and a twirl of the finger indicating the bird was ready to fly.

"Roger that, Chief," Sawyer confirmed. And now there was no time for anything but the mission. With no corpsmen for the return trip, she and Phyllis would cover all the other patients, leaving Dara to watch the fresh postop. Compared to the acutely injured troops she was used to transporting in the field, these patients were mostly stable and, other than close monitoring, shouldn't require much in the way of active treatment on the trip home. The weather worried her way more than the medical challenges at the moment.

"Strap in, Ms. Winchell," Norton said.

Sawyer glanced over Dara's shoulder as Norton assisted Catherine in climbing aboard, looking windblown but a lot more comfortable in the helicopter than she had previously.

"Of course." Catherine took her previous seat, and Norton moved forward, speaking into her headset. Everyone pulled on their headgear.

"Prepare for liftoff," Norton said.

The bird shuddered to life with a familiar roar, rose almost straight up, and headed off into the gray morning.

Landfall minus 34 hours, 5:55 a.m.
In flight over the Gulf of Mexico

Thirty minutes into the flight, Dara checked her patient's vital signs for the third time. His blood pressure was a little higher than it had been the last time she checked, and his heart rate a little faster. The neurosurgeons had opted not to insert an intracranial bolt to measure the cerebrospinal pressure. Myers explained they were worried about the probe being dislodged since he needed to be moved immediately. Luckily, he hadn't shown any signs of brain injury or swelling on his preoperative MRI. Dara was glad not to have a sensitive pressure probe going through his skull and directly into his brain while they were flying through rough weather, but it also left her guessing as to what exactly was going on inside his head. He was heavily sedated, and checking his pupillary reflexes really didn't help her. As far as she could tell with the limited access she had available, all his extremities were well perfused and neurologically intact. Still, his vital signs weren't going in the direction she'd like to see.

Her radio crackled and Sawyer said, "Something wrong?"

"I'm not sure." Dara was past being surprised when Sawyer seemed to read her moods or her mind, even when most of her body was covered up with a helmet and bulky flight suit. If she'd been that transparent to anyone else, it would've bothered the hell out of her, but she was inexplicably pleased that Sawyer was so tuned in to her. That's what it was, tuned in. Not reading her so much as *sensing* her. Sawyer, for all her outward appearances of being stoic and unemotional, was unbelievably sensitive, a trait Dara hadn't realized she was searching for in a woman until now. And what the hell was she doing thinking about that in the middle of all this. "Nothing I can put my finger on, but his vital signs are just a little rickety. How much longer?"

"Forty-three minutes."

Dara would have smiled at the precise answer if she hadn't been so worried. Of course Sawyer would be precise. "All right. There's nothing to do but keep an eye on him for now."

"Keep me apprised."

"Roger, Colonel."

She heard a faint chuckle and then her headset quieted again.

Ten minutes later, she repeated her vital signs check. His systolic pressure was definitely elevated now, and his pulse rate was 20 percent above normal. Something was going on. She checked his temp. Most postoperative patients ran a temperature, but his had kicked up half a degree as well. Sepsis? Too soon for that. Probably pulmonary, and not a damn thing she could do about that in this helicopter. Bleeding? That would account for the increased pulse rate but not the blood pressure, unless…unless his pressure spike was causing him to bleed and his healthy heart was kicking up to compensate for the diminishing volume. A paradoxical situation that could fool some into thinking there was no bleeding problem until his pressure dropped out in a heartbeat. She cautiously increased his intravenous fluids. With any postoperative patient, but particularly one at risk for spinal or cerebral swelling, taking care not to fluid overload them was key. Damn, how did Sawyer and Jones and the rest of them do this on a wild flight over a battlefield, with bombs exploding and bullets tearing through the helicopter, and people bleeding to death in front of them? She was riding a relatively calm wave right now, and her pulse rate was probably 150.

"We've got a bit of a snafu," Sawyer said.

"Not what I want to hear right now," Dara said. "What is it?"

"The pilots had to detour around a significant squall system, probably Leo's calling card, and we're running low on fuel."

"We're going to have to land somewhere?"

"Not the best option. If we land and can't take off again when the storm moves closer, we'll have to transfer all these folks to ground transport."

"Not good," Dara said. "Way too much delay, especially for this guy."

"Copy that. So we're going to refuel midair as soon as we can get a refueling tanker to intercept our course."

Dara's stomach tightened. She knew what that meant, she'd seen it on TV or in a movie or something, and it always seemed to be really difficult. "Is it going to work?"

"It's going to have to."

CHAPTER SEVENTEEN

"Rendezvous with the tanker, two minutes," Chief Norton said. "Strap in and prepare for refueling."

Dara clipped her harness to the nearest hook in the safety rigging so she could remain by her patient, trying not to be annoyed she couldn't move as freely as she had before. Better to be mobile enough to work than to be strapped in and practically held captive like Catherine. And, wow, *really* not fair to feel a bit of perverse pleasure at that thought, all because Catherine was shamelessly pursuing Sawyer at the same time she was prying into Sawyer's private life. Once they landed, Catherine would head back to her warm, safe studio and the whole irritating matter would disappear. She hoped.

By craning her neck, she could get a look out the rain-spattered cargo bay window at a narrow patch of gloomy gray sky. A knife-edge section of wing angled into view followed by a portion of the body of an airplane that had to be three or four times the size of the helicopter. Her view was suddenly obscured by the gunmetal gray side of the really big airplane. She understood the gist of what was about to happen—the tanker would drop a flexible tube of some sort, the Black Hawk pilots would miraculously slot the thing into a receptacle somewhere, and fuel would flow into their helicopter. That couldn't really be such a great idea, could it? Even on a good day in clear skies? And how exactly was that tanker, considering it resembled an elephant trying to sidle up to a Labrador retriever that never held still, supposed to get close enough to accomplish that without knocking them out of the sky?

She probably should be a lot more nervous, but Norton and Sawyer seemed totally unconcerned, and her adrenaline was running so high all she registered was excitement. She experienced the same exhilaration every time she was in the midst of a medical crisis. Every thought came through as sharp and clear as a beacon, every impulse crystallized into pure sensation. The combination was addictive—hell, even good sex didn't compare. Or maybe the sex had never been that good—something else to ponder sometime.

"You holding up okay?" Sawyer's voice sounded in her headset.

Oh yeah, just great. I'm just comparing this near-death experience with your typical, sort of forgettable sex and deciding this was more fun. And how come I think you know that? Dara nearly laughed and just barely stifled the impulse. Way to project a solid, professional image. "Fine. How is it going?"

"The HC-130 is in position. They'll drop the drogue to connect with our probe as soon as we get a little closer. There might be some tight maneuvering while the pilots get us lined up. Don't let it worry you."

"I'm okay."

"Never doubted it."

The confidence in Sawyer's voice went a long way toward calming the nerves Dara hadn't realized were making her twitchy. She probably ought to be embarrassed, but nothing about Sawyer made her self-conscious, even when she was a little shaky.

"How's the patient?" Sawyer asked.

"Not as stable as I'd like but nothing I can quite put my finger on. I'll be happier when we get him in the ICU, though."

"Me too. Everyone else here is good."

"Good. Thanks."

Sawyer clicked off. The helicopter turned and circled, seemed to slow, and Norton said, "Stand by. Engaging drogue."

A bump followed by a shudder streaked through the metal decking beneath Dara's knees, and then nothing but the unrelenting roar of the motor. Across from her Catherine clutched the shoulder straps of her harness, a wide-eyed stare the only sign she was anxious. Phyllis, the seasoned Navy nurse, calmly continued checking vital signs, adjusting lines, and changing IVs. Dara hoped she looked as cool. Hopefully Sawyer couldn't detect her racing pulse and jittery stomach.

"We're coming around for a second pass," Norton reported in a flat, unemotional tone.

Dara realized she was holding her breath and forced herself to breathe. Getting light-headed right now was a really bad idea. The helicopter twisted and turned some more. The shudder and shake kept up. Sweat trickled down Dara's back. Wasn't it supposed to be cold in these damn helicopters?

"We're breaking off," Norton said, still sounding as if she was reading a phone book. She was nerveless, and that was somehow very reassuring. "Too much turbulence for a safe deployment of the drogue."

"Copy," Sawyer said on the comm-wide channel. "Any adjustment to flight plans?"

"Negative, Colonel. We're heading to Miami," Norton said. "Mission objective unchanged."

"Copy, Chief."

As the Black Hawk wheeled away from the tanker plane, Dara caught a final glimpse of the hose with the basketlike nozzle on the end twisting back into the underbelly of the aircraft. The plane grew smaller until nothing was visible outside the square window but the unrelenting rain.

Dara went back to her routine. No point asking Sawyer whether they'd actually have enough fuel to reach Miami, which she noted Sawyer had not asked about. No matter what happened next, Sawyer couldn't change it, and neither could she. Expecting Sawyer to be responsible for all of them as well as everything that might befall them simply wasn't fair. Sawyer didn't think of it that way, that was clear, and of all the things that Dara admired about her, that was one of the greatest. That sense of responsibility, that willingness to be accountable, was something she'd come to mistrust when her father had betrayed her family. Not everything about that lesson had been bad, and looking back on those last years of childhood after he'd left, she was grateful in a way. She'd learned very quickly the only person she could hold accountable for anything was herself, and she clung to that when she was disappointed or afraid or lonely.

Now, flying into the face of a hurricane, unable to change whatever her fate might be, she was, if not accepting, at least content to know she was here by her own choice, by her own will, and responsible for whatever might happen. She suspected Sawyer would argue the point, reminding Dara she wouldn't even be here if Sawyer hadn't allowed it. Dara heard the words in her mind, saw the flash of confusion in

Sawyer's eyes when she laughed at that. As if Sawyer's permission was necessary for anything she did. Certainly, Dara accepted Sawyer's command in a crisis, just as Sawyer supported her when appropriate, but personally? When it came down to Dara doing what she believed was essential—no, she followed no one's orders. Which made it a good thing she wasn't wearing a uniform. She'd make a lousy soldier. Fortunately, she and Sawyer weren't likely to clash over those kinds of black-and-white issues—they each had their own fields of battle—for which she was grateful. She could admire and respect Sawyer's sense of duty and responsibility without being on guard against it. She'd much rather get closer to her. And now *there* was a thought she needed to put aside for a later time—a much later time.

She might've been imagining it, but the helicopter seemed to be rocking and swaying more than it had before. Perhaps her imagination also, the howl of wind rising above the rotors. She couldn't possibly be hearing that. Memory, perhaps, of the sound of the storm out on the tarmac before they'd taken off. No matter. The wind could scream and the rain could cut at them, and all she could do, all she needed to do, was take care of the young man entrusted to her. She ran his vital signs again. His systolic pressure was all over the place now, up the first time she checked it, down, then up again. His heart rate had climbed to 160. His temp was at 101.5. He was in trouble, and waiting until she was back in the safe, secure confines of the hospital with every modern diagnostic test available to her was not an option.

She hadn't trained for the battlefield, but she was on one now. She slid her gloved hand behind his neck and gently palpated around the edges of the surprisingly small bandage the neurosurgeons had left over the linear incision over his spine. She couldn't see behind the external fixation frame encasing his head, but she wouldn't be able to until she got him onto a revolving bed where she could flip his whole body 180 degrees without moving his spine at all. That would be his routine every four hours so the ICU staff could check his incisions and make sure he wasn't developing pressure ulcers. Now she was left with only her senses, and her fingertips told her the slight sponginess of the tissue around the outer edges of the bandage was normal postoperative swelling. If he was bleeding, it wasn't there. Lucky for him, so far. Bleeding around the spinal cord could rapidly produce paralysis.

She inched lower, wincing as her knees absorbed the pressure from the unforgiving metal floor, and opened the thermal wrap encasing him from the upper chest down. Myers reported they'd taken the bone grafts from his posterior hip area, where it was easy to reach when he'd been lying on his stomach for the surgery. Dara wasn't going to be able to see that area now either, but after changing to a new pair of surgical gloves, she carefully worked her hand beneath him. She couldn't feel much but found the bandage over the graft site, and when she removed her hand, the fingers of her gloves were streaked bright red. He was bleeding through his bandages. How much, she couldn't tell.

She pressed the button on her headset with a knuckle. "Colonel?"

A second later, Sawyer answered. "Kincaid here. Over."

"He's bleeding. I can't tell how much for sure, but I'm afraid his pressure's going to drop out any minute. What do you have in the way of plasma substitutes?"

"We've got cryo. The fresh frozen plasma would take forty-five minutes to thaw."

"I know. Get me two units of the cryo. We'll be on the ground before the FFP would be ready." She hesitated. "Right?"

"Right." Sawyer edged around the stretchers in the tight confines, opened a storage container, and extracted two units of cryoprecipitate, a condensed version of plasma filled with blood-clotting agents. She passed one to Phyllis and the other to Dara to plug into his IVs.

Norton said, "Fifteen minutes to the LZ. It's going to be bumpy."

Dara said, "Can someone radio ahead and get the OR ready. He'll need to go back STAT to find out what's causing this bleeding."

"Copy that." A minute later Norton said, "The OR will have a team waiting for us at the hospital LZ. They'll take him straight down from there."

"Thank you."

"Everyone else is stable," Phyllis said, the first communication from her the entire trip. She'd simply worked economically and proficiently as if they'd still been in the ICU on a normal night. "I'll stay and help you transfer the rest of these patients to the unit."

Technically, Phyllis wasn't covered by the hospital malpractice insurance and didn't have privileges to practice at Miami Memorial. And Dara couldn't care less. "That would be great. Thanks."

The helicopter shuddered and plummeted, taking Dara's stomach along with it. She grabbed for the nearest thing to steady herself, which turned out to be Sawyer's arm.

"Turbulence," Norton said unnecessarily. "We don't have enough fuel to go around the weather. The ride's going to get a little rough."

Dara gave herself a minute to regain her equilibrium, the hard strength of Sawyer's forearm under her grip an unyielding comfort. When she trusted herself not to topple over, she let go of Sawyer's arm, even though a part of her wanted to hold on just for the contact. She wasn't fatalistic and did not want this trip to be her last.

She'd never been one for meditation, so she had no mental calming tricks in the face of the unknown. Instead, she'd had years of dealing with crisis situations. Panic was not in her nature. Gritting her teeth, she ignored the rocking and rolling and pitching of the helicopter and focused on the patients, checking and rechecking, just as Phyllis and Sawyer were doing.

She caught her breath when the helicopter slammed down, jolted up again, or so it seemed, and slammed again.

"Sorry about that." The pilot's voice came through the headset. "Welcome to Miami."

Dara gasped, almost laughing with relief, and glanced at Sawyer.

Sawyer grinned back. "Welcome to the Guard, Dr. Sims. You're a SAR medic now."

CHAPTER EIGHTEEN

Landfall minus 29 hours

When the helicopter doors opened, Chief Norton climbed out and, a few seconds later, signaled the okay to disembark. The engines continued to rev and the rotor kept up its steady whir above Dara's head, a sound she was going to have echoing in her brain for a long time. A cold wet wind strafed the inside of the Black Hawk, and she reflexively bent over her unconscious patient as she released the clamps on his stretcher and pushed it toward the open hatch. Sawyer jumped out and, when Dara crouched in the doorway to follow, reached up a hand. Dara grasped it and swung down to the rooftop of Miami Memorial. Even through the gloves, she felt Sawyer's firm grip, and the tension from the chaotic, seemingly endless flight drained away even before her feet planted on the solid surface of the helipad. She had the strange sensation of being home, and for an instant couldn't distinguish whether it was because she was back at the hospital, or holding Sawyer's hand.

More questions she had no time to ponder.

"Thanks," Dara murmured as the OR team hurried across the rooftop toward them. Within seconds she was going to be too engrossed taking care of the transfers to talk, but she didn't want Sawyer to disappear before she said good-bye. She expected Sawyer to jump back on board, and letting go of Sawyer's hand took real effort. "Are you leaving?"

"We'll give you a hand getting all these patients inside. As soon as we get everyone off-loaded, I'm sending the helicopter back to Homestead."

"What about you?" Dara said.

"I'll rendezvous with my battalion at the operational command post here in the city. I've got to review the provision status in the local evac centers and deploy troops to assist in civilian transport wherever the locals need us." Sawyer looked out over the city as if she could see through the wall of rain to the streets below, a frown creasing her forehead. For her, that little bit of expression signaled real worry. "At this point, we're in a support capacity only."

"Of course." Dara knew her well enough now to appreciate how hard it was for Sawyer to stand on the sidelines when she wanted to be taking charge. She'd have felt the same way. She had only a second to decide how much she wanted to say. "I know you're going to be swamped—" She grimaced. "Literally…but if you get a chance—"

"I'll call you," Sawyer said with the slightest question in her voice.

"Yes." Dara smiled. "Not good-bye, then. You have my number?"

Sawyer patted her phone in her shirt pocket. "I do."

Dara foolishly thought she looked as if she was touching her heart—and the only thing worse than her instant chagrin was the bolt of pleasure that shot straight through her. What was the matter with her? Tired, that was it. Tired and stressed. And out of time as the anesthesiologist and the trauma fellow arrived, heads down in the drenching rain, already reaching for the stretcher with her patient.

"What have you got?" Wen's senior trauma fellow asked.

"A fresh postop neurosurgical patient," Dara said as Phyllis and Sawyer lifted the second patient down from the helicopter. Three more hospital staff in scrubs and green cover gowns she recognized from the ICU descended on the next stretcher. "He's bleeding somewhere. I think his graft site or something in the vicinity. BP's been bouncing, and he's got a temp. We've given him two units of cryo…"

She jogged along beside them, filling them in on the other relevant details, aware that behind her, Phyllis and Sawyer were seeing to the rest of the patients. Once she'd handed her patient off to the trauma surgeons in the OR, she called Myers. "It's Dara. You might want to talk to the guys here—we're taking your postop back to the OR. I think he's bleeding somewhere around the graft site. He spiked a temp too."

"Well, hell," Myers grumbled. "He was juicy when we closed but I couldn't find anything active. You think it could be DIC?"

Dara's stomach twisted. Disseminated intravascular coagulation was a disastrous and often end-stage event, frequently related to severe infection. "I don't know. They're getting fresh labs now."

"Okay. Who do I call?"

Dara gave her the OR number and the name of the attending surgeon, then headed to the ICU to check on the other transfers. By the time those five were all settled and she'd discussed their cases with the ICU attending *and* called Randall with an update, two hours had passed and Sawyer was long gone. She missed seeing her nearby, missed the surety of her presence, missed her fleeting and uncensored laugh. She was just really tired.

She slipped down the stairs to the ER back entrance, cowardly avoiding the main desk and the rack of pending case charts, and hid out in the break room to have a cup of coffee and catch up on the last twenty-four hours' worth of messages.

She'd taken one sip of fresh hot coffee—praise all the powers that be—and before she could even open her mail, her phone blared with its emergency message tone.

1:05 p.m.

Florida State Disaster Management Division
Evacuation Update

Storm tracker models now predict Hurricane Leo will make landfall in the direct vicinity of the Miami metropolitan area. Mandatory evacuation orders are now extended to all Zone A, B, and C regions.

Dara's breath caught. The new evacuation orders changed everything and, really, nothing at all. Her job remained the same— to coordinate the emergency medical relief efforts between civilian emergency response teams, the National Guard, and Miami Memorial. But the hospital was also filled with patients and staffed by hundreds of individuals, all of whom were now in immediate danger. In addition, many had family in the evacuation zone. The protocols for this crisis situation weren't open to debate, and she didn't plan on wasting time with more meetings. She texted the department heads in a group message:

Per the latest state mandate, an emergency evacuation order is now in effect. Any patient deemed medically stable should be discharged within the next twenty-four hours. Elective surgical, interventional radiology, and diagnostic procedures are immediately canceled. Non-mandatory personnel duties are suspended as of the end of first shift today.

The hospital would go to minimal function over the course of twenty-four hours. The emergency room would remain open, as would all critical care units—medical, cardiac, surgical, trauma, and neonatal. Staff members covering those units would most likely be working double or triple shifts until the emergency situation resolved.

As Dara finished the text, exhaustion swept through her like a dull gray curtain dropped over her senses. She sipped the coffee, leaned back, and squeezed the bridge of her nose. She was running on less than four hours' sleep in the last several days, and she'd need to crash soon to catch up before further rest became an impossibility.

"You ought to get out of here," Penny said, sliding into a seat across from her.

Dara jumped, sighing wanly as she opened her eyes. "I was just thinking the same thing myself. I'll try in a little while."

"How was the helicopter trip?"

Dara grimaced. "Rough ride with no parachute. Not something I want to repeat right away." She smiled a little, remembering the sense of being part of something unique, of the teamwork—of being challenged and winning. "Although, I have to admit, now that it's over, parts of it were fun."

"The part having to do with the super-hot colonel?"

Dara blushed and knew it. "I certainly won't deny she's hot."

Penny snorted. "Well, yeah. Anyone with eyes could see that. How was working with her?"

"Oh, she's good. An excellent medic, cool in a crisis, and knows how to lead."

"Sounds like your kind of woman."

"I think I just described a highly skilled professional, so, yes. The kind of associate I respect."

"And that's it?"

"What more were you looking for?" But she knew. Penny wanted her personal opinion—did she like her, enjoy her sense of humor, find her interesting, attractive. Yes, yes, yes, and very much yes. So she kept quiet. Too soon to say all that out loud.

"She watches you, you know."

"How on earth would you know that?" Dara asked.

"I only had to see the two of you together for about thirty seconds. No matter what she was doing, you were on her radar."

"Penny," Dara said, pleased but disbelieving, "we were dragging patients out of the helicopter across the roof into the elevator in a torrential downpour. There was hardly any time for…anything."

Penny shook her head. "You obviously have not dated in too long a time. You can't even read the signals anymore."

"Sawyer is not the kind of person to send signals," Dara said. "For God's sake, Catherine Winchell—" She frowned. "Where did she get to?"

"The blonde?" Penny said. "I noticed her with a camera. I think she went up to the OR, but I'm not sure. What was she doing with all of you, exactly?"

"She's a reporter for Channel 10 on assignment with the National Guard. She's following the storm preparations and breaking weather developments. She joined us at Homestead and went with us to Key West."

"She's pretty interested in your colonel too."

Dara might've snarled because Penny laughed. "That's just my point about the games people play. Catherine has been hitting on Sawyer since the minute they met, apparently. Sawyer said no and that was it as far as she was concerned. Now she doesn't even notice Catherine's innuendos. Sawyer doesn't play games. I'm not even sure she knows how. It's just not in her makeup. She's all about the job."

"Sounds like someone else I know."

"No—the difference is I know how to play the games, I just don't want to." The familiar bitterness and faint self-recrimination that usually followed thoughts of all the many ways she'd been taught to use her money and position and power to her advantage were oddly absent. Being around Sawyer, being free to be herself, had purged a wound she hadn't realized was still festering.

Penny squeezed her hand and said softly, "Where'd you just go?"

Dara shook her head. "You're my best friend, right?"

"Have been for—okay, let's not go there, it makes me feel old and tired. A lot of years."

Dara laughed. "There's something about Sawyer. I've never met anyone like her before."

"So it's not just she's hot?"

"That's just it." Dara sighed. Sawyer was charming without realizing it, sexy with absolutely no clue about the impact she had on women, and so charismatic when she focused all that intensity on you, she was spellbinding. And the very fact she had absolutely no idea just made the whole package a million times more exciting. "Damn it. Everything about her is hot."

"Ooh," Penny said with a teasing lilt. "Somebody's finally got your attention."

"Okay, maybe. Yes. And could it be any worse timing? I might not even get to see her again."

"Honey," Penny said, "these things don't follow a timetable or punch a clock or tick off days on a calendar. It's not about time, it's about…connection. God, the first time I saw Sampson, other than thinking he was sex on a stick, I noticed his laugh. And his energy, and the way he looked at me like he'd just discovered a big ole shiny present under the tree. I was hooked, and it took all of about twenty seconds. After that, time didn't mean anything."

"I'm not like that—I'm not emotional that way." Penny just smiled, and Dara insisted, "I'm not! I like to know what I'm getting into with a woman. I'm a head person, not a…a heart person, I guess."

"Okay. You know best." Penny's expression said she didn't agree, but she sighed and her face grew serious. "I think you'll be seeing the colonel again, all the same. We're in for a rough ride, aren't we."

"I'm afraid so," Dara said, still thinking of Sawyer. Where was she now—was she out in the storm, in danger, or warm and dry finally, and grabbing a few hours' sleep? Was she thinking of her? Dara blinked and pointed a finger at Penny. "There's no *we* in this. I want you out of here at the end of this shift, and I don't want to see you again until Leo is history."

"That would be a no. I'm not going home until this is all over." Penny handed her tablet to Dara with a spreadsheet open. "I've worked through the call schedule, and we've got all the shifts covered with staff who aren't absolutely needed at home—the single parents or ones with special-care dependents. Everyone has an on-call room assigned so we can sleep when we need to—"

"Absolutely not. You're pregnant, if you recall?"

"Oh, believe me, I haven't forgotten it." She patted her stomach and made a face. "I might be queasy now and then, but that doesn't make me infirm. Women have managed all kinds of chores over the millennia while pregnant. At least I'm not pushing a plow."

"Sampson will kill me."

"He knows already. The hospital is one of the safest places to be, right? We're flood-proof, we've got generators, we're a goddamn fortress."

"Pen," Dara said, trying to sound reasonable rather than dictatorial, "we've got other people who can pick up the extra shifts. You and Sampson should head to your place in South Carolina or his mother's place or somewhere. There's an evacuation order, remember?"

"Honey, Sampson's a firefighter. He's not going anywhere. All the first responders are on emergency status now."

"Of course he is." Dara rubbed her eyes. "I must be more tired than I thought. I just want you to be safe."

"Well, I'll be right here where you can keep an eye on me." Penny scooted her chair closer and hugged her. "You need to get out of here for a little while. We're all going to need you sharp."

"I know. I will."

Penny hesitated. "What about your mother?"

Dara sighed. "I'm just about to call her."

CHAPTER NINETEEN

Landfall minus 22 hours

National Hurricane Center Atlantic Ops
Storm Advisory

Tropical storm winds are likely to arrive in the Florida Keys and south Florida in less than twenty-four hours. Some locations may be uninhabitable for weeks or months due to damage from extreme winds, structural impairment, and coastal flooding. Preparations for evacuation, relief, and rescue should be rushed to completion.

Stan read the advisory as it went out with a sense of helpless futility. The closer Leo approached, the more rapidly he was being delegated to the role of observer, shouting out warnings and helpless to act on them. He couldn't even get his own wife to heed his urgings to evacuate.

"You okay, boss?" Bette asked quietly as she swiveled in her chair and regarded him with a weary sigh.

"Yep." Stan forced an upbeat note into his voice. He needed to bolster his people's spirits, to keep them sharp and committed despite lack of sleep and decent food, and a pervasive sense of doom that was hard to shed looking at the weather maps. Tracking Leo was a bit like watching a train coming full-on while tied to the tracks. Landfall was just the beginning of another battle for them. Their job wouldn't be done until Leo thrashed himself out and passed on by, and not for quite a while after that. "All good here."

Channel 10 News Report, 7 p.m.
Miami Beach, Florida

"This is Catherine Winchell reporting live from Miami Beach, Florida. Hurricane Leo is now only four hundred miles offshore. Earlier today a National Hurricane Center bulletin reported Leo swept through the Turks and Caicos Islands as a Category 5 hurricane with winds in excess of one hundred eighty-five miles per hour on its path toward the southeastern Bahamas and Cuba. Early photos depict widespread devastation, with over eighty percent of homes, businesses, and municipal structures destroyed. Power outages throughout the islands have left communities without communication networks, fresh water, or sanitary facilities. At least twelve people have died, and the death toll is expected to rise.

"Behind me you can see the first ominous signs of the impending waves predicted to threaten coastal regions, including downtown Miami. Storm surge is expected to reach fifteen feet or more in height. The governor has now ordered mandatory evacuations throughout south Florida, including coastal communities in Miami, Palm Beach, and cities south of Lake Okeechobee. Residents are advised to seek shelter locally to avoid the projected gas shortages and highway congestion. Six thousand Florida Air and Army National Guard under the command of Colonel Sawyer Kincaid, supported by troops from adjoining states, are on hand to assist local emergency response teams in transporting citizens to area shelters. If you are in an evacuation zone and do not know how to locate the nearest shelter, call Channel 10 News at 555-LEO-HELP.

"Follow me on Twitter, Channel 10 Facebook, and here on Channel 10 News for live updates and interviews with those in charge of our emergency crisis response."

National Guard Command Center
Miami, Florida

A sharp rap on the door roused Sawyer from her uneasy doze. She hadn't really been sleeping. Her mind was still working, running through the lists of things she needed to do, a part of her body and brain alert to the slightest change in the sound of the hundreds of Humvees and high-water vehicles pulling into the huge lot behind the warehouse the Guard had commandeered as its staging arena. The blare of horns and the muted thunder of voices reverberated through the metal walls separating her quarters from the general billet area.

She'd spent an hour, before grabbing a little rack time, getting passed from one bureaucrat to another at Florida National Grid, trying to get a recovery projected for the anticipated power failures, before she finally connected with someone willing to give her a straight answer. The answer wasn't pretty. Despite the intense development of their network in the Miami metropolitan area, the power company projected massive outages if the storm struck as currently predicted, with repairs and rebuilding of the grid likely to take weeks. Any facility without generator capability or the fuel to run it was likely to be without lights, air-conditioning, refrigeration, clean water, sanitation, and basic communications.

She sat up on the side of her cot, ran both hands through her hair, and felt her energy level rise. She didn't sleep much and she didn't need to. Her body was acclimated to a constant state of readiness, and she only heeded the normal urge to rest when absolutely necessary.

"Enter."

The flimsy, windowless metal door grated open and Rambo's big frame filled the doorway, the light behind him silhouetting his features, but she'd recognize him anywhere.

"Hey." Seeing who it was, she rose, unbuttoned her uniform shirt, pulled it off, and tossed it onto the bottom of her bunk. Rambo had seen her in her tank top a few hundred times. "Give me a minute."

Rambo let the door close behind him, leaned against it, and waited.

As the commanding officer, she rated private quarters in what had once been a small office that had probably been used to process the manifests for the goods coming into the warehouse. She was happy to have a bunk of her own, a tiny sink, and a private toilet. Downright luxury accommodations. The rest of the battalion shared the common space out on the vast warehouse floor, sleeping on cots fifty to a row and showering in container units behind the building. The mission support company had already taken care of the essentials—sectioning off a coffee and food section and even designating a quiet corner where men and women could connect to the internet and communicate with their families.

Running cold water in the sink, she splashed her face, dried off, and pulled a clean pressed shirt from the footlocker at the bottom of her bunk. She buttoned her shirt and tucked it in. Two high windows let in enough light for her to read his expression. "Problems?"

"We've brought in twelve thousand pallets of bottled water and MREs. We've got the trucks loaded up and ready to roll. I'm worried about the fuel situation. We're commandeering as much of the local supplies as we can, but the evacuation has pretty much tapped out the sources. Gas stations all up and down the corridor are out of fuel already. Depending on how long we'll have to distribute supplies, and how far, we could run into a supply chain problem."

"What about tankers?" Sawyer asked.

"That's what I wanted to talk to you about. Can we get the Navy to get us some fuel offshore?"

"I'll make some calls. They've got five warships on maneuvers in the Caribbean in support of the areas already hit, but they're shutting down the bases at Jacksonville and Miami. Homestead is moving out their aircraft too."

"We could ferry fuel in from a distance by barge, maybe," Rambo said.

"Maybe." Sawyer doubted smaller vessels would be able to handle the high seas once Leo got closer, but they might be able to off-load fuel ahead of the storm if they acted quickly. "I'll push them. Have your storage depots ready to receive."

"Roger that. Thanks. How's the evacuation going?"

"The city public transit system is overloaded already—huge wait times—so we're kicking in transport vehicles." Sawyer shrugged. "We've got three thousand troops on the streets on around-the-clock shifts conveying homeless, seniors, and those with no means of travel to shelters. We've got another five hundred filling sandbags along the seawall. Hell, we're even moving pets."

"Well, yeah." Rambo laughed. "Mika would have my ass if we left her cat behind."

"How's Mika holding up?"

He smiled, that smile he always got when his wife was mentioned, one of self-satisfaction and incredulity, like he couldn't believe his luck. Sawyer'd never quite understood what was behind that expression before, but she thought she might be starting to. Sometimes a person walked into your life, someone you never expected or were even looking for, and changed everything. That was crazy, she knew. She wasn't that kind of person. She didn't have those hidden needs, those well-concealed vulnerabilities. When her family had fractured, her mother broken and chronically depressed, her siblings too young to console her and more in need of consoling themselves, she'd had to grow up fast. She'd gone to half a dozen schools by the time she was twelve. Friendships never had the chance to cement. She'd learned not to count on relationships, fragile things that splintered and blew away like the trees had surrendered to Andrew.

Then she'd found the home she'd always been missing in the military, with a family that would not desert her, that she could count on. And that had been enough. More than she'd ever had, more than she'd ever thought she needed, until lately. She rubbed her chest, conscious of the ache that persisted deep inside.

"You okay?" Rambo said.

"What? Yeah, fine."

"You look like something's bothering you."

Sawyer shook her head. They all had one mission, one focus, but a significant percentage of her troops also had families in danger. Her scattered siblings should be safe somewhere inland or out of state altogether, but for the first time, she experienced the kind of gnawing worry many of her troops had dealt with during deployments when they couldn't be present for a loved one who needed help or support. She kept thinking about Dara. The newest storm projections put Miami Memorial, and Dara, directly in its path. She hadn't yet figured out how to handle that.

"No, I'm good." And the weird thing was, she was good. The ache wasn't actually painful. If she had to put a word to it, she'd call it more anticipation, a sense of excitement that was wholly new for her. "I'll get on those calls."

Sawyer glanced at the time. 1900 hours. And wondered where Dara was.

7:40 p.m.

Dara tried her mother again while watching Catherine on the news loop that had been running every three or four minutes for the last forty. Catherine managed to look fashionably attractive in a navy-blue windbreaker and tailored tan pants. To give her credit, she didn't shirk from getting soaked. Her blond hair was definitely waterlogged and tangled, the disheveled effect adding to the seriousness of her message while making her seem professionally undauntable. Annoying, how hard it was to dislike Catherine when she was so obviously doing a necessary and difficult job.

"Hello, darling," her mother said.

Caught by surprise after failing to connect the last dozen times she'd called and still mildly irritated over Catherine, Dara didn't bother hiding her annoyance. "You're not answering your phone."

"I just did."

Dara heard the familiar distracted note in her mother's voice that usually indicated she was doing three things at once, all of which were more important than talking to her daughter. "I thought we agreed when I called, you'd answer. You know when I do, it's not to chat."

"Believe me, darling, I know that. You've never been one for maintaining social niceties." Her mother still sounded unperturbed, but the message was an old and pointed one. Dara had failed to be the daughter her mother had expected.

Dara's molars were starting to hurt, a sure sign she was grinding them. She consciously relaxed her jaw. "Mother, have you been watching the news?"

"You know I rarely do. There's so much false reporting these days."

"You *are* aware we are in the direct path of Hurricane Leo."

"Oh, heavens, I've lived in Florida all my life. Hurricanes hardly excite me."

"Well, this one should. It's a massive storm, and we're in its direct path. You should have already left by now."

Her mother laughed. "You can't be serious. I wouldn't have evacuated for Andrew if your father hadn't been worried about invalidating any insurance claims we might have needed to make. Really, that was a ridiculous and wholly unnecessary trip. The house was fine except for a few loose tiles on the roof."

Dara closed her eyes, trying not to think about what had happened just a few miles away to Sawyer's family. She was assailed by guilt over something she couldn't have changed—she'd been five years old, after all. Still, the image of Sawyer struggling in the floodwaters only to lose her father and her home hurt. She concentrated on convincing her mother to deal with reality, a not inconsequential challenge. "This one is likely to be every bit as big as Andrew, if not even more powerful, and playing Russian roulette with nature is ridiculous. You're not going to be able to drive out of the area at this late date, but I've checked the shelters in your—"

"Oh my goodness." Her mother laughed. "Why on earth would I leave my home to spend days sleeping with strangers in some un-air-conditioned building with no toilets, no decent coffee, and no privacy."

"Maybe because you might end up wading through water up to your chin if you don't?"

"You're an alarmist. I have no idea who you got that from."

Dara had expected that response, but she'd had to try. "Domestic flights out of Miami International are all full, but you can get a charter out of Miami-OPA if you hurry."

"I'll do no such thing. I know exactly what will happen. I'll spend two days traveling to some city I don't want to visit so I can be stuck in a hotel where I don't want to stay, only to discover that I can turn around and come back home four days later, and then I'll have to reschedule God knows how many appointments. It's a lot of bother over nothing."

"Why are you being so stubborn?"

"I'm not being stubborn—I simply know how things would look if I turned tail and ran away in the face of a little bad weather."

"Look bad to whom? Who are you trying to impress?" Of course she knew—appearances counted for everything with her mother. Her social status was her most coveted possession.

True to form, her mother said icily, "I hold a position of some importance in the community, whether you believe that or not. Since there's a crisis, as part of the board of the local Red Cross, I should certainly be here to help make decisions. In fact, I'm going to call them as soon as I get off the phone with you."

"I can't do anything to change your mind, can I?"

"It's absolutely not necessary." Her mother paused. "Are you leaving the city?"

"What?" Dara closed her eyes. "No, Mother, I'm not leaving. I'm a doctor, remember? This is an emergency management situation and...I'm working."

"There, you see? We're just the same."

"Please answer your phone from now on," Dara said quietly.

"Yes, darling. I really must go now."

"Be careful," Dara murmured as the call ended. Leaning back, she clicked off the television. She really didn't want to watch Catherine any longer. Profound sadness welled in her chest, and she chided herself for still being disappointed every time she and her mother failed to communicate. When her phone rang, she answered automatically. The hospital again. Of course.

"This is Dr. Sims."

"Were you sleeping?" Sawyer asked.

Dara's energy returned with a swift jolt to her midsection. A very nice warm jolt. She had to smile. "I tried. You?"

"Tried. Are you going back in tonight?"

"Probably not until morning. Everything is on autopilot at the moment, but I'm on call. So...who knows."

"Hungry?"

The rest of Dara's fatigue dropped away on a wave of anticipation. "Famished."

"Chinese or pizza?"

"Chinese—no octopus."

Sawyer laughed. "Roger that."

"I'm at—"

"I have your address."

CHAPTER TWENTY

Dara slid her phone onto the glass-topped coffee table in front of the sofa and did a quick scan of her living room. She hadn't had a visitor in weeks. Now that she thought of it, possibly months. Her mother never dropped by, and when she saw Penny outside work, it was usually at Penny's for a meal with her and Sampson. She really ought to return the favor and have them over, but then she'd have to cook. Wow—Penny was right, she really did need to up her social game. Not that she really felt anything lacking. She had friends—at least, she had Facebook friends—and they counted, didn't they? Her college roommate, her friends from anatomy class, forever bonded over their first-year med student experience with a cadaver, her fellow residents scattered now around the country. She followed what was happening in their lives, took note of their children, and birthdays, and family events—even posted a response once in a while. She didn't really have much to share, but she wasn't avoiding having a social life. Not really. Most of her personal interactions centered around her work—she spent twelve hours a day with other people, people she considered not only colleagues but friends. In the brief moments between seeing patients and running the department, she talked to them about what she'd read or seen on television or might see at the movies if she ever got the time. The hospital was her world, and her condo was just the place she went to sleep and, occasionally, when she wasn't too tired, to read a book. Her connections with Penny and the ER staff fulfilled her need for human contact. Okay, maybe not *all* her needs, but she wasn't lying awake at night worrying about her lack of a sex life. Sex required at least a basic relationship with someone she would want to say hello to in the morning, and she hadn't met anyone who stirred her up enough to want to go there.

Stirred up. Like she was right now. Totally different. She was rusty at the face-to-face social end of things. Not the end of the world. No reason to panic. So she was a little out of practice entertaining. She hadn't grown up in her mother's house without knowing exactly what should be done, even if they'd had staff to do it. The mental checklist appeared, and she ran down it. Sawyer was bringing food, check. Drink. Wine.

Hell, did she even have a bottle of wine? Did Sawyer drink wine? She didn't know. She didn't know a lot of things about her, really. What she did know seemed to be the important things—Sawyer had a sense of humor, she was fiercely dedicated to her work, she had no problem being in control but also was willing to listen to others who knew what they were doing. And Sawyer had the most disconcerting way of surprising her. Like right now. Calling out of the blue, making the first move. Dara stopped short.

Was that what Chinese food was, a first move? A move toward what? She wasn't a stranger to dating, just because she didn't spend much time thinking about the next one or why she hadn't met anyone she really wanted to see more than once. She couldn't fit Sawyer into the usual dating picture—she already knew more about Sawyer, and had told Sawyer more about herself, than she'd ever revealed to another woman after half a dozen dates. Nothing about any of the countless moments she'd shared with Sawyer felt remotely date-like.

So this wasn't a date.

She thought about that as she raced around, straightening the few things that were actually in the same place they'd always been in. She barely made a ripple in her own life outside the hospital. From the moment they'd met, Sawyer made more than ripples—she made waves. And Dara liked it.

Fine. She admitted it. Terrible timing or not, she liked the way Sawyer sharpened the colors in her life, the way she made her skin tingle, the way she looked at her like she was fascinating and special. Thank goodness the sheets were clean.

Dara laughed out loud. Okay—getting way ahead of herself. But even that foolishness felt good. No one had to know what pictures she entertained in her head.

One last look around. The place was neat. The refrigerator was woefully bare.

But, thankfully, she had three bottles of wine, one red and two white, and that should work. She had one other big problem.

She was standing in the middle of her kitchen in sweatpants and a ratty T-shirt she'd pulled on when she'd stripped off her scrubs earlier. And she'd been wearing those scrubs for longer than she cared to remember. Well, she was an expert at the three-minute shower.

The shower probably took two and a half, which was good because she needed that time to apply just the teeniest bit of makeup so she didn't look like the walking dead. Or at least like she hadn't been dead for six months before she reanimated.

When the doorman rang up to say that Sawyer was in the lobby and to ask if he should send her up, her hair was dry if loose and a little on the wild side, her makeup, what there was of it, hid the smudges under her eyes, and she was wearing skinny jeans and an open-collared cobalt silk shirt that Penny always told her made her eyes look like the ocean on a summer's day. She always laughed when Penny said that, but tonight she hoped it was true.

She was ready for a date, and maybe Sawyer was here to talk about work.

Well, no matter. She could look good all the same. She hoped. "Thanks, Ernesto. You can send her up. And, Ernesto—you should be thinking about leaving before the hurricane hits."

"Not me, Doc. I have a job right here taking care of the building and all of you. I'm not going anywhere."

"Your family?"

"My wife and kids are staying with friends inland."

"You be careful, then."

"You too, Doc. Your friend is on the way."

When the knock came on her door, she didn't even pretend that she wasn't waiting for it. She opened it instantly.

"Hi," she said, all of a sudden uncertain. Sawyer carried a big brown paper bag under her arm that looked like it was full to the brim with containers, and she was wearing a tan T-shirt stretched sinfully tight over her chest and stomach, tucked into camo pants with a web belt cinched with a bronze metal clasp, and rough leather brown boots. Uniform. Working dinner, then?

Sawyer raised an eyebrow. "Hi. You sure I'm not barging in?"

"No, of course not. Come on in." Dara held the door open so Sawyer could enter. *Good going, Dara. Way to get awkward right away.* "I appreciate you bringing dinner."

"I don't know about you, but I've had enough of canteen food and MREs." Sawyer handed Dara the bags. From Dara's expression when she'd opened the door, she was as surprised to see Sawyer as Sawyer had been when she'd decided to call her. She'd found a slim window of time when she'd done all she could do for a few hours at least, and her first free thought had been of Dara, followed by a powerful urge to see her. And here she was. She wanted an excuse to see her, and dinner seemed like a good one. She wasn't sure where she was going to go from there, especially if Dara expected they'd be having a working dinner. She could do that, probably had to do that at some point, but right now, she wasn't thinking about anything except the thunder of pleasure that rumbled inside her. No point pretending otherwise. "Besides, I didn't know when I might get another chance to see you—when we weren't both in the thick of it."

"Oh. Well then, I'm glad you're here. And the food—that's good too." Laughing, Dara added, "Kitchen's this way."

"Nice place," Sawyer said, taking in the gleaming stainless-steel appliances, and glass-fronted cabinets, and a white quartz-topped island that separated the kitchen from a dining area big enough to seat six at a natural wood table and chairs. Through a wide archway, she got a glimpse of a living room with sliding glass doors opening onto a balcony. A million-dollar condo overlooking the ocean.

"Thanks," Dara said offhandedly.

Sawyer'd never given much thought to Dara's family, or what that meant. Even faced with the subtle elegance of Dara's condo, she still couldn't see Dara in the role of heiress. Dara might have been born to privilege, but the Dara she knew was driven by something wholly personal—a sense of responsibility and obligation.

Dara was the substance. All the rest was meaningless. Besides, nothing in the condo was as captivating as Dara, who'd look amazing in a tent in the middle of the desert. Sawyer came around the side of the island into the space where Dara worked. Dara looked good in scrubs, hell, she looked gorgeous soaking wet with her hair in crazy tangles and rainwater dripping off her chin. But tonight, she looked spectacular. "You look great, by the way. I mean, you always do, but tonight…I've kind of run out of words fancy enough to say what I mean."

Dara paused with plates in her hand and studied Sawyer. "You're doing just fine. And thank you. You look very good too."

"I'm sorry I'm not dressed for dinner." Sawyer shrugged. "I don't have any civilian clothes packed, in case you were wondering."

"I happen to like the way you look." Dara laughed. "Do you ever actually wear civilian clothes?"

Sawyer grinned. "Sometimes. If I'm at the beach."

"You actually go to the beach?" Dara set the plates down and paused before pulling silverware from a drawer. "Are you a chopsticks person?"

"Definitely chopsticks." Sawyer unpacked the food containers and put them on the place mats spread out on the countertop. "Sometimes I make it to the beach. I was there on my leave, like I told you. I was wearing shorts and a tank top, but come to think of it, they were army issue too."

"Of course they were." Dara's brows drew down. "Right. That's where you met Catherine."

Sawyer grinned. "She's something, isn't she?"

"She's something, all right," Dara muttered. "Do you like wine? I've got a cabernet, a sauvignon blanc, and a white burgundy."

"The red is good."

Dara handed her a bottle and an opener. "You do that, and I'll get glasses."

"Sure. Anyhow, if Catherine gets the word out, and that gets people moving, gets them out of the danger zone, I won't have much complaint."

"I suppose you're right." Dara stared at all the food. They were obviously expecting an army. "This looks great, by the way. And you *are* right about Catherine. What she's doing is important, and I'm being petty."

"Nah. That's not really like you," Sawyer said, opening containers. "I wasn't sure what you like, except not octopus, so I got a lot."

"You hit it with the moo shu and the cashew chicken." Dara sighed. "Oh, and that's not true about me not being petty. I have my moments."

"So what's bugging you?"

Dara stalled for time and fiddled with preparing her pancake. "Catherine is very good at what she does, but I dislike the way she keeps getting personal with you. For a story."

"Thanks." Sawyer hesitated. "I'm not used to people worrying about my feelings that way. So, ah—I appreciate you caring."

"Well," Dara said, "I know you can take care of yourself, but I could see she was bringing up things that hurt you and I...well, that and other things just made me a bit crazy."

Dara was blushing, and Sawyer was intrigued and a little pleased. She'd never seen Dara the slightest bit off her stride before. Somehow they'd ended up just a few inches apart, and even that felt like too far. She put her plate down and leaned an elbow on the counter. She wanted to touch her, and because she did, she waited. This was no time to hurry. "What other things?"

Dara arranged food on her plate, carefully not looking at Sawyer. If she took the step, there'd be no going back. They had critical work to do, and injecting the personal into it was a mistake. "Would you like to eat in the living room? There's always a great breeze at night."

"I would, yes." Sawyer left her empty plate where it was. "First, though, what other things does Catherine do that annoy you?"

Dara licked her lips, and Sawyer instantly forgot about dinner, forgot about being tired, forgot about being worried about thousands of troops and ten times that many civilians. She was fascinated, captivated, by the moist pink tip of Dara's tongue sliding over her lower lip. The hunger that welled inside her now had nothing to do with food. She raised her eyes, found Dara's gaze on her face, saw that Dara's eyes were just a little hazy, like the swirling gray-blue of the ocean after a storm. After its depths had been riled up and its tides hurled against the shore, after the wild seas had calmed but riptides still seethed beneath the surface. Something ancient and powerful stirred in Dara's gaze. "What, Dara?"

"Catherine annoys me because she's trying to get you into bed," Dara said softly. There. She'd said it. Sawyer could laugh it off and they'd have dinner and that would be that. Or not. She hoped not.

Sawyer grinned. "You think?"

Surprise, surprise. Again. The amusement in Sawyer's voice carried a hint of a tease. A whisper of a dare. Well, this was a game she didn't mind playing. Dara rested her hand very lightly on Sawyer's waist, just above the top of her pants. "Yes, I think. And, as I mentioned, it annoys me."

Sawyer sucked in a breath. Dara hadn't moved any closer, but the touch connected them with the force of an electric field. Sawyer's heart triple-timed. She'd had women touch her when she'd been naked that hadn't felt a tenth as good. Right now she'd carry a hundred pounds on a fifty-mile forced march in the Everglades if it meant Dara would keep her hand where it was. Dara had sent a signal. Her move next. "Not interested."

"I told you it was petty," Dara murmured, one finger tracing the top edge of Sawyer's camos.

Sawyer's vision narrowed. "I kind of like it."

"Like what?" Dara asked.

Sawyer swallowed. Desert dry. As light-headed as if she'd been baking in the African heat for a week with no water. "I like that you don't like her coming on to me."

"Mmm. Good." Dara tapped a fingernail on the bronze buckle at the top of Sawyer's button fly. Sawyer twitched and Dara's stomach flipped. She should slow things down. Her cell was on the counter. The outline of Sawyer's was clear in her front pants pocket. Any second they could both get a call. Have to go. Have to say good-bye again. Running out of time again—always running out of time with Sawyer. Not this time. "Do you have a girlfr—"

"No." Sawyer's voice was a low growl. "You?"

Dara shook her head. "No."

"Good," Sawyer murmured. "Then you won't mind if I kiss you."

"I would mind very much if you didn't," Dara said.

Sawyer leaned just close enough to kiss her, letting Dara's palm on her stomach set the distance between them. She was only a little bit taller, and she only had to bend her head a fraction, angle her mouth ever so slightly to cover Dara's. When her lips glided over Dara's, she lingered over the path Dara's tongue had traced when she'd licked her lip. Sawyer focused every sense on capturing the feeling of Dara's mouth, eager and warm and unbelievably soft. She wasn't much for going slow doing anything, but this—this couldn't be slow enough.

Carefully, Sawyer clasped Dara's waist, conscious of smooth silk and firm muscles beneath her palms, and drew Dara closer without lifting her lips from Dara's.

She wanted the kiss to last her through whatever was coming, to carry her beyond the chaos and the inevitable destruction and danger and death. She needed to believe this kiss, so completely untarnished and sublimely powerful, would somehow survive through all of that.

CHAPTER TWENTY-ONE

Dara's legs felt just the teeniest bit shaky. More than a teeny bit. She clenched her fist in the fabric of Sawyer's T-shirt and turned to steady herself with her butt against the counter. She didn't let go, though, dragging Sawyer with her, keeping Sawyer's mouth over hers. Somewhere in the last remnants of her still-functioning brain she knew she'd been kissed before, but for the life of her, she couldn't remember another woman's mouth that fit so well, another woman's lips so insistent and sure, another woman's breath mingling with hers as if she was being stroked from the inside out. A flood of sensations too overpowering to define stole through her. Awareness of excitement pulsing deep inside, awakening of a desire so acute she ached, amazement at the sure and certain knowledge she'd been searching for this feeling without even being aware of it. The kisses brought warmth where she'd been cold, light where there'd been shadows, and answers to questions she'd been asking forever.

Too much to process, too good to need words. Thoughts too fleeting to grasp, her body registering rightness in every cell. Her mind was ablaze, burning reason to ash, but she could feel. Oh, could she ever. She slid her free hand around the back of Sawyer's neck, and the dark strands of hair curled through her fingers like silk and satin, sunlight and shadow, and every mysterious force she'd ever imagined. Now she knew hunger in a way she'd never been hungry before. She ached for Sawyer's touch to fill her, take her, satisfy her.

She swept her tongue over Sawyer's lower lip, letting her teeth graze ever so lightly over the indescribably sensuous surface. Tasted something tangy and strong, like Sawyer.

"You taste like…" Dara murmured against Sawyer's mouth. "Damn. Something really good."

"Wintergreen."

"Mmm. I now love wintergreen."

Laughing through the kiss, Sawyer cupped Dara's hips and pulled her closer, keeping her mouth exactly where it should be, covering Dara's.

"Don't stop," Dara whispered.

"Not going to," Sawyer said, deepening the kiss again, sliding the tip of her tongue more insistently between Dara's lips, demanding more. She wasn't stopping even if she couldn't breathe and her vision was hazy and she might be having a heart attack. As long as Dara kept kissing her back, she'd hold her ground. Dara's tongue darted into her mouth and she teased back.

Dara released her grip on Sawyer's shirt and stroked the ridge of her collarbone with her fingertips, letting her palm splay over the muscles below. Sawyer sucked in a breath, and Dara pressed a little harder, making Sawyer's grip on her hips tighten. Oh, Sawyer liked that, did she? Heady with the power of pleasing, Dara caressed the angle of Sawyer's jaw and nipped at her lower lip. "You have a fabulous body." She sucked the spot she'd just bitten. "I have wanted my hands on you since…mmm, day one."

"All yours," Sawyer muttered, pressing closer.

Sawyer's hard muscles and hot, demanding kisses pulled Dara back into the whirlwind. She wasn't going to be able to hold it all in much longer. She murmured in the back of her throat, a plaintive note of need escaping on a rush of pleasure. "*Oh.*"

If Sawyer had heard that faint cry, half groan, half whimper, at any other time, she would've thought it was pain, but she knew it wasn't. No, definitely not pain, not with the way Dara's hands raced over her body, the way she answered kiss for kiss, touch for touch. Sawyer got the message, reveled in it. Approval, welcome, invitation. The kiss exploded into the rest of Sawyer's body, almost too much, too good, to absorb. The firmness of Dara's thighs fitted to hers, the softness of Dara's cheek beneath her fingertips, the fullness of Dara's breasts against her chest. Everywhere the fire. Too many barriers between them, cotton and silk, irritating and distracting. She wanted skin, wanted deeper than that.

Grumbling impatiently, Sawyer caught the back of Dara's shirt between two figures and tugged the tail free of her pants, sliding just the tips of her fingers underneath, tracing a slow circle in the hollow at the base of Dara's spine. So much better, sweet and seductive, like Dara's mouth. She eased her leg between Dara's, trapped her gently but inescapably against the counter. Dara arched her back, exposing the sensuous column of her neck that tantalized and taunted. Sawyer kissed her way from the angle of Dara's jaw down her throat, breathing in the intoxicating scent of sunshine on white sand.

"You feel amazing," Sawyer whispered, frustrated with no way to describe how touching Dara had somehow become everything, the *only* thing, she needed to live. Air, water, food—she could survive without them, but some hidden well within her had suddenly been tapped and need rushed forth, a flood that defied boundaries. "I don't want to stop." She closed her eyes tightly, kept her hands very, very still. "I think I have to stop."

Dara pressed her forehead against Sawyer's cheek and let out a long breath. "Are you being all responsible now?"

"Hell no—practical."

"Worse." Dara laughed shakily and leaned back, her body still pressed to Sawyer's, both arms around her neck. "You're a hell of a kisser."

Sawyer grinned. "I think I'm highly motivated to perform well."

"Oh, really?" Dara nibbled at her chin. "Why is that?"

"You're the most amazing woman I've ever kissed."

Dara's gaze grew heavy. "Careful what you say if you intend to stop kissing me."

"I don't intend to stop. Just delay a little." Sawyer kissed her quickly, just a little to stave off the choking need. "Because honestly, if we keep going, it's going to get really hard to stop. If my phone rings, or yours does, I still want enough sanity left to answer it."

"I don't suppose I have to mention this is terrible timing," Dara said, laughing wryly. "Like maybe the worst ever."

"Maybe not." Sawyer clasped Dara's waist lightly, fingers curling just above her hips. She probably ought to step back. Dara hadn't argued about putting on the brakes, and she agreed—at least her head did. Her body wasn't entirely on board. But the clock was ticking, and even though she could be reached in an instant for any kind of problem, and everything that needed to be done was under way, she still was stealing a little bit of space for herself when she had no right to it. But now that she was here, now that she'd touched her, now that she'd kissed her, she wasn't going to let go until she had to. "I've never paid much attention to timing, but I never really had to. I don't have much in the way of moves, so I haven't perfected much in the way of a bedroom campaign."

"Believe me, your lead-up to the frontal assault is stellar." Dara tapped the center of Sawyer's chest with a closed fist. Gently, but enough to pull all the excitement into one hot ball in the middle of Sawyer's stomach. "You, Colonel Kincaid, have moves you don't even know about."

Sawyer closed her hand over Dara's fist. "Is that right?"

"Oh, that's very right. And I'm not about to tell you any more than that. I prefer to be the only recipient of said moves."

"Are we discussing rules of engagement?"

Dara took a breath. She hadn't intended to go there, certainly didn't have any right to, or maybe not even any reason to. But there it was. In fact, there it had always been, since she'd first seen Sawyer and wanted to know who she was, since she'd become addicted to the wry grin and intense flash of intelligence and passion in her eyes, since she'd detected the gleam in Catherine Winchell's eyes when she looked at Sawyer and known exactly what it meant. She hadn't liked the idea of all that heat and power and too-sexy-to-live focus being directed anywhere else when there'd only been professional interest between them. Now there was a kiss—and if she was going to be totally honest with herself, even in secret, more than a kiss. So yes, she was going there. Foolish, possibly. Premature, probably. But time was not on their side, and she couldn't turn back the rising tide of desire and surprising possessiveness that came over her when she so much as looked at Sawyer.

Carefully now. No matter how crazy Sawyer's kisses made her, or how reckless, she still had enough sense left to maintain boundaries, even her own.

"Nothing too complicated," Dara said lightly. "But since I don't usually kiss women I'm not serious about…" She shook her head. "No, let me clarify. I've kissed women for a lot of reasons, many of them not very serious reasons either, but I've never kissed anyone the way I just kissed you. I'm not asking you to tell me how many women you've kissed—"

"Not all that many, and not a single one I can remember," Sawyer said, her throat tight and her belly tighter. "If I didn't need to be back soon, I'd kiss you again. And then I guarantee I'd want a lot more than kisses."

Dara trembled. She couldn't have hidden how wired her body was even if she'd wanted to, and she really didn't see any point after what she just said. "If I didn't have calls to make, family to check up on, and staff to follow up with, I'd invite you to get started on the more-than-kisses right now."

"So the rules?" Sawyer said huskily. "Just to be clear?"

Dara tapped Sawyer's chest again, this time with one finger, then touched a place between her own breasts. "If there are to be more kisses, I'd prefer they stay between us until we can decide if there will be a *more*. Then I won't have to kill Catherine."

Sawyer laughed. "I can assure you, I have no desire to kiss Catherine Winchell. Or any other woman. And I'm patient."

"*That* I haven't noticed."

Sawyer dove in for a quick kiss that she let linger for a second too long. When she pulled away, her vision was hazy. "I can be very patient about some things."

"Good to know," Dara murmured. "I guess for now we say this was nice, and let that be."

"Do you mind if I say it was a lot better than nice? Like amazing." Sawyer pulled her close, hip to hip, and kissed her again, longer and harder than the last time. "And that I'm going to be thinking about kissing you a whole hell of a lot until I can do it again?"

"Mmm. No argument." Dara clasped Sawyer's hands and gently pulled them away from her body. Every instinct screamed for her to reverse course. She slid out from between Sawyer and the counter, grabbing on to the little bit of space like a lifeline. Her control still fluttered like a torn sail in a gale wind. One touch and she was going to forget all the rational things they'd both just said. "We ought to eat something. Especially if all we have to look forward to is vending machine food and MREs."

"Okay. You're right." Sawyer grabbed a container and scooped out noodles. "Where's your family? You said you had to check on them."

"My grandmother is in an extended care facility—Shoreline Residential. They've assured me they're well prepared, but you know, I just want to touch base."

Sawyer pulled out her phone and made a note. "I'll keep an eye out for the name if anything comes up."

"Thanks." Dara squeezed her arm. "How about you? I know you mentioned siblings."

Sawyer shook her head. "We don't keep in touch, but they're not in the area—as far as I know."

"I'm sorry."

"Long time ago." Sawyer sighed and caught Dara's hand. "But thanks. Your mother left already?"

Dara snorted. "Heavens, no. She wouldn't leave when there's anything newsworthy happening." She closed her eyes. "Argh, listen to me. Let's just say Mother and I don't agree on what's important. So she's sheltering in place. Which probably means the staff are as well, so she won't be alone."

"Better give me her address too." While Sawyer was tapping in Priscilla Sims's address, her IM alert sounded.

Dara's followed a second later.

NOAA weather alert, 8:35 p.m.
Hurricane Leo is currently projected to make landfall in the Miami metropolitan area in fifteen hours as a Category 5 hurricane. Storm surge is likely to reach record heights and extend inland in many coastal areas for as much as half a mile. Wind speeds of 185 mph are predicted to extend hundreds of miles in advance of the storm. Shelters within the affected areas may be compromised.

Dara looked at Sawyer. "We're talking about thousands of people who are sheltering in place."

Sawyer nodded grimly. "We need to consider relocating the medical command center outside the Miami area. Jacksonville, maybe."

"What? We're right here—we can handle the load."

"Maybe you ought to evacuate. If you ramp up now, we can help you transfer the criticals you have in house still. I've got resources I can give you before Leo lands that I won't be able to give you in another eighteen hours. This whole area is going to be devastated. We both know that. No power, and all that that means. The hospital could be in trouble."

Dara sat back, the faintest chill racing down her spine. "You want me to just up and leave?"

Sawyer wanted to say yes. She'd seen what was coming, knew that no matter what they did, people were going to die. Her chest seized, a vise clamping around her heart. "It might be the safest thing for everyone."

"And what about emergency care for all the people who are not evacuating, and even the ones who have moved inland who are going to have injuries?"

"That's what the Guard is here for. We have the resources to provide critical care in the field, and then we'll—"

"You can't really think I would leave?"

Sawyer blew out a breath. "Ten days ago we expected the storm to come up the west coast, or even across the southern end of the state. But now you're right in the path. This isn't about personal obligations any longer."

"Sawyer," Dara said carefully, "I have a job to do, just like you. My patients would be at higher risk transferring them out now, especially given the logistical challenges, than taking care of them right where they are. And I'm certainly not going anywhere."

"In light of this last bulletin, the governor and my commander will expect an update from the field about our state of readiness—including our medical support lines."

"Then you'll have to do what you think best," Dara said, "just like me."

CHAPTER TWENTY-TWO

Landfall, zero hour
Roc Hotel
Miami Beach, Florida

Harry stood in the open doorway of the balcony on the hotel's fifth floor, enjoying the complimentary food and beverage service the Roc had provided for any staff who'd volunteered to stay during the storm and assist management in getting the place back up and running after Leo passed. He'd heard some fifty or so guests still remained too, mostly foreign tourists who hadn't been able to get flights out in time and couldn't go anywhere else. He wouldn't mind playing at being a bellman or a porter for a few days—beat the hell out of being crammed into some high school gym with a few hundred strangers or sweltering in his rent-by-the-month room with no AC. He swirled the ice cubes in his margarita and braced himself as the wind and rain picked up, flinging darts of cold water at his face. The palm trees down by the pool bent away from the oncoming gale, their fronds streaming out behind them like the long hair of the girls in high school who'd crammed into his old Caddy convertible when he'd put the top down and gone tearing down the strip, them screaming into the night. He smiled, almost hearing their high-pitched, excited squeals now. Wait a second. Hell, that *was* screaming—a banshee wail he finally recognized as wind. Goose bumps rose on his skin. Weird how the shore looked even wider than it had a few minutes ago—weren't the waves supposed to be getting higher? It looked like the water was being sucked out to sea.

His pulse raced, and he gulped the rest of his drink. He wanted a refill, but he couldn't stop watching, like glancing into the rearview mirror at a red light and seeing a car barreling down, knowing he was going to get hit and not being able to look away. The thatched roof on his poolside cabana bar rose and fell like it was breathing, straw strands breaking free and shooting away like darts from a blowgun. The air filled with the roar of a runaway freight train barreling down on a curve, and out to sea, a huge black swell appeared, frothing and spuming like a giant creature unleashed from the deep. The sea raged ashore devouring everything in its path, pushed along by a wall of wind so powerful the building swayed and trembled.

"Holy sh—" Harry jumped back as a tree limb as big as his arm flew by the open doors. He was on the fifth floor, for crap's sake. Rain slanted in and slashed at his face, pounding his body with the force of a dozen baseball bats. Wincing at the beating, he shouldered the slider closed, just catching a glimpse below that damn near stopped his heart. The storage sheds he'd helped fill with poolside tables and chairs upended and spewed twisted furniture into the waves. His bar came apart like a wet cardboard box and sank beneath water that had to be higher than the first floor already. The palm trees gave up the fight and swirled away like a bunch of abandoned pick-up sticks tossed in the gutter.

Somewhere overhead a terrible rending sound was accompanied by a nauseating tilt of the floor. Harry grabbed for a nearby end table and managed to slow his fall as the balcony doors shattered and Leo stormed inside.

Miami Memorial Hospital
Emergency Services Department

Dara and every staff member who wasn't actively caring for patients crowded into the break room and huddled in front of the television. Catherine Winchell, microphone in hand, stood on a downtown Miami corner. The ocean two blocks away was barely visible as a thin slice of gray a shade or two lighter than the battleship-gray sky down the avenue behind her. She'd braced her back against a sculpted steel lamp pole, one arm looped around it as her body swayed at a forty-five-degree angle, her yellow rain slicker billowing behind her like a parasail.

"That woman has some stones," someone muttered.

You have no idea, Dara thought, silently urging Catherine to forget the story and retreat to higher ground.

"Hurricane Leo has just made landfall here in Miami," Catherine shouted into her microphone, eyes nearly closed against the stinging pellets of rainwater propelled by a force so strong she barely managed to keep her feet. Her cameraman clung to the door handle on the media van, gamely filming what he probably couldn't even see at this point. She only hoped he didn't let go or come to his senses, jump in the van, and leave her stranded out here. "As you can see, ocean water has already breached the seawall and is beginning to flood the streets. If you are in the area, do not try to drive. The major thoroughfares are already impass..."

Catherine's words seemed torn from her throat and the camera wavered, panning madly over buildings that were quickly becoming islands in the rapidly rising storm surge. A studio anchorman could be heard yelling in the background, "Catherine, Wade—get out of there now!"

Dara held her breath, watching Catherine's form flicker as the live feed faded in and out. The water was already up to Catherine's hips—higher than many adults, and certainly a small child, could survive if pulled under. And yet Sawyer had jumped into those waters to help save her family. Dara pictured a seven-year-old Sawyer trapped in a flimsy mobile home as the floodwaters rose around her, scrambling for safety with two younger children and a terrified mother. She knew without a doubt Sawyer would be out in those waters in seconds if another's life hung in the balance. That's what Sawyer did—risked her life to secure the safety of others. Dara's heart hammered wildly. "Come on, Catherine," she whispered, "haul your butt out of there."

The TV feed switched back to the studio, where an anchorman who was trying hard not to look worried sat at the ubiquitous curved console in front of a projection of a map of Florida covered by a huge red circle that encompassed the whole lower two-thirds of the state.

"You're watching up-to-the-minute live updates from Channel Ten Storm News Central. Our on-the-scene reporter Catherine Winchell will be back with further updates as they unfold."

Penny leaned over and murmured, "Bet she wins awards for this gig."

"She ought to," Dara said. "If this is the beginning, we're in for an ugly time."

"Sampson said not to expect any word from him, maybe for days," Penny said quietly. "I made him promise to check in whenever he could, but he said they expected cell service to go out when the power did, and the power company's saying it could be weeks before they get the grid up again."

"I hope they're all wrong." Dara's stomach dropped. She hadn't been able to sleep after Sawyer'd left the night before—the kiss alone would have kept her awake, and their debate over keeping Miami Memorial open for business just added a shot of adrenaline to her already humming system. Her body wanted one thing, and her head warned her to reverse course. She was letting her attraction to Sawyer get out of control—kissing was all well and good, and damn, that *had* been good, but kissing for her did not usually lead to a near-simultaneous desire to drag a woman off to her bedroom and stay up all night exploring her admittedly fabulous body while offering herself up like the main course at an all-you-can-eat banquet. Which she had most definitely wanted to do—and still did, even if Sawyer was the wrong woman at the wrong time and might not even be the right woman at the right time. Sawyer was used to being in charge, used to giving orders, and used to assuming responsibility for everyone and everything that crossed her path. She'd been indoctrinated to put herself at risk for the greater good when she'd been just a child, and despite how valorous that might be, it did not necessarily make for smooth relationships. Not with a woman like Dara, who needed to be firmly in charge of her own decisions and her own destiny, right or wrong. No, she'd met Sawyer in the midst of a crisis when every interaction, every action and reaction, was heightened by the tension and danger, and that went a long way toward explaining why she was acting so out of character.

All of that rolling around in her head while her body was amped up to the point of exploding was not conducive to falling asleep. Since trying to rationalize away the disturbing need to hear Sawyer's voice, to know where she was and what she was feeling, did not make for a restful night, she'd stopped trying to sleep shortly after midnight. She'd emptied what little food remained in her refrigerator and dumped it along with the leftover Chinese down the trash chute, checked that all her electronics were unplugged, packed a go bag with necessities, and returned to the hospital. She'd slept fitfully and every time she'd surfaced, she'd checked her texts. Nothing from Sawyer. Finally at six a.m. when she'd figured Sawyer had to be awake too, she texted, *Be careful out there. Call if you can.*

"Have you heard from the colonel?" Penny asked.

"Not since a quick text this morning. She said one of the designated shelters had flooded from a backed-up sewer line and they were moving people to another facility on airboats."

"She probably won't have much more in the way of communication access than Sampson once we really get hit."

"I know," Dara muttered.

Penny cocked her head and pursed her lips. "Uh-oh. Something's up."

"What? No, nothing," Dara said way too fast.

"Oh, don't even try that with me." Penny poked her arm. "You weren't even gone very long last night—what happened?"

"Just as I said. Nothing." Dara sighed. "Much. We were having dinner and—"

"Wait—what dinner? Where and how?"

"Sawyer brought Chinese over—"

"To your apartment?"

Dara shot her a look. "If you want the story, you'll have to be quiet."

Penny made a zipping motion over her lips.

"Yes—she called and offered to bring takeout. I said yes—we could eat and catch up at the same time."

Penny rolled her eyes and made snorting sounds.

"Stop." Dara grinned. "We got the alert and never ended up eating much."

"What else happened?"

"There might have been a kiss."

Penny sat up straight, the same predatory glint in her eye Catherine Winchell got when she smelled a story. Dara wondered why she'd never noticed that before. That probably explained why she could never keep a secret from Penny. Relentless. Before Penny could pounce, Dara added, "A long, very nice…exceptionally nice…brain-melting…kiss."

"Nice," Penny said on a long exhalation.

"Yes, well, we all have too much to do to dwell on that," Dara said.

Penny snorted again. "You just keep telling yourself that."

"No choice." Dara knew better than to expect Sawyer to keep in touch in the midst of a developing crisis, but she could still hope.

An ER nurse stuck his head in the room. "We've got a drowning and a blunt force trauma coming in. ETA five minutes."

Dara jumped up. "Like I was saying, no choice."

Halfway to the door, the room plunged into darkness.

Landfall plus 22 minutes
National Guard Crisis Command Center

Sawyer grabbed for her phone as the lights went out. While searching for a cell signal, she counted the seconds in her head. At twenty the emergency generators kicked in and the perimeter lights below the ceiling in the warehouse came on. Her computer monitor flickered back to life and she keyed in the URL for the FPL power grid. Everything for hundreds of miles surrounding Miami was dark.

"Major," she called to her XO.

"Ma'am," Rodriguez said, appearing in the door of her cubbyhole office. He was a slender thirty-year-old who'd been activated for the current crisis and assigned as her executive officer due to his experience with disaster response in his civilian role as a Florida department of environmental conservation officer. So far he'd managed to keep track of all the various state and local civilian responders and their military counterparts while updating Sawyer on traffic on the emergency channels.

"Secure communications with the county and local law enforcement. If they're offline, reroute all emergency calls to us."

"Yes, ma'am. What about medical 9-1-1 calls?"

"I'll contact fire-rescue dispatch and confirm readiness."

"Miami Memorial is in the blackout zone," Rodriguez pointed out.

"They'll have backup power, and unless or until they can't handle any new patients, they will be our primary delivery point." Sawyer shunted aside the twist of worry in her gut. Dara would be fine. She involuntarily glanced at her phone. No text from Dara. No time. That's all that meant.

"Yes, ma'am." Rodriguez halted, pulled out his phone, and frowned. "Charlie Company reports structural damage to the evac center at the Tamiami Fairgrounds. Part of the roof went."

"Casualties?"

Rodriguez pressed his phone to his ear. "Say again," he shouted. "Roger that." He looked to Sawyer. "No troop casualties. Minor civilian injuries—cuts and bruises mostly. Several possible extremity fractures—Charlie Company is transporting."

"Carry on." Sawyer waited until he'd cleared the doorway and texted quickly. *Keep me updated. S*

She hesitated, wanting to say more, but nothing she could condense into a text would say what she needed to say, or do anything to dull the gnawing fear building in the pit of her stomach as the wind howled and the metal sheets of roofing screamed and tried to break lose. Finally she added, *Be careful.*

Words as impotent as she felt in the face of Leo's wrath.

Landfall plus 86 minutes
National Hurricane Center Atlantic Ops

Stan snatched his phone off his desk when it vibrated and he saw the number. "Anna? Is everything all right?"

"My God, Stan, I've never seen anything like this. Even Andrew didn't come in so hard."

His wife sounded more awestruck than frightened, which was like her and not necessarily a good thing. Knowing her, she'd try going outside to take photos. "Where are you?"

"In the closet."

Stan covered his other ear and pressed the cell to his left. "Say again? This connection is iffy."

"I know—the lights went out here a while ago and we don't have power back yet. I don't know how long I'll have a cell signal." Anna huffed. "I have the battery backups to the computer I can use to charge my phone if the signal lasts."

"Did you say you were in the closet?"

"I thought that was best after the hurricane sheets blew off the windows and then the glass shattered." She laughed. "There are palm fronds in the living room. From the look I got outside, the water must be into the lobby, probably the stairwells."

Stan's chest tightened. If the first floor flooded, the generators would be swamped too. No power, no food or water. "How many people are still in the complex?"

"At least half."

Stan cursed under his breath.

"You know a lot of them are seniors and wouldn't want to leave. We're okay above the first floor, I think."

"You might not get power back, Anna." Stan kept his voice steady, but he had to sit down. "You're going to need to evacuate—you and everyone there."

"I really don't know how we can do that, Stan," Anna said softly.

Chapter Twenty-three

Landfall plus 13 hours
Miami Memorial Hospital

Dara finished wrapping the preformed fiberglass splint with an ACE wrap. "You need to see an orthopedic surgeon within the next three days. The break looks clean to me, but you're probably going to need a cast for another six weeks."

The firefighter grunted, and she looked into his soot-smeared face. "Was that a yes, Lieutenant Julio?"

He grinned. He must've been in his early fifties, a little salt-and-pepper streaking the stubble on his chin and cheeks, crow's-feet from years of Florida sun radiating from the angle of his eyes, and creases circling the corners of his wide mouth. His shoulders were broad and his frame muscular looking even under layers of clothes that made Dara sweat just looking at them. His turnout coat was draped over a chair nearby. He still wore his heavy Kevlar turnout pants and flame retardant boots, and she pitied him needing to work in ninety-plus-degree weather in sweltering protective gear. Although the gear probably had kept his injury on the less serious end of the spectrum.

She could tell he wasn't listening. He wasn't the first firefighter, cop, or other first responder she'd seen in the last thirteen hours, and every single one of them said the same thing.

It's nothing, Doc. Regulations require me to get clearance. So could you put a Band-Aid on it and sign off on me so I can get back out there.

Every single one of them was eager to get back into the fray and seemingly unconcerned for their own well-being. Like Sawyer, she was sure. With most of them, their injuries had been minor enough she'd been able to grant their request with a clear conscience, but one paramedic had been swept under by a rush of water into a basement where she'd been assisting the apartment building manager in shutting off a gas leak. She'd hit her head on something when she'd been pulled below the surface, sucked in a lungful of muddy water, and nearly drowned. She was upstairs in the ICU on a ventilator. As soon as Dara got a minute she'd go up and check on her.

Treating the steady stream of civilians and emergency workers gave her a pretty good idea of how bad things were out there already, and they had days to go before Leo was done thrashing them. And then weeks of rebuilding and recovery. Knowing Sawyer was trained and experienced didn't help calm her worries—she was an ER doc. She'd seen every kind of injury under just about every circumstance imaginable. And Sawyer was not the kind of commander who led from the rear. Oh no—she'd be at the front, no matter the risk. Dara tried her best not to panic when she hadn't heard from her. She just kept working and checking her cell. Sawyer would get in touch soon.

Right now, she had a reluctant firefighter to talk some sense into.

"You realize, if you ignore my advice, you could convert what would be a straightforward fracture into something a lot worse."

"Not my first rodeo, Doc."

She rolled her eyes. "How about your first hurricane, Lieutenant?"

He shrugged. "Not that either, but I've never seen a mess like we've got out there. Electric lines down, power out everywhere, cars sitting upside down on hotel patios—" He shook his head. "I'm surprised you don't have people stacked twenty deep out there in your waiting room."

"Don't we?"

He snorted. "Looked like it might be getting close. Give it another twelve hours if the rain don't ease off and you might. Still hundreds of people trapped in their houses who are gonna need help getting to shelters."

"Just try to use your judgment out there, and remember to go easy—and take care of that arm."

"Sure thing, Doc. Thanks for the quick work."

He hopped down, grabbed his bright yellow turnout jacket, and slung it over his shoulder. She realized he'd never taken off his helmet. Maybe he slept in it. He looked happy to be heading back out into miserable weather to face another emergency.

"You're welcome," Dara called as he hurried out of the cubicle. "Don't forget to sign out before you go."

Another grunt was her only answer. Shaking her head, she quickly checked the room to make sure all the sharps had been disposed of and pushed the curtain back. She jumped when she came nose to nose with Penny on the other side.

"Don't tell me—another critical?"

"Not yet. Thought you'd want to know Sawyer's on TV again," Penny said.

"Catherine?"

Penny nodded wryly. "Yep."

Dara sighed. Catherine had obviously caught up with Sawyer somewhere and was reporting on the National Guard's rescue efforts with regular broadcasts. "I suppose I should watch. I need to know what's going on out there."

"And it doesn't hurt to catch a glimpse of the colonel, either."

"No," Dara murmured, "it doesn't." She paused for a second and pointed at Penny. "And you—you need to get off your feet for at least six hours. I mean it. You've just worked a twelve-hour shift."

"So have you."

"Not pregnant." Dara pointed to herself.

"Just you wait," Penny said peevishly. "Someday you'll be in this situation, and I'm going to mother-hen you to death for revenge."

"That day is a long way off," Dara said. "Now go."

Penny, looking pale and tired, said, "All right. Six hours. You need a break too."

"I will. Shoo." Dara trusted that Penny would follow instructions. She was stubborn, but not reckless. As Dara hurried toward the break room to catch the last of the news report, she thought about what Penny had said. She'd never really considered the issue of children. She was single and had a demanding job and, if she was honest with herself, had never really pictured herself in the kind of relationship where children might be part of the plan. She'd need someone she could count on for the long term before she'd consider children. Someone she loved, and who loved her. Though maybe the pictures she'd been letting herself consider hadn't been everything she wanted. Maybe.

The break room was empty—everyone who wasn't seeing patients was trying to catch some sleep.

Catherine was in her now-familiar position of standing in the rain with some destroyed part of the city as a backdrop, a microphone held between her and Sawyer as the two of them leaned close together to form a windbreak around the mic. This had to be Catherine's sixth or seventh live update since Leo made landfall, and each one played every few minutes until a new one took its place. Catherine had traded her civilian clothes for a camo jacket, one Dara was happy to see didn't have Sawyer's name on it anywhere. She would've been really annoyed if Catherine was wearing Sawyer's clothes. Sawyer was in full uniform and looked as alert and energetic and in command as she had twelve hours before in her first news feed. If you didn't know her, you wouldn't see the strain in her jaw or the shadows in her eyes.

"…situation in the Keys?" Catherine said.

"We've deployed four hundred troops, including engineers and construction crews, and twenty heavy trucks from our ground transport company to assist in securing the bridges between the islands, but the lower portion of the Keys is inaccessible by road. Along with the Navy and Air National Guard we're assisting local authorities in evacuating residents who either are unable to return to their homes from shelters or have had to abandon their residences due to severe damage."

"What does that mean for the relief efforts in our area?"

"We now have eight thousand troops actively in the field. Due to the profound flooding extending throughout the metropolitan area, most of our rescue efforts are being carried out in high-water vehicles and boats."

"What can we expect over the next few days?"

Sawyer looked directly into the camera. "The National Hurricane Center predicts rain will continue for the next thirty-six hours at least, adding significant water to the flooding already present. Wind will be less of a problem as Leo moves past, but the flooding will worsen. Vehicular traffic will be impossible, and anyone in residences or business establishments cut off by high waters can expect no improvement in their condition for at least three days." Sawyer's expression grew more intense. "If you are without fresh water or food or suffering from severe heat conditions, it's essential that you evacuate. We have troops ready to assist. Call the number on your TV screen or 9-1-1 if you have access to cell service. If not, signal your need for relief with a white flag of some kind. Hang it out a window or from any object that can be sighted from the air. We are patrolling the entire region by helicopter, and we *will* find you."

Dara listened to Sawyer's orders and wondered how many times today Sawyer had remembered climbing into a tree, tying a tattered cloth to a branch, and waiting to be rescued. She wondered when she would see her again, recognizing that the ache in the pit of her stomach wasn't hunger or fatigue or fear. She needed Sawyer, a glimpse, a brief touch, a smile to let her know her world was still all right.

Landfall plus 20 hours

Dara's door opened, a slash of light cut across her face, and she sat up blinking. "What is it?"

Her voice sounded used up and empty, a lot like she felt. How long had she been asleep? It felt like only a few minutes.

"Sorry," Penny said in a rush. "We've got five on the way—all multiples, two critical."

Dara pushed herself to her feet. A wave of dizziness threatened to capsize her and she steadied herself with a hand on the bedside table. The flow of emergencies had been unrelenting, occasionally surging to the point where the injured backed up in the waiting area despite the PAs, residents, and nurses triaging as quickly as they could. Then they'd almost be caught up and the tide would ebb, only to repeat the cycle a few minutes later.

"Who do we have?" Dara asked in the shorthand that was second nature to her and Penny after years of working together.

"You, a couple of first-year residents, and Vincie. Both PAs are already tied up with an MI and an acute appendicitis."

Dara made a mental note to check on those patients later. Even in a crisis, ordinary medical emergencies still kept coming. "Trauma room?"

"Two is open."

"How soon?"

"Five minutes out."

"What do we know?"

"Not much. It's weird, a guy who said he was a cameraman with Catherine called it in. All he could tell me was part of a road collapsed and a vehicle flipped over."

"Catherine's cameraman?" Dara's body trembled with a jolt of adrenaline. Catherine was with Sawyer, wasn't she? Why hadn't Sawyer called? "Did he say anything about the victims? Who they are?"

"No, sorry. He didn't have much in the way of details. He sounded pretty shook up."

"Right. I'm coming." Dara struggled to make sense of the chaotic story. Sawyer and Catherine weren't necessarily together. If they were, Sawyer would've been the one to call in any kind of mass casualty alert. Sawyer wasn't there. Sawyer wasn't hurt. Still, Dara's heart pounded anxiously. "I'll take the residents, you assist Vincie."

"Right. I'll see you there."

Dara stuffed her phone into the back pocket of her scrubs and jogged toward the trauma bay. Two first years and the chief ER resident waited for her. She nodded to Vincie. Even when Vincie ought to have been as exhausted as Dara, she radiated calm. If Dara had to deal with a major crisis with minimal help, Vincie and Penny would be the ones she would've chosen. "Hi, Vincie."

"Morning." She smiled wryly. "I suppose we could call it that. It's almost four."

"Wonderful." Dara took a quick inventory of the two treatment tables side by side, the overhead lights already turned on and focused downward, instrument packs on trays, gloves and gowns by the door. She pulled on a fresh cover gown, grabbed a pair of disposable gloves. Her two very green residents waited off to the side, a mixture of panic and excitement in their eyes.

"I want the two of you to assist in transferring and getting monitors on and lines in."

"Okay," Kirk said briskly, the current crisis apparently having purged his previous laid-back attitude.

"Roger that," Naomi muttered.

Dara pointed a finger at her. "Let me guess. Reserves?"

"Yep. Coastie," she said, smiling.

Dara smiled back. "All right then. Get going."

Both residents hurried out into the hall as a familiar commotion signaled the imminent arrival of the trauma patients. Wheels clattered over the tile floor, a mishmash of voices talked over one another, growing louder as the first responders tossed bits of information to the trauma team like confetti on the wind. The double doors burst open and the first gurney rocketed through. For just an instant, Dara's heart stilled, and her breath stopped in her chest. Sawyer's face was streaked with blood, and for the blink of an eye, that was all Dara could register. She took half a step forward and her brain registered the rest of it. Sawyer ran alongside the gurney, both hands pressed to the thigh of a small woman in a military uniform, barely visible beneath the jumble of equipment sharing the stretcher with her. Sawyer's hands were bloodied, as were the dressings and everything else in the vicinity. But despite the fresh blood trickling down Sawyer's temple, she was moving, *alive*, and Dara breathed again.

"Colonel?" Dara said, finding her voice.

"Blunt penetrating trauma to the thigh," Sawyer said tersely. "Probably a fractured femur and something big torn up in there. Blood loss is barely controlled."

"Let's get her over here."

Kirk stepped up quickly to assist Sawyer in the transfer, and out of the corner of her eye, Dara saw Vincie and Naomi moving the next patient onto the other bed. When Penny reached over to help, Dara called, "Penny, don't."

Penny shot her a look but nodded and set about getting the IVs hooked up. The door opened again and Catherine entered, a cameraman beside her.

Dara moved to intercept her. "Not in here."

Catherine looked as if she was about to protest, then nodded once and backed out, saying, "I'll want an update as soon as you're free."

"That will be a while," Dara muttered, quickly assessing the young troop. BP 60 palpable, heart rate 150, extremities cool. "She's hypovolemic, all right. Going into shock. How many more?"

"Three more beside Amal over there," Sawyer said, indicating Vincie's patient. "These two are the most serious. The others are all extremity fractures. I've got my team lending an assist to yours in the ER."

"Good, fine." Dara carefully lifted one corner of the dressing

Sawyer held in place in the patient's left upper thigh. The entry wound was a small, almost innocent-looking clean puncture, the edges of the two-inch circular wound almost surgical in precision.

"Kirk, get surgery down here. Any surgeon, I don't care who it is. No, wait. If you can't get trauma, get general surge, and if you can't get them, get plastics."

"All right."

"Tell them we need them *now*."

"Yep. I'm on it."

"What the hell did that?" Dara asked no one in particular.

"Piston rod maybe," Sawyer said. "We took a nosedive into a fifteen-foot crater when a sump hole opened up under us."

Dara's stomach clenched. It could so easily have been Sawyer lying there. "Have you seen the exit?"

"No, once we got her extracted, there was too much blood. All we could do was try to control it."

"So we may have a foreign body in there." Dara raised her head and caught sight of one of the ER nurses who'd just walked in. "Christie. X-ray."

"We've been calling," Christie said, "but one of the portables is down, and the other tech is—"

"I don't care. If they're not down here, that's where they need to be. Call them again."

"Okay. Calling."

"We're getting really thin on staff," Dara muttered as she accepted four units of blood from a blood bank tech. "Is it getting any better out there?"

"Some," Sawyer said. "Mostly now we're dealing with walking wounded, heat exposure, and minor traumas. Plus the usual medical emergencies."

"How bad is your head?"

"Looks worse than it is," Sawyer said offhandedly.

Dara narrowed her eyes. "Don't do that."

Sawyer blew out a breath, nodded. "I never lost consciousness. Hurts like hell. Probably need some stitches."

"Vision?" Dara hung a unit of blood.

"No problems. Dara," Sawyer said softly, "I'm okay."

"Do you need me to get someone to take your place holding compression on that wound?"

"I got this." Sawyer's jaw tightened. "She's my senior NCO. Her husband's down in the Keys with our ground transport company."

Dara nodded silently. Sawyer would not leave one of hers.

The X-ray tech arrived with a portable machine and Dara motioned him over. "We need a PA of the left thigh. There may be a foreign body in there. You have to be quick. We need to keep pressure on the wound."

"Just keep holding while I get the plate underneath," he said.

"Hey, Dara," a woman in surgical scrubs said as she bounded into the room with a harried-looking young guy in scrubs behind her. The woman halted at the side of the stretcher, hands on her hips and a frown creasing her forehead. "This does not look like a facial trauma to me—although you've got a dandy jaw fracture just down the hall. I was about to book an OR room when your resident corralled me to come down here."

"Hi, Gabby," Dara said. "That jaw will have to wait. We've got a major vascular injury here and you're it so far."

"Huh." The woman edged in next to Sawyer at the side of the stretcher, and Sawyer gave way. She was a head shorter than Sawyer, full-bodied, with quick, almond-shaped brown eyes. Wisps of ebony hair escaped from beneath a surgical cap, and gray streaked her temples. In another setting, Sawyer would have thought her strikingly beautiful. Right now she found her unmistakable self-assurance even more appealing.

"It's been a while since general surgery for me," Gabby said.

"You never forget, do you?"

"Not yet." Gabby eyed Sawyer with interest, taking in her uniform and bloody face. "Gabby Hernandez. Plastics. Anything else I need to know about this troop?"

"Good to meet you, Doc. Sawyer Kincaid." She shifted her hand as the surgeon lifted the compression pack to survey the wound. "Sergeant Meadows was alert for a few minutes after our vehicle flipped. She was pinned in but was able to tell us she wasn't injured anywhere else. Blood loss was brisk, and she lost consciousness pretty quickly. Other than a big vessel torn up in there somewhere, she's been stable."

"Well, most of the vessels I sew together are about the size of a hair. A big one ought to be easy." Gabby replaced the bandage and motioned to her resident to take over the compression. "I'll get her upstairs, get this open, and if the vascular boys get free they can take over. If not, I can still do a vascular anastomosis."

"Thanks, Gabby." Dara stripped off her gloves and tossed them at a nearby trash can. "How's the family?"

"Manny got his mother to evacuate. They're in a hotel in Vegas."

"Good for him," Dara said, thinking he'd done a lot better than she'd managed to do with her mother. "Thanks for staying."

"Wouldn't have missed it."

"Are you set over there, Vincie?" Dara called as Gabby's team pushed Sergeant Meadows's stretcher out the door.

"Fractured ribs and a pneumothorax. I put in a chest tube, and the blood gases are good."

"Good. Send him up to the SICU. I'll be down the hall." Dara pointed at Sawyer. "Come on. You're next."

CHAPTER TWENTY-FOUR

"Look, you've got more important things to do than patch up a superficial laceration," Sawyer said. "Just get one of the residents to stick a couple staples in it."

Dara slowed and pointed to the first empty treatment room they passed. "In there. I just need to get a suture tray."

"Dara," Sawyer said quietly. "Come on. You know—"

Dara spun around and poked a finger that stopped just short of Sawyer's breastbone. "Listen to me. You matter. You're not just someone who takes care of everyone else. You need to learn that part of taking care of people is letting them take care of you. Now, if you don't mind, I have a lot to do, and I would like to take care of you so I can get on to the rest of it."

Sawyer sucked in a breath. Shadows smudged the pale skin beneath Dara's eyes and she looked ten pounds thinner than the last time she'd seen her. Sawyer wished she could get her out of the line of fire, someplace safe, and knew she couldn't. Knew Dara wouldn't want her to and would be royally peeved if she tried. What she didn't need to be doing was adding to Dara's worries to lessen her own. "Hey, I've missed you."

With a shake of her head, Dara pressed her hand flat against Sawyer's chest. "And that's why you get away with so much. Because you say the perfect thing at just the wrong time and somehow make everything seem right again."

"I'm glad I've got something going for me." Sawyer covered Dara's hand, curled her fingers lightly around the edge of Dara's wrist.

"You know what? I haven't said this before, but I like it when you take care of me. When you worry about me. I like mattering to you."

Some of the weariness lifted from Dara's shoulders as she brushed her fingertips slowly back and forth over Sawyer's chest. Sawyer's uniform shirt was stiff, but it didn't prevent the heat from seeping through, from warming her all the way down inside. "You are an incredibly frustrating woman. You know, when I heard we had injured troops coming in, and I saw you with the blood…" She drew a shaky breath. Too late to worry if she was revealing too much. "I was terrified."

"I'm sorry."

Dara leaned in and kissed the tip of Sawyer's chin. "I don't want you to be sorry for being who you are. As a matter of fact, I don't even want you to change anything—except the part where you remember that you are not alone."

"Dara, I—"

"I'm sorry I don't have my camera rolling," Catherine said from a few feet behind them. "There's nothing like a budding romance to humanize a crisis. Not exactly the personal story I was going for, but it might work even better. When did you—"

Sawyer's eyes darkened when she looked past Dara. "This is off the record and private."

Dara turned, her hand drifting down Sawyer's arm as she faced Catherine. "Every shot you take of Sawyer and the others out there risking their lives is personal. You're risking your life too, and people know it. We're not a *story*, and it's time to back off."

"You know, I suppose you're right. Pity," Catherine said with a smile that almost looked regretful. "You both look so good on camera."

Dara rolled her eyes and muttered, "Impossible. Come on, Sawyer. Let's get back to work."

Sawyer said, "Be right there. Catherine, you and your cameraman can take a break. I'll be coordinating from here until my people are stable and I get a chance to see them."

"I could use some time in the editing booth," Catherine said. "Can I count on you to let me know if anything urgent comes up?"

"Somehow you always seem to get the word," Sawyer said dryly. "But yes, I'll keep you updated."

Catherine patted Sawyer's shoulder. "It pays to have good sources, darling." She brushed her thumb over Sawyer's jaw. "You have blood on your face."

"Catherine," Dara said lightly, holding the curtain open so Sawyer could enter the treatment room, "that's a no-fly zone from now on."

Laughing, Catherine waved and headed away in the opposite direction.

Dara shook her head. "She's unbelievably aggravating and I rather like her."

"I'd like her more if she didn't turn up at the worst possible times," Sawyer grumbled. "I'd give a lot for a couple of hours—hell, a couple *minutes*—alone with you and no interruptions."

"So would I." Dara gave her a little push. "Go inside and sit down. You need anything? Coffee, something to eat?"

"Let's get this over with." Sawyer hopped up and sat on the edge of the stretcher. "When we're done, I'll grab a cup of coffee and something hot to eat. I'm waiting to see how my sergeant does."

"I can offer you an on-call room if you want to grab a little sleep."

"I wouldn't mind."

"Good. Sutures first. Be right back. Stay put."

Sawyer chuckled. "Roger that."

Dara hurried down the hall and pulled an instrument pack and some local anesthetic from the med cart. As she headed back to the treatment room, Penny came around the corner, and she paused. "Any word from Gabby?"

"Not yet," Penny said. "She said she'd call down with a report when she could. You need some help?"

"No, I can handle it. How are you doing?"

"My shoes are three sizes smaller than they were twenty-four hours ago, but I feel fine."

"You need to get off those feet for a while. How's your blood pressure?"

"It's fine."

"When was the last time you took it?"

Penny rolled her eyes. "A couple of hours ago."

"Uh-huh," Dara said. "As soon as I'm done with Sawyer, I want to check you out. Don't disappear."

"Like there was anyplace I could go. Oh…" A smile lit up her face. "Sampson checked in. He's all right, but he said everything's a mess. He and his team were called out to the Roc. One of the outside stairwells collapsed and part of a wall came down. They've got some occupants trapped. He doesn't know how many. We're probably going to get them soon."

"Wonderful. All right. I'll be here. See if you can get everyone who is not actively with a patient to get something to eat and some sleep."

"What about you, Chief?" Penny said.

"I'm good."

Penny dipped her head toward the curtained-off cubicle. "How's the colonel?"

"Stubborn, but manageable."

Penny grinned. "Atta girl."

"I heard that," Sawyer said as Dara slipped inside the curtain and opened the instrument tray on a portable stand.

"Which part?"

"The stubborn part."

"I thought that was mild considering some of the things I could've said."

"Really?" Sawyer caught her hand before Dara could open the pack of sterile gloves and tugged her over to the stretcher.

She suddenly found herself between Sawyer's legs, and in the next breath, Sawyer's mouth was over hers. Everything dropped away—the anxiety, the never-ending concern for her patients, for her family, for Sawyer. Fatigue melted like snow in the spring sun, and every fiber within her sprang to life. She wrapped her arms around Sawyer's shoulders, her fingers finding the nape of Sawyer's neck. She pressed into Sawyer's chest, her breasts responding to the subtle curves of Sawyer's body as if Sawyer's hands had closed around them. She moaned softly, instantly aroused. Gasping, she clutched Sawyer's shoulders and pushed away. "You have no idea what you do to me."

"I might," Sawyer said, her voice husky and her eyes dark and devouring. "I know what you do to me, and it's a craving like I've never felt before. Like if I don't have you soon I'm going to burn up from the inside out."

Dara stroked Sawyer's cheek. "I can't look at you without wanting your hands on me, without wanting to feel you everywhere."

"When I get the chance, I want to take my time," Sawyer murmured, stroking the swell of Dara's hips. "And I never have any at all."

"Listen," Dara murmured, brushing her mouth over Sawyer's, "I don't care if it's fast. All I care is that it's you."

Sawyer let out a breath and kissed her back. "It's the very first thing on my to-do list."

Dara laughed. "I'll hold you to that."

Taking a second to steady herself, Dara stepped back and wrapped her professional cloak around her erratic emotions and runaway body. She pulled on gloves, drew up the lidocaine, and motioned for Sawyer to lie back. "You know the drill."

"I'm all yours, Doc."

"Are you now," Dara said quietly as she began injecting the long, deep laceration just behind Sawyer's hairline.

"I am."

Dara looked down, met her eyes, and found Sawyer's gaze steady and absolutely sure. "Good."

She worked quickly and efficiently and within a few minutes was done. She smeared some antibiotic ointment over the laceration, sealing it until the wound would seal itself in a few hours.

"You're good to go, Colonel."

"Thanks." Sawyer sat up as Dara started to dispose of the instrument tray. "Where will you be?"

"Penny says fire rescue is bringing in some patients any minute, so"—Dara shrugged—"I'll be here."

"How do I find out about my sergeant?"

"I'll tell Penny to page you as soon as the OR lets us know. Gabby will call down."

"You're sure?"

"I promise. I know how important it is to you." Dara stroked Sawyer's jaw. "Let me show you the on-call room so you can grab some sleep, okay?"

"Okay. How about you?"

"I'm pretty good for now."

"Come find me when you get a break?" Sawyer said.

Dara turned to go, turned back, and kissed her. "I will."

Landfall plus 30 hours

"Sawyer," Dara murmured softly, placing her hand lightly on Sawyer's shoulder so as not to startle her. She hadn't turned the room lights on when she'd come into the on-call room, and she didn't knock either. For some reason, she wanted the dark and the solitude to shut out the chaos that permeated the brightly lit hallways, to still the cacophony of voices, to silence the constant demands for her attention and her energy. She wanted, *needed*, just these brief free moments to recharge. To grab something for herself, to restore what she had never realized before she needed. The calm, the certainty, the warmth that radiated from the connection to this one unique woman.

"I heard you coming," Sawyer said.

"How could you?" Dara said lightly, sitting on the side of the bed, her hip touching the outside of Sawyer's. Like the first time when they'd shared an on-call room, there was just enough light so Dara could see Sawyer's eyes, the shape of her face, the length of her body. She'd stretched out on top of the covers in her clothes, her boots standing at attention near the foot of the bed, perfectly aligned, ready to be stepped into. Her shirt was unbuttoned, her belt loosened, but otherwise she was completely clothed. She was a second away from being ready for action, probably how she always slept when she was in the field. Possibly how she always slept. Dara filed the thought away with the many other fascinating images that made Sawyer so captivating.

"I recognized your footsteps." Sawyer reached up and grasped Dara's hand, their fingers intertwining easily. She tugged until Dara had to lean down. With her mouth just a whisper away, Sawyer added, "I smelled you too. The second the door opened. You smell like sunshine, you smell like life."

"You make me feel alive," Dara whispered.

Sawyer's arm came around Dara's shoulders, dragged her down, and her kiss was hard and hot and fast and what Dara had secretly been hoping for, but she was still taken by surprise. Surprised by the power and possessiveness of Sawyer's mouth and her own eagerness to be possessed. Dara dug her fingers into Sawyer's shoulders, not to push her away, not to escape, but to cleave even more tightly. Sawyer's hands, her mouth, her body were hard and tight with tension. Dara shifted closer onto the narrow single bed, and Sawyer turned until their bodies touched along their lengths. Heat flared between Dara's thighs and she moaned softly.

Sawyer's hand pushed beneath the back of Dara's scrub shirt, stroking the length of her spine, sending electric shocks into the pit of her stomach. She readied faster than she'd ever soared to the pinnacle before—trembling, amazed, terrified, and beyond reason. She found Sawyer's free hand, dragged it between them, pressed it between her thighs. She might've heard Sawyer chuckle, a deep, supremely satisfied sound, and she didn't care how desperate she might seem. Not one little bit. She tugged at the strings on her scrubs, and finally, finally, Sawyer's hand was on her skin, her palm hot against the base of her belly, her fingers streaking downward, stroking, finding the pounding pulse point.

Dara arched when Sawyer stroked her clit, one heartbeat, two heartbeats, and stretched tight to the breaking point, she shattered. She muffled her cry against Sawyer's shoulder, fighting to absorb the explosion that racked her body.

Chest burning from holding her breath, afraid to miss one single incredible second, Sawyer wrapped her arms around Dara and held on tightly. She kissed Dara's temple and buried her face in her hair.

"That was…" Dara's voice faded and she sighed.

"Dara, I…" Sawyer blinked, struggling with too many feelings to contain.

"Perfect," Dara gasped. "In case you were wondering. Perfect. Not too fast, not too slow. Just right. Just exactly right."

Sawyer laughed. "You're amazing. I think I'm going to need CPR in another second."

"Are you all right?" Dara asked, trying and failing to rise up on one elbow. She settled for resting her cheek on Sawyer's shoulder.

"All right? Hell no. I'm totally blown away. Totally crazy about you."

Dara laughed shakily. So much, so fast. Too much? How could she tell? She could barely think. "I just want you to know—oh hell, what does it matter what happened in the past. That was amazing. And I've never, ever come like that in my life."

Sawyer sat up with her back against the wall and tugged Dara until she was curled in her arms. "We don't have much time, do we?"

"No. We don't. I'm sorry." Dara pressed her hand to Sawyer's abdomen and felt her tense. "Are you sure you're all right?"

"You mean, am I going to walk around in a state of constant arousal?"

"That would be it, yes."

"Probably, but since that's kind of been the case every time I've been anywhere near you lately, it's not much different." She tilted Dara's chin and kissed her. "Besides, I like it. I like the way you make me feel."

"I like *that*," Dara muttered.

"How about you? Are you okay?" Sawyer asked.

"You mean, how do I feel about coming in here and practically attacking you?"

"If you want to call it that. I sort of thought of it like giving me a present."

Dara laughed, and lightness flooded her heart. "Did you now? Well then, I'd say we both got a fabulous present and I feel…like I've never felt before. Satisfied, content, happy."

"Happy. Yeah, that's what it is. Crazy how that can be with all that's going on."

"I know." Dara's feelings went far beyond what her simple words could convey, and she didn't even try to resist. She closed her eyes, breathed her in. Smiled. "You somehow still smell like wintergreen."

"I ought to smell more like a swamp in high summer," Sawyer said dryly. "I need to shower and get a change of clothes. Gabby should be done by now, right?"

"I'll call up and get you a progress report." Dara sensed their time running out, and God, she didn't want to let her go. And she couldn't ask her to stay. With a sigh, she sat up. "I'm going to have to grab a change of clothes and get back out there too. I'm waiting on some X-rays on a patient who might have a broken forearm."

Sawyer caught Dara's arm just before they reached the door, pulled her close, and kissed her again. "Thanks again for the present."

Dara gripped her shirt. "Well, next time I want my own."

Laughing, Sawyer whispered, "My pleasure."

CHAPTER TWENTY-FIVE

Landfall plus 46 hours

Dara pushed the stack of files away with a long sigh. It didn't matter how shorthanded she was or how many patients waited to be seen—fortunately, right now, the emergency room wasn't full—she still had to do paperwork. It didn't help that Gretchen, from the safety and comfort of her Manhattan pied-à-terre, had sent her a ream of forms to review and sign off on documenting for the state just how much it was costing the facility to function as the medical emergency command center; or that the pharmacy needed override clearance because they'd run out of several key drugs and other critical supplies and would have to special order them at twice the normal delivery costs; and that requests from half a dozen other departments had somehow filtered through to her in the absence of much of the management staff. *Most* of the management staff, really. In all fairness, everyone was a lot better off with the administrators high and dry somewhere, so the rest of them could get on with handling the medical emergencies.

And as of right now she was done with paperwork, and the hospital would just have to manage to run without the proper forms for a few more days. Just as she was about to head back to the intake area, her cell rang and she snarled. Her snarl died abruptly when she saw the caller ID.

"Hey," she said quickly, "everything okay?"

"Better than okay," Sawyer said. "I might have some good news for you."

Leaning back in her chair and closing her eyes, Dara let the sound of Sawyer's voice soothe her frazzled nerves and caress that place inside her where she desperately needed to be touched. "What news? I could use something good right about now."

"You sound pretty beat. Did you get any sleep?"

"I feel like I'm back in my residency days," Dara said, trying to inject a little levity into her voice. Sawyer sounded worried and was no doubt as worn down as her. No point in spreading around the misery. "I remember lying down a few hours ago and closing my eyes, and I think I was sleeping, but I might've been sleepwalking. It's been pretty steady around here. I'm okay, though. I escaped for a while to dig out from under the paperwork, and honestly, I'd rather be running a code."

"I hear you." Sawyer laughed.

"So come on," Dara prodded, "what's your news?"

"We've cleared one of the major thoroughfares, and we're going to let essential civilians come through. Essential meaning public works employees, city officials, and hospital personnel. You should be getting some relief very soon."

"That would be great." Energized, Dara sat up. "If I can get a few more staff in here, I can put together some kind of reasonable call schedule. I really need to send Penny home. She's coming up on two days straight."

"Where is she going? Most of the residential areas are without power, even the ones that aren't still blocked off by fallen trees and building debris, or underwater."

Dara laughed. "Penny's husband is a firefighter—the belt and suspenders kind of guy. They have a generator, and so does Penny's sister Cissy, who lives a few houses away. Cissy says their road is passable, and Penny is going to stay with her. I wouldn't let her leave if she wasn't headed somewhere safe."

"Huh. Is she driving?" Sawyer sounded dubious. "She'll still have to navigate some pretty iffy areas to cross the city. Probably not a good idea for her to go alone."

"I'm due a few hours' break. I can drive her."

Sawyer was quiet a few seconds. "How about this. I need to do recon and check in with some of our squads. As soon I clear things at my end, I'll come by and take you both to Penny's sister's. Your area still has no power."

"And I have no food." Dara's first instinct was to say no, to say she could take care of things herself, but Sawyer was right. She couldn't risk running into trouble with Penny along, and she couldn't be foolish either. Sawyer had the means and the experience for this situation, and oddly, she didn't find letting Sawyer take care of her the least bit uncomfortable. Warning bells didn't sound either. "Only if you can take the time to do it."

"How does three hours sound?" Sawyer said. "We're moving into the recovery stage. We've still got civilians who need to be transported to secure locations and the usual emergencies, but that's why we call it mobile command. I'm always available, no matter where I am."

"Then I'll see you when you get here."

"Good. I want to see you."

"Same here," Dara murmured. "You have no idea how much."

National Hurricane Center Atlantic Ops

"Stan," Bette called. "It's Anna on two."

Stan yanked his cell out of his pocket and swore when he saw that it was dead. He kept forgetting to charge the damn thing. Somehow, he'd completely lost his sense of time in the last few days. He grabbed the landline off the counter where Bette had left it. "What's the matter? Are you all right?"

"This is the part where you get to say I told you so," Anna said with a hint of laughter in her voice.

"I'll hold that in reserve. You're okay?"

"I'm fine. What about you? You sound stressed, and you never do."

Stan barked out a laugh and rested his rear against the counter. "Well, I suppose that's a matter of opinion. I'm okay. I'm damn tired of being here, and"—he lowered his voice—"I miss you."

"Me too. And I'm sorry you've been worried," Anna said. "I really should've listened to you, as it turns out."

"That's not important now. What's going on?"

"We're marooned. Our block, really, the whole neighborhood, is an island. The best I can tell from the news reports which, to tell you the truth, are about as confused as most of us feel right about now, is that it's something to do with the sewer system not being able to handle the volume in some parts of the city."

"How deep is it out there?"

"About knee high, still. I haven't ventured out, I'm not that crazy, but from what I see, people are using boats for the most part. There's a tremendous amount of debris in the streets. But that's not why I'm calling."

"Really?" Stan shook his head. "All that isn't enough?"

"You're really not going to believe this, but I'm honestly not lying." Anna laughed. "One of the building maintenance crew managed to get here this morning in a fishing boat with an outboard motor on it because the generators have been going in and out for the last twelve hours, mostly out."

"Damn it, I was afraid that was going to happen. You're flooded on the first level, aren't you?"

"Into the stairwells. And it's hot inside. I'm okay, but some of the older residents in particular are starting to suffer. To give him credit, he got here, but he only made it as far as the front door."

Stan's stomach cramped. "Is debris blocking you in? Anna, that's a fire hazard. That building needs to be evacuated."

"I agree with you—the power situation is just too unstable. But it's not debris. Stanley…there's an alligator in the lobby."

"You're not just saying that to lift my spirits, are you?" Stan said slowly.

"You know I'd do anything to help you through this, darling," Anna said dryly, "but even I couldn't come up with that. It's big too. So the maintenance guy is not going to venture inside."

"Can't say I blame him. Did he call someone?"

"I suspect they probably heard him yelling without the phone. We're waiting for the National Guard."

"Where are they taking you?"

"No one knows, but I imagine one of the local shelters. I'll call you when I land."

"I'll do my best to get you some kind of transportation to a hotel, if we can find one that's operational yet."

"You know, Stan," Anna said, "I'll be fine at a shelter for a few days. You just worry about Leo."

Stan glanced at the weather map. Leo liked Florida and didn't look like he was going anywhere soon.

Landfall plus 50 hours

"And I don't want to see you for twenty-four hours," Dara said to Penny as Sawyer pulled the Humvee to the curb in front of Penny's sister Cissy's house in Miami Springs. Dara was happy to see Cissy's house had fared better than many others in the same neighborhood, even though the yard was littered with tree branches, and here and there a stray piece of siding. Most of the areas they'd driven through had been like that—some blocks devastated, others surviving with fairly minor damage. The rain had finally abated to a light drizzle, and some streets were passable. The state emergency management division had still not opened the city for the return of the general population, but in sporadic patches residents could be seen clearing the roads and driveways of wreckage. Many streets were only passable in specialized high-water vehicles or boats, and people could be seen transporting bags of clothing and animals in fishing boats, kayaks, and canoes, and even the occasional rubber raft.

"You *will* call me if you get short," Penny said, her forehead wrinkling.

Dara leaned over and kissed her cheek. "I'll keep you updated, I promise. But really, with Rod coming back this morning and Kim Lee and Raul both checking in, we're going to be a lot better off than we were up until now. You deserve a break."

Penny squeezed her arm and glanced over at Sawyer. "The both of you do too. Make yourself at home at our place. The freezer is stocked. There's even a bottle of wine on the counter, and you know I'm not going to be drinking it, so feel free to break it open."

Sawyer laughed. "Thanks."

"I hope you get a little time to unwind." Penny climbed out, waved to them, and hurried up the sidewalk as the front door opened and her sister came out to engulf her in a hug.

Sawyer turned the vehicle around, backtracked to the adjacent block, and pulled in where Dara directed her. Happily, Penny's modest coral-pink bungalow had fared as well as her sister's. The yard had taken the brunt of the wind damage with uprooted shrubs and a toppled tree that had missed any of the vital structures, but the house had escaped with only a few missing shingles and a detached rain gutter.

Sawyer shut off the engine and stretched. "I think we might've earned a glass of wine."

"I think you're right. I don't even know what time it is, and I don't care." Dara leaned across the wide compartment and slid her hand onto Sawyer's leg. "How tired are you?"

"Who said I was tired?" Sawyer murmured.

"Good. Let's go open that wine."

Sawyer stopped to open the hurricane shutters on the front windows, and once inside the single-story house, with the generator running, life seemed almost normal. They had lights, fresh food in the refrigerator, and the promised bottle of wine sitting on a sideboard in the cozy living room.

"I think there's a corkscrew in one of those drawers by the sink," Dara said, searching one of the overhead cabinets for wineglasses. "How do you feel about drinking wine out of water glasses?"

Sawyer laughed. "Right about now, I'd drink it out of anything, so that sounds fine."

"Done." Dara turned, held out the bottle, and Sawyer swooped in for a kiss.

Dara reached blindly behind her and set the bottle on the counter before wrapping both arms around Sawyer's neck. "God, you feel so good."

"Is there a guest room?"

"Down the hall, second room on the right."

"Grab the wine."

"What—oh!" Dara made a grab for the bottle.

Sawyer picked her up and started down the hall.

"You're really doing this, aren't you," Dara said, relaxing into Sawyer's arms. "Carrying me."

"Hundred pounds of equipment, twenty-mile marches, remember? You feel positively light."

"I feel positively amazing." Dara kissed Sawyer's neck and secretly reveled at the feeling of being swept away. She laughed at the silliness of the thought.

"What?" sawyer asked.

"Nothing. Just…happy."

"Good." Sawyer took the turn into the bedroom, gently deposited Dara in the middle of the bed, and unlaced her boots as Dara kicked off her shoes. Leaning over, Sawyer kissed her. "I'm hoping to make you feel even better than amazing."

"Mmm, not so fast," Dara said when Sawyer tugged on the zipper of her jeans. "I think I have a present coming."

Straddling Dara on her knees, Sawyer opened Dara's jeans. "I sort of thought—"

"I think I have a pretty good idea what you have in mind." Dara grasped Sawyer's wrists, twisted her hips, and Sawyer let herself be tossed over onto her back.

Dara could have anything she wanted.

"But I'm getting my present first." Dara shimmied out of her jeans and pulled her shirt off over her head. In just her bra and panties, she sat astride Sawyer's middle and started working on the buttons on Sawyer's shirt. When Sawyer went to help her, Dara pushed her hands away.

"I always like to take my time opening my presents," Dara said conversationally. "I'm very careful not to tear the paper when I loosen the tape. I even fold up the wrapping paper and keep it if it's especially pretty."

Parting the fabric on Sawyer's uniform shirt, Dara let her fingertips trail down the center of Sawyer's body. By the time she got to Sawyer's belt, Sawyer's thighs were trembling and her hands were clenched in the soft cotton quilt that covered the guest bed.

"Sometimes, I don't even open the actual present for a while. I just leave it so I can see how pretty it is." Dara unbuckled the brass buckle on Sawyer's belt, then unbuttoned the fly of her BDUs.

Sawyer groaned.

Dara's throat was dry and her hands trembling, but she would not hurry this most incredible moment. She pushed up Sawyer's T-shirt, bared her stomach, and felt everything inside her clench. Muscles starkly etched beneath satin skin, elegant planes and strong curves. She leaned down, kissed the hollow above the top of Sawyer's briefs.

"Dara," Sawyer said dangerously, her voice low and hoarse.

"This might be the best present I've ever had." Dara grasped the top of Sawyer's pants and pulled them down. Her legs were long and lean, as she knew they would be. She brushed her palms up the inside of Sawyer's thighs, over skin so incredibly soft, until her hands disappeared inside Sawyer's underwear.

Sawyer's hips came off the bed, and Dara laughed. "Maybe I'll just enjoy looking at my present for a little while—"

"If you don't—" Sawyer jackknifed upright, her arms circling Dara's waist, and kissed her. One hand slid into her hair, holding her head as she plundered her mouth.

Dara raked her hands down Sawyer's back, heard her moan. Oh, she liked Sawyer undone, the iron control fracturing, the power breaking like waves against the shore. For her. Before her own need drove her under, she braced her hands on Sawyer's shoulders and pushed. "Lie down."

Grumbling, Sawyer obeyed.

Dara stripped off Sawyer's briefs and stretched out between her legs. "Now I'm going to have the rest."

Sawyer knew it wasn't going to be long. Dara's mouth was too hot, her lips too sweet, her tongue too knowing. She slipped her fingers into Dara's hair, silky as the pleasure streaking through her. When she had nothing to hide, nothing left to fear, she came.

"We forgot the glasses," Dara said lazily.

"Uh-huh. And the corkscrew." Sawyer rolled onto her side and kissed her. "I'll get them."

"Really? You can move?" Dara frowned. "I'm losing my touch."

Sawyer laughed. "Not unless you can top the best sex ever in the universe."

Dara propped her chin in her hand and smiled contentedly. "Hmm. Something to shoot for, then."

"I love a woman with an agenda. I'll be right back." Sawyer paused on the way out to the hall and gestured to the wall screen. "I hate to suggest it, but I ought to scan the news. The governor has a way of making announcements to the press before we hear about it."

"Politics," Dara said. "Sure, turn it on. As long as there's wine."

"This is Catherine Winchell reporting from Jorge Middle

School, one of the forty shelters being managed by the Florida Red Cross. I'm here with Ms. Priscilla Sims, one of the Miami Red Cross board members, and Ms. Anna Oliver, whose husband—"

Dara shot up in bed. "I can't believe my mother is on the news. Wait, yes I can—but at the shelter?"

"You look like her," Sawyer said, sliding an arm around Dara's waist, "only happier."

"Oh," Dara said, relaxing against Sawyer's side, "I most definitely am. Shh—I want to hear this."

Sawyer grinned and kissed the tip of Dara's shoulder.

Catherine was talking to an attractive redhead wearing a Tampa Bay Rays baseball shirt and blue jeans.

"Anna," Catherine said, "I understand you and a number of residents were evacuated from your condominium early this morning."

"Yes, unfortunately a number of buildings on our block were completely isolated by high floodwaters that have yet to recede. We had power for the first twenty-four hours, but the last day and a half has been pretty difficult, especially for older residents."

"Absolutely. The heat wave following so quickly after what we've just been through is making the recovery efforts much more difficult." Catherine looked earnestly into the camera. "We urge anyone without power and air-conditioning at risk for heat-related complications to seek refuge at a local shelter. If you need transportation, call the number on your screen or 9-1-1, or make efforts to contact local rescue teams."

Catherine turned back to Anna. "Tell our viewers about the surprise visitor you discovered in your lobby."

Anna smiled into the camera. "I think in this case, a picture might be worth a thousand words." An obviously amateur video came on. "I took this when the National Guard arrived this morning to relocate our friend."

Sawyer appeared in the frame along with several other

national guardsmen and a man wearing a blue windbreaker with yellow block letters proclaiming Animal Control. The camera cut away to the corner of the building lobby, flooded with several feet of water, and the unmistakable snout of an alligator breaching the surface.

"Rest assured," Catherine said with a smile, "the alligator was captured uninjured and is even now on his way back to his natural habitat." She turned to Dara's mother. "And with the tireless aid of the Red Cross, the recovery efforts continue."

Priscilla said, "We respond here and abroad for just such emergencies, and your generous supp—"

Dara clicked off the TV and glanced at Sawyer. "Catherine never misses anything, does she? Especially not if you're involved."

Sawyer snorted. "She's got an open link to our comm channels. She knows where the emergencies are. And seriously, who would pass up the chance for the alligator story?"

"True." Dara laughed.

"So how was it, seeing your mother on television?"

"Oh, it's not the first time. When I was a teenager, it used to be rather humiliating. But now..." She shrugged. "She actually does a lot of good with her humanitarian missions. And you have to hand it to her, she did stay, although I doubt she was ladling out food in a shelter. That took some courage."

Sawyer took her hand and kissed the backs of her fingers. "You take after her in a big way where that's concerned."

Dara tapped Sawyer's chest. "Look who's talking. You're the hero of everybody's day."

"I'm not trying to be."

"I know. It's just the way you're made." Dara leaned over and kissed her. "And I love you for that."

Sawyer took in a slow breath.

Dara stared.

"That's the nicest thing anybody's ever said to me," Sawyer finally said.

Dara framed Sawyer's face. "You know what? Nothing has ever

made me happier than saying that." She kissed her. "So let me try again. I love you."

Sawyer grinned. "It's even better the second time."

"Well, wait'll you've heard it a few hundred times, maybe then you'll be used to—"

Sawyer drew Dara down onto the bed. "Never. I will never get tired of hearing that." She kissed her, sliding her leg between Dara's, kissing her way along the angle of Dara's jaw down to her throat. She murmured against the pulse that beat deep in the fragile tissues, "I love to hear you say it. I love everything about you." She raised her head, found Dara's hazy gaze fixed on her face. "I love you, Dara."

CHAPTER TWENTY-SIX

Landfall plus 57 hours

Dara's phone rang, pulling her from a dreamless sleep, the first jolt of adrenaline bringing her instantly awake. She had her cell in her hand as Sawyer stirred beside her, the sudden tension in Sawyer's leg where it rested against Dara's signaling she was ready for action. Dara caressed Sawyer's bare shoulder in the dim room. Early evening.

"Dr. Sims."

"Doc," a low, husky voice said, the urgency plain, "this is Brian at Shoreline. I'm sorry to bother you—"

"You're not, Brian." Dara's breath hitched. "What is it? Is it my grandmother?"

"No, no, at least—*she's* doing pretty well compared…to everybody."

Dara jumped out of bed and grabbed her clothes from the floor. She'd known Brian for years, and he'd always been steady and cheerful. Now he sounded scared. "What's happening?"

"I'm not supposed to be calling. They're monitoring everybody's calls, but I…I'm in the john on my cell and I don't have much time…"

Dara bit back an impatient remark. Slow and easy, just like when she was calming down an anxious family. "Take your time, Brian. Just tell me as best you can. Is there an emergency?"

"Yes…no? I think…" He took an audible breath. "Yes, there's a problem. We don't have any power, and the generators can't handle the load. The AC's been out for over two days."

"What?" Dara ordered herself not to shout. They were in the middle of a heat wave with temps over 100 degrees. In these conditions, everyone was at risk, but especially the elderly and infirm. "Has the director called the power company and told them about the emergency?"

"That's what they say. They keep telling us not to worry, somebody's coming, but nobody ever does. There's some really sick folks here, and…I don't think some of them are doing so well."

"What about the on-call doctors who cover the facility? When were they last by to check the residents?"

"Not since before Leo—they were due yesterday, but then I heard their group had closed their practice until the evacuation was lifted. All we've got are a few LPNs, two RNs, and a few non-medical staff."

For eighty residents.

Dara closed her eyes. Shoreline had a major breakdown in the emergency management system, and right now, how that had happened or who was at fault didn't matter. What mattered was getting them some help. "All right. I'm coming."

"Thanks, Doc. You won't tell them I called you?"

"No. You just try to keep everyone cool and hydrated as much as you can. Make me a list of the most critical patients so I can see them right away."

"Right. We're trying to do that, but we're running out of everything."

"Don't worry about your inventory—just use what you have. We'll get you resupplied."

"Right. You'll be here soon?"

"As soon as I can." Dara tossed her phone onto the bed and grabbed her scrub shirt, pulling it on as she searched for her pants. "I've got to go. There's an emergency at Shoreline, the facility where my grandmother is a resident."

"I heard." Sawyer had her pants and boots on and was buttoning her shirt. "I've been keeping tabs on Shoreline. We haven't seen any changes in their status. No reported emergencies."

"That was one of the nurses. He said they have no AC and the power company hasn't been responsive."

"Shoreline's not on the FPL priority list of facilities. They're within a critical radius of the nearest hospital, and they have backup generators. Even if they called about a power outage, they might not get service right away unless they told someone their generators were failing."

"Why haven't they, then? You know what the temperatures are like out there, and with no AC...That's insane." Dara scanned the room to be sure she hadn't left anything behind. She doubted she'd be coming back anytime soon. She might not have another chance to be alone with Sawyer like this again anytime soon. "I'm sorry."

Sawyer frowned. "Why?"

"I was hoping..." Dara sighed as she pulled the covers straight on the bed. "I just wish we had more time."

"We will," Sawyer said.

The certainty in her voice was all Dara needed to hear. "I should go. Can you take me back to the hospital for my car?"

"No," Sawyer said, "I'll take you right to Shoreline. Come on."

Dara hesitated. "Sawyer, I don't want you to get caught in the middle of some kind of political nightmare, and this has all the earmarks of one. You haven't been officially notified, and—"

"Hey," Sawyer said, grabbing Dara's hand. "This is family. Come on."

Dara kissed her. "Thanks."

Once in the Humvee, Sawyer called her XO. "Rodriguez, check the logs for any emergency calls from residential care facilities in a fifty-mile radius. I need to know how many of them have reported power outages and how many the power company is handling as priority."

"Yes, ma'am. Might I ask the colonel why?"

"I'm on my way to Shoreline Residential. They apparently have an unresolved heat situation which hasn't been logged or addressed by us or FPL."

"Scanning now, Colonel. Nothing from Shoreline on our logs. It will take me a while to cross-check with FPL."

"Let me know when you do."

"Might I suggest calling a few places on the priority list in the zones where the grid is down, Colonel? We might get a better assessment of response and resolution."

"Good idea. See to it."

"Yes, ma'am."

Sawyer detoured around an area where her sector maps showed the roads were impassable. "Either Shoreline didn't report a problem or the power company hasn't gotten to them yet."

"After forty-eight hours?" Dara said, dismissing the panic that threatened to cloud her judgment. This was personal in a way that ordinary emergencies weren't, but she was prepared to deal with it and she would. She just needed to get there. "I appreciate what you're doing."

Sawyer glanced over at her. "Even if I wasn't wearing this uniform, I'd be doing the same thing. I'm not letting you handle this one alone."

"I'm more than happy for the assist." Dara stretched her hand between them and Sawyer grasped it. "And I'm glad you're here."

Dara tried to keep calm as the trip that should've taken them forty-five minutes took almost three hours. By the time Sawyer detoured around blocked or flooded highways, backtracked to find a semipassable route, and pulled the Humvee into the turnaround in front of the sprawling one-story structure, Dara's nerves were jangling.

As they walked up the sidewalk to the main entrance, Dara said, "I should probably take the lead here since there's no official callout."

"Understood."

The lobby was empty and no one staffed the reception area, the first sign of trouble. The air inside was as stifling as outside with a stale, oppressive odor. Dara immediately started to sweat and checked the thermostat on the wall by the corridor down to the residence section. "God, it's a hundred and ten degrees in here."

Sawyer felt the overhead vents. "They have no working air-conditioning."

"Hello?" Dara walked down the hall. "Hello?"

An aide in a tank top, shorts, and a soiled smock appeared in the doorway. "I'm sorry, we're closed to visitors." Her lank blond hair was sweat soaked and her pale face damp and drawn. She looked to be in her thirties and very frightened.

"I'm Dr. Dara Sims," Dara said. "My grandmother is a resident here. I'm going down to check on her. Do you have other residents who need medical assistance?"

The aide looked left and right, an anxious expression on her face. Dara walked closer. "What's going on?"

"If I talk to you," the blonde whispered, "I might lose my job. I can't afford to lose my job. I haven't been home for five days, and I've got three kids. My mother's watching them. Please."

"I'll make sure nothing happens if you talk to me. Who do I need to see?"

"Oh God, I'm really worried about some of the patients, especially Mr. Mirabelli in room 114."

"Dara," Sawyer said, "I'll check on him. You check your grandmother."

"Yes," said Dara, already jogging away. Usually half a dozen staff were moving about the hallways delivering meds and meals, or transporting residents to activities, but Dara didn't see anyone on her way to her grandmother's room. Even Brian was MIA.

"Gran?" Dara said, hurrying into her grandmother's room. Her grandmother was in bed, wearing only a light nightgown. Her pillow was sweat stained, her face shining with perspiration. Dara bit her lip and waited until her voice was steady.

"It's Dara, Gran."

"Dara," her grandmother said, turning amazingly clear eyes toward her. "I think you might need to do something about the heat, dear."

Dara choked back a sob of relief as she took her grandmother's pulse. One twenty. The skin on her arm tented when she gently pinched it. She was dehydrated and would be in serious condition in just a few more hours.

"When's the last time you had something to drink?" Dara said, pouring tepid water from a half-full pitcher into a glass and holding it to her grandmother's lips. The question was automatic and she didn't expect an answer. Of course she wouldn't remember. Her grandmother drank until the glass was empty and Dara refilled it. "Go slowly, now. Are you hungry?"

"I'd really rather wait for brunch, Priscilla," her grandmother said, leaning back to the pillows with a sigh.

"Mom's not here right now, Gran, but I'll get you something to eat as soon as I can. I have to check on some of the other residents, but I'll be back, I promise. Then we're going to move you somewhere more comfortable."

"All right, that sounds just fine."

Dara spot-checked several rooms on her way toward 114, her shirt already soaked through from the hot, heavy air. Most of the residents appeared to be sleeping, or unresponsive. Here jaws ached from the effort not to start shouting for someone in authority to explain what the hell was going on.

Sawyer stepped out of room 114 and closed the door, her expression grim. "We've got a problem. I'm calling for a squad to evacuate the building."

Dara's chest tightened. "Mr. Mirabelli?"

"Deceased"—Sawyer nodded—"and he's not the only one."

"Oh my God," Dara whispered.

"Dr. Sims." Brian raced toward her. "I'm so glad you're here."

"Brian, I need you to get all available staff together in the lobby immediately. We'll be evacuating the establishment as soon as possible."

"Yes, yes. Thank you. Thank you."

Dara called the emergency room to put them on notice. "I'm at Shoreline Residential Center with at least a dozen criticals, mostly dehydration, respiratory failure, possible cardiac complications. ETA…" She glanced at Sawyer, her brows raised.

"I'll have trucks here in twenty-five minutes."

"Less than an hour," Dara said.

When she finished briefing the ER, she ran a hand through her hair and stared at Sawyer. "I think this is your operation now."

Sawyer grasped her hand. "How's your grandmother?"

"I'm going back to check on her and the others, but she's stable."

Sawyer nodded. "I need to contact the local authorities since we have a mortality. And, Dara, I think we need to brief Catherine."

"Yes. This is a story that needs to be told," Dara said.

Landfall plus 60 hours
Channel Ten Breaking News

"This is Catherine Winchell outside the emergency room at Miami Memorial Hospital. We've been following the evacuation of Shoreline Residential Center, located only three miles from the hospital itself. Eight residents have succumbed to heat-related complications as a direct result of Hurricane Leo, despite the facility having been one of several dozen in the area approved to remain in operation throughout the crisis. Apparently the facility did have generators but was unable to obtain enough fuel to keep them running once the power failed. Many of the staff remain on duty despite personal and family hardship. The governor has instituted an investigation and is even now in the process of ensuring that no other facilities suffer the same crisis.

"If you have family members in a similar situation and have been unable to reach them or a responsible individual, please contact the hotline emergency number."

"Dara," a familiar voice called as Dara rounded the corner from her office.

Dara stopped in her tracks. "Mother!"

"I really wish I didn't have to learn about these things on television," Priscilla said. "How's your grandmother?"

"She's fine. She's upstairs in the step-down unit. She'll be here a few days until…" Dara shook her head. "I'm not sure Shoreline is going to reopen anytime soon. But we'll worry about that when we come to it."

"According to the news report, you're responsible for saving all those people's lives."

"Not just me, Mother. I had a lot of help."

"Well"—her mother looked around the ER, the first time she'd ever been there—"it does seem this job turned out to be useful after all."

Laughing, Dara shook her head. "I guess you're right."

The doors behind her mother opened and Sawyer came through. Dara smiled and her mother followed her gaze.

"Oh yes," her mother said, "I saw her at the shelter a few days ago. She rescued that poor woman from the alligator."

"Yes," Dara said, "she's quite good at that sort of thing."

"I tried to find her after the news interview, but she'd vanished."

Dara motioned Sawyer over. She would've taken her hand, but they were both on duty. "Colonel Kincaid, I'd like you to meet my mother, Priscilla Sims. Mom, Colonel Kincaid is in charge of the National Guard's relief and rescue efforts."

"Very pleased to meet you, Colonel," Priscilla said, extending her hand. "I do hope you have an opportunity to attend one of the Red Cross benefit dinners when all of this unpleasantness is over."

Sawyer smiled. "I'll certainly try to do that, and we appreciate all the work your organization has put into the relief efforts."

Priscilla preened and glanced at Dara. "Well, darling, seeing that everything is under control here, I'll be on my way. I think Ms. Winchell wants to interview me about this latest tragedy."

"I'm sure she does. Bye, Mother," Dara called as her mother swept away. Shaking her head, she regarded Sawyer and almost laughed out loud at Sawyer's incredulous expression. "Do you really plan on attending a fancy benefit dinner?"

"Only if you'll be my date," Sawyer said.

Dara laughed. "Oh, that might be fun."

CHAPTER TWENTY-SEVEN

Landfall plus 15 days
Miami Memorial Hospital

Channel 10 Weather Forecast
Clear and sunny
High temperature 98 degrees
Ocean temp 85 degrees

Penny rapped on the partially open door and stuck her head into Dara's office. "Hey, I thought you were leaving early."

"I've got a couple of minutes still. I'm going to get these damn requisitions done if it kills me." Dara waved Penny in while surreptitiously surveying her with a critical eye. She looked rested, her color was good, and her eyes were bright. "Do you feel as good as you look?"

Penny laughed. "Better. Believe me, a ten-hour shift feels like nothing after...you know."

Dara nodded. Two and a half weeks after the crisis began, they were almost back to normal. Ninety-five percent of the staff had returned, except those unlucky ones whose homes were still uninhabitable. The emergency room census had fallen to normal levels, and if she didn't look at the devastated properties and demolished shoreline and destroyed foliage while driving to work, life almost seemed normal. But it wasn't, and probably never would be completely again for anyone who'd just lived through Leo. An element of fragility had been injected into the sense of daily life, the feeling that nothing could ever really be taken for granted because circumstances beyond one's control, situations beyond the human ability to fight, could come along and uproot one's existence. Time, always something she understood to be fleeting, was even more precious now.

"I feel guilty leaving after a regular shift still."

Penny laughed, but her eyes held the memory of the tragedies they'd witnessed. "Good news about your grandmother, though. I saw Millie when I stopped by to visit. She said she'd worked out a placement for her."

"Yes, we got really lucky, and Millie got her a spot at one of the SunView places," Dara said. "The whole social service department has done an amazing job considering how many displaced patients we have. Shoreline won't reopen for six months, maybe not even then if they can't replace the administration, and who knows what the sanctions are going to be. I explained it to my grandmother...but..." She sighed. "The best thing is, Brian is going to be working there, so when she's aware, she'll have someone around she knows."

"That's wonderful."

"Yeah." Dara pushed the requisition forms away. "Screw it. I'm going home."

"That's right," Penny teased, "big date tonight."

Dara shrugged, a little self-conscious and a little embarrassed to admit she was nervous. "Not exactly. Well, I guess it could be considered a date. I'm having dinner with Sawyer and her best friend and his wife at their house. It's a barbecue."

"Sounds like fun."

"It's pretty much akin to meeting the family," Dara said slowly, just then realizing why she'd been anxious about something so simple. She was getting to see a new and important part of Sawyer's life. "He's a little more than her best friend."

"Aha," Penny said, leaning back against the door, looking as if she planned to stay awhile. "Sawyer wants the special people in her life to meet. That's nice."

"Yeah." Dara smiled. "It is."

"So...how is everything?"

Heat rushed up Dara's throat and she suspected Penny could see her blush. "Everything is fine, thanks."

"That good, huh?" Penny laughed. "Good for you. So, serious then?"

"Yes," Dara said, "pretty much." She caught Penny's eye roll and grinned. "Okay, yes, totally. I'm...she's the one."

"Mutual. I'm sure. I've seen her look at you."

"Yes," Dara said quietly. Sawyer made her feel loved every time she looked at her, every time they touched.

"How long will the Guard be stationed down here?" Penny asked. "I still see them everywhere."

"The recovery efforts are going to go on for months, especially with so many areas still without power. A lot of the out-of-state Guard have pulled out, except from the Keys, where the engineers are working on the bridges, but the Florida Guard will be here in some capacity for six months."

"Sawyer too?"

"Sawyer too."

Penny tilted her head from side to side. "So, um, where's she sleeping?"

"Penny," Dara said with a mock sigh.

"Aw, come on. Give a little."

"Most of the time with me."

"And after her duty here is over?" Penny asked.

Dara nodded. "We haven't made any definite plans, but I've got a pretty big apartment and Sawyer has enough seniority to request a posting at Homestead, so..."

"Woo-hoo. Sounds like a plan to me. I think she's great, by the way."

"Yeah, me too." Dara bit her lip, shrugged. "I suppose it seems fast, but I know...*we* know..."

"No, it doesn't. It seems right," Penny said, "and you should get out of here soon."

"Fifteen more minutes," Dara said, "I just want to check on a couple of the residents."

"They're all doing great," Penny said.

"Yes, nothing like a disaster to help them mature."

Penny shook her head. "Too true. Have fun tonight and be prepared to report tomorrow."

Dara laughed. "Thanks. You go home too. Your shift was over thirty minutes ago."

"Right behind you."

Dara left everything just as it was on her desk and walked out into a sunny late afternoon. The skies were nearly cloudless, the air hot and clean. Her phone rang as she got to her car, and she answered when she saw Sawyer's number come up.

"Hi."

"I might be a little bit late," Sawyer said. "We've got a call to assist the Coast Guard in a civilian rescue op—fishing trawler taking water and likely going down."

"That's okay. I'll see you when you get there," Dara said.

"I'll call you." Sawyer paused. "I love you. I'll be there."

Dara smiled. "I know. Me too."

When Dara got home, she took a shower, dressed for a casual night out, and settled in to read a book. Sooner than she thought, a knock came on the door. She set her book aside and hurried to answer it. Her heart gave a little jump as it did every time she saw Sawyer. She took her hand as she came in.

"You weren't that late," Dara said.

Sawyer threaded an arm around her waist, pulled her close, and kissed her. "Nope. Benefits of command. I delegated."

Dara laughed and kissed her back again. "How much time do we have?"

Sawyer chuckled. "How much of a hurry are you in?"

Dara squeezed her hand and tugged her toward the hall and the bedroom beyond. "Plenty of time."

"I'm glad I wasn't later, then."

"You never have to worry about that. I know you'll be here."

Sawyer slowed her down and turned her around to face her. Her eyes grew suddenly serious, her expression steady and strong. "I always will be. I love you."

"I know. I love you too," Dara said. "It seems I'm learning that need is not a weakness."

"And I'm learning that in some parts of my life, I don't need to be in charge," Sawyer said. "All I need to be is a good partner."

"Thank you," Dara said as she kissed her. "For being exactly the woman I need."

"I'm feeling pretty lucky. Because I'm pretty sure you could have had anybody in the world."

"I don't know if that's true or not," Dara said, "but I can tell you this. You're the only woman I want. Today, tomorrow. Every single one of them."

"And I can promise you I'll be right here."

"Like I said, just what I need." Dara tugged her down the hall. "Now come on, Colonel, time for a little R and R."

About the Author

Radclyffe has written over fifty romance and romantic intrigue novels, dozens of short stories, and, writing as L.L. Raand, has authored a paranormal romance series, The Midnight Hunters.

She is an eight-time Lambda Literary Award finalist in romance, mystery, and erotica—winning in both romance (*Distant Shores, Silent Thunder*) and erotica (*Erotic Interludes 2: Stolen Moments* edited with Stacia Seaman and *In Deep Waters 2: Cruising the Strip* written with Karin Kallmaker). A member of the Saints and Sinners Literary Hall of Fame, she is also an RWA/FF&P Prism Award winner for *Secrets in the Stone*, an RWA FTHRW Lories and RWA HODRW winner for *Firestorm*, an RWA Bean Pot winner for *Crossroads*, an RWA Laurel Wreath winner for *Blood Hunt*, and the 2016 Book Buyers Best award winner for *Price of Honor*. In 2014 she was awarded the Dr. James Duggins Outstanding Mid-Career Novelist Award by the Lambda Literary Foundation. She is a featured author in the 2015 documentary film *Love Between the Covers*, from Blueberry Hill Productions.

She is also the president of Bold Strokes Books, one of the world's largest independent LGBTQ publishing companies.

Find her at facebook.com/Radclyffe.BSB, follow her on Twitter @RadclyffeBSB, and visit her website at Radfic.com.

Books Available From Bold Strokes Books

A Country Girl's Heart by Dena Blake. When Kat Jackson gets a second chance at love, following her heart will prove the hardest decision of all. (978-1-63555-134-1)

Dangerous Waters by Radclyffe. Life, death, and war on the home front. Two women join forces against a powerful opponent, nature itself. (978-1-63555-233-1)

Fury's Death by Brey Willows. When all we hold sacred fails, who will be there to save us? (978-1-63555-063-4)

It's Not a Date by Heather Blackmore. Kade's desire to keep things with Jen on a professional level is in Jen's best interest. Yet what's in Kade's best interest...is Jen. (978-1-63555-149-5)

Killer Winter by Kay Bigelow. Just when she thought things could get no worse, homicide Lieutenant Leah Samuels learns the woman she loves has betrayed her in devastating ways. (978-1-63555-177-8)

Score by MJ Williamz. Will an addiction to pain pills destroy Ronda's chance with the woman she loves, or will she come out on top and score a happily ever after? (978-1-62639-807-8)

Spring's Wake by Aurora Rey. When wanderer Willa Lange falls for Provincetown B&B owner Nora Calhoun, will past hurts and a fifteen-year age gap keep them from finding love? (978-1-63555-035-1)

The Northwoods by Jane Hoppen. When Evelyn Bauer, disguised as her dead husband, George, travels to a Northwoods logging camp to work, she and the camp cook Sarah Bell forge a friendship fraught with both tenderness and turmoil. (978-1-63555-143-3)

Truth or Dare by C. Spencer. For a group of six lesbian friends, life changes course after one long snow-filled weekend. (978-1-63555-148-8)

A Heart to Call Home by Jeannie Levig. When Jessie Weldon returns to her hometown after thirty years, can she and her childhood crush Dakota Scott heal the tragic past that links them? (978-1-63555-059-7)

Children of the Healer by Barbara Ann Wright. Life becomes desperate for ex-soldier Cordelia Ross when the indigenous aliens of her planet are drawn into a civil war and old enemies linger in the shadows. Book Three of the Godfall Series. (978-1-63555-031-3)

Hearts Like Hers by Melissa Brayden. Coffee shop owner Autumn Primm is ready to cut loose and live a little, but is the baggage that comes with out-of-towner Kate Carpenter too heavy for anything long term? (978-1-63555-014-6)

Love at Cooper's Creek by Missouri Vaun. Shaw Daily flees corporate life to find solace in the rural Blue Ridge Mountains, but escapism eludes her when her attentions are captured by small town beauty Kate Elkins. (978-1-62639-960-0)

Twice in a Lifetime by PJ Trebelhorn. Detective Callie Burke can't deny the growing attraction to her late friend's widow, Taylor Fletcher, who also happens to own the bar where Callie's sister works. (978-1-63555-033-7)

Undiscovered Affinity by Jane Hardee. Will a no-strings-attached affair be enough to break Olivia's control and convince Cardic that love does exist? (978-1-63555-061-0)

Between Sand and Stardust by Tina Michele. Are the lifelong bonds of love strong enough to conquer time, distance, and heartache when Haven Thorne and Willa Bennette are given another chance at forever? (978-1-62639-940-2)

Charming the Vicar by Jenny Frame. When magician and atheist Finn Kane seeks refuge in an English village after a spiritual crisis, can local vicar Bridget Claremont restore her faith in life and love? (978-1-63555-029-0)

Data Capture by Jesse J. Thoma. Lola Walker is undercover on the hunt for cybercriminals while trying not to notice the woman who might be perfectly wrong for her for all the right reasons. (978-1-62639-985-3)

Epicurean Delights by Renee Roman. Ariana Marks had no idea a leisure swim would lead to being rescued, in more ways than one, by the charismatic Hudson Frost. (978-1-63555-100-6)

Heart of the Devil by Ali Vali. We know most of Cain and Emma Casey's story, but Heart of the Devil will take you back to where it began one fateful night with a tray loaded with beer. (978-1-63555-045-0)

Known Threat by Kara A. McLeod. When Special Agent Ryan O'Connor reluctantly questions who protects the Secret Service, she learns courage truly is found in unlikely places. Agent O'Connor Series #3 (978-1-63555-132-7)

Seer and the Shield by D. Jackson Leigh. Time is running out for the Dragon Horse Army while two unlikely heroines struggle to put aside their attraction and find a way to stop a deadly cult. Dragon Horse War, Book 3 (978-1-63555-170-9)

The Universe Between Us by Jane C. Esther. Ana Mitchell must make the hardest choice of her life: the promise of new love Jolie Dann on Earth, or a humanity-saving mission to colonize Mars. (978-1-63555-106-8)

Touch by Kris Bryant. Can one touch heal a heart? (978-1-63555-084-9)

A More Perfect Union by Carsen Taite. Major Zoey Granger and DC fixer Rook Daniels risk their reputations for a chance at true love while dealing with a scandal that threatens to rock the military. (978-1-62639-754-5)

Arrival by Gun Brooke. The spaceship *Pathfinder* reaches its passengers' new homeworld where danger lurks in the shadows while Pamas Seclan disembarks and finds unexpected love in young science genius Darmiya Do Voy. (978-1-62639-859-7)

Captain's Choice by VK Powell. Architect Kerstin Anthony's life is going to plan until Bennett Carlyle, the first girl she ever kissed, is assigned to her latest and most important project, a police district substation. (978-1-62639-997-6)

Falling Into Her by Erin Zak. Pam Phillips, widow at the age of forty, meets Kathryn Hawthorne, local Chicago celebrity, and it changes her life forever—in ways she hadn't even considered possible. (978-1-63555-092-4)

Hookin' Up by MJ Williamz. Will Leah get what she needs from casual hookups or will she see the love she desires right in front of her? (978-1-63555-051-1)

King of Thieves by Shea Godfrey. When art thief Casey Marinos meets bounty hunter Finnegan Starkweather, the crimes of the past just might set the stage for a payoff worth more than she ever dreamed possible. (978-1-63555-007-8)

Lucy's Chance by Jackie D. As a serial killer haunts the streets, Lucy tries to stitch up old wounds with her first love in the wake of a small town's rapid descent into chaos. (978-1-63555-027-6)

Right Here, Right Now by Georgia Beers. When Alicia Wright moves into the office next door to Lacey Chamberlain's accounting firm, Lacey is about to find out that sometimes the last person you want is exactly the person you need. (978-1-63555-154-9)

Strictly Need to Know by MB Austin. Covert operator Maji Rios will do whatever she must to complete her mission, but saving a gorgeous stranger from Russian mobsters was not in her plans. (978-1-63555-114-3)

Tailor-Made by Yolanda Wallace. Tailor Grace Henderson doesn't date clients, but when she meets gender-bending model Dakota Lane, she's tempted to throw all the rules out the window. (978-1-63555-081-8)

Time Will Tell by M. Ullrich. With the ability to time travel, Eva Caldwell will have to decide between having it all and erasing it all. (978-1-63555-088-7)

Change in Time by Robyn Nyx. Working in the past is hell on your future. The Extractor series: Book Two. (978-1-62639-880-1)

Love After Hours by Radclyffe. When Gina Antonelli agrees to renovate Carrie Longmire's new house, she doesn't welcome Carrie's overtures at friendship or her own unexpected attraction. A Rivers Community Novel. (978-1-63555-090-0)

Nantucket Rose by CF Frizzell. Maggie Jordan can't wait to convert a historic Nantucket home into a B&B, but doesn't expect to fall for mariner Ellis Chilton, who has more claim to the house than Maggie realizes. (978-1-63555-056-6)

Picture Perfect by Lisa Moreau. Falling in love wasn't supposed to be part of the stakes for Olive and Gabby, rival photographers in the competition of a lifetime. (978-1-62639-975-4)

Set the Stage by Karis Walsh. Actress Emilie Danvers takes the stage again in Ashland, Oregon, little realizing that landscaper Arden Philips is about to offer her a very personal romantic lead role. (978-1-63555-087-0)

Strike a Match by Fiona Riley. When their attempts at matchmaking fizzle out, firefighter Sasha and reluctant millionairess Abby find themselves turning to each other to strike a perfect match. (978-1-62639-999-0)

The Price of Cash by Ashley Bartlett. Cash Braddock is doing her best to keep her business afloat, stay out of jail, and avoid Detective Kallen. It's not working. (978-1-62639-708-8)

Captured Soul by Laydin Michaels. Can Kadence Munroe save the woman she loves from a twisted killer, or will she lose her to a collector of souls? (978-1-62639-915-0)

Under Her Wing by Ronica Black. At Angel's Wings Rescue, dogs are usually the ones saved, but when quiet Kassandra Haden meets outspoken owner Jayden Beaumont, the two stubborn women just might end up saving each other. (978-1-63555-077-1)